# JOANNA NADIN

## the RACHEL RILEY Diaries

### THE TIME OF MY LIFE

OXFORD
UNIVERSITY PRESS

LIBRARIES NI
WITHDRAWN FROM STOCK

D0262576

# OXFORD
UNIVERSITY PRESS

Great Clarendon Street, Oxford OX2 6DP

Oxford University Press is a department of the University of Oxford.
It furthers the University's objective of excellence in research, scholarship,
and education by publishing worldwide in

Oxford   New York

Auckland   Cape Town   Dar es Salaam   Hong Kong   Karachi
Kuala Lumpur   Madrid   Melbourne   Mexico City   Nairobi
New Delhi   Shanghai   Taipei   Toronto

With offices in

Argentina   Austria   Brazil   Chile   Czech Republic   France   Greece
Guatemala   Hungary   Italy   Japan   Poland   Portugal   Singapore
South Korea   Switzerland   Thailand   Turkey   Ukraine   Vietnam

Oxford is a registered trade mark of Oxford University Press
in the UK and in certain other countries

Copyright © Joanna Nadin 2014
Inside illustrations © Sarah Jane Coleman 2014
The moral rights of the author and illustrator have been asserted

Database right Oxford University Press (maker)

First published 2014

All rights reserved. No part of this publication may be reproduced,
stored in a retrieval system, or transmitted, in any form or by any means,
without the prior permission in writing of Oxford University Press,
or as expressly permitted by law, or under terms agreed with the appropriate
reprographics rights organization. Enquiries concerning reproduction
outside the scope of the above should be sent to the Rights Department,
Oxford University Press, at the address above

You must not circulate this book in any other binding or cover
and you must impose this same condition on any acquirer

British Library Cataloguing in Publication Data
Data available

ISBN: 987-0-19-279278-5
1 3 5 7 9 10 8 6 4 2

Printed in Great Britain

Paper used in the production of this book is a natural,
recyclable product made from wood grown in sustainable forests.
The manufacturing process conforms to the environmental
regulations of the country of origin.

LIBRARIES NI
WITHDRAWN FROM STOCK

*For small-town girls everywhere.*

I'm RACHEL RILEY
– welcome to my so-called life.

January

# Thursday 1
*New Years Day*

This is typical. I spend months eschewing fiction and fairy tales in pursuit of cold, hard, facts, only to realize I am, in fact, still in love with Jack. And so I rush to the Stones' superhero-themed 'Jack is back/we're adopting an ethnic minority (i.e. Irish) baby' New Year's Eve party to tell him this joyous news, only to discover the following devastating fact: Jack is in love with someone else.

This time it is someone called Maya who he met when he was digging wells in Guatemala. She is probably a willowy indigenous beauty with almond eyes and cascading hair. While I am a midget with borderline ginger hair that has never done anything remotely resembling cascading. Mostly it just sits on my head looking mental.

I cannot believe I ever said being me was brilliant. It is the utter opposite. I lead a pointless and fruitless existence. Like a leaf blower. Or a nun. I am not even going to bother making any New Year's resolutions. They will only end in tears and disappointment.

And possibly a ban and a shouting from Mum. She has already vetoed several of James's and Dad's before they have even begun, e.g.:

1   I will become the world's first merboy (James).
2   I will rearrange the bookcase on a new points-based system, according to number of killings, and presence of mythical creatures (ten points for *Lord*

*of the Rings*, nul points for *Five on Kirrin Island*) (James).

3    I will do more of what I like on Sundays, as it is, in fact, the Day of Rest (Dad).

4    I will teach the dog to sniff drugs and revive the fortunes of the House of Riley by renting it out to PC Doone (James).

5    I will have a well-earned beer when I get in from work even if it is only Tuesday and not yet six o'clock (Dad).

Mum is right about number 4 though. There is no way the dog is going to be able to identify drugs. It will only eat them. And the thought of the dog having swallowed a kilo of amphetamines is mind-boggling.

Uncle Jim is wise to stay out of the hoo-hah. He is still too depressed over his wife Marigold leaving him halfway up a Himalaya for an accountant from Chipping Sodbury. He had better find his mojo soon (lust for life kind, not normal pants-based lust kind) or Mum will do some resolving for him. She has done one for Dad, i.e. 'Make more effort at work.' She is worried that Wainwright and Beacham will be next in line for cutbacks and will be separating the wheat from chaff. She is definitely of the opinion that Dad is chaff. Am leaving before she can impose anything on me. Will go round to Sad Ed's house. However Sylvia Plath-like I feel, Sad Ed is always worse. Oooh, maybe he has revived his resolution to die an untimely tragic death and go down in music legend. Though he should probably try to work

a bit more on the music side of this equation first. At the moment his Bontempi-playing is less than legendary.

4 p.m.
Yet more proof that I am doomed. Sad Ed is not depressed at all. In fact he is utterly jubilant. He snogged Scarlet at the party last night and it turns out his mojo (pants one, not lust for life one) was right all along and she is his ONE. I asked if his feelings were reciprocated. He said he is not sure because then she passed out due to excessive consumption of something called a Flaming Mojito. I said it is amazing Bob and Suzy are being allowed a baby when they have utterly failed to advise their eighteen-year-old daughter of the perils of alcohol. Sad Ed said it was Suzy who gave her the drink in the first place, and, *au contraire*, she is the very definition of earth motherhood and he cannot wait until he weds Scarlet and she adopts him as a son-in-law (this is because his own mum is practically a pensioner and Deputy Chair of the Aled Jones fan club (Essex branch)). I said this is unlikely to happen given Scarlet's feelings on marriage, i.e. it is the province of small-minded right-winged suburbanites whose only ambition in life is to perpetuate the same tedious mistakes of their parents. Sad Ed was undeterred though (which is completely out of character. Usually he is deterred before he even thinks of what it is he doesn't want to do) and begged me to go to Scarlet's to find out if her mojo is similarly excited. I said I will go tomorrow. When she has stopped vomiting. And when Jack

is back in Guatemala being reunited with his irritatingly worldly and exotic girlfriend and cannot look down on my tragic normality and small-town hair.

## Friday 2

Ugh. I knew it. Sad Ed's kissing was more potent than I thought. Scarlet says she has found her ONE too. Though interestingly she does not actually know who her ONE is, or was, due to there being too many Flaming Mojitos inside her and too many Batmen at the party. I said surely she could tell who was who inside the unforgiving Lycra suits (one is gargantuan for God's sake) but she says no, it is a complete mystery, but she is pretty sure it must have been her ex, i.e. Trevor Pledger (head goth, owner of floor-length vegetarian leather coat, currently on gap year at the shuttlecock factory). I pointed out he was still going out with minigoth Tamsin Bacon according to Melody Bean (also a minigoth, has a tarantula called Arthur, once engaged to Sad Ed), but Scarlet says details like that are meaningless in the face of true love. Asked if she had considered for a minute that her true love might in fact be an enormous manic depressive with upper arm issues and an obsession with drowning himself in the shopping-trolley-clogged River Slade. She said no, if it is not Trevor, which it is, then it is more likely to be the third, as yet unidentified, Batman, as there is no way Sad Ed is the key to her fulfilment.

Left at the mention of fulfilment. This is what having a TV sex guru and an abortionist as parents does to you.

On the plus side, there was no sign of Jack so can assume he is safely back in Chichicastenango. His absence can only aid my getting over him, i.e. out of sight, out of mind. Although right now he is very much contaminating my mind with missed-opportunity love thoughts. Why, oh why has his fickle pelvis fallen at the first sight of exotic non-Walden-based beauty? If only he had stayed here for his gap year, and dug wells for impoverished people on the Whiteshot Estate we could very well be in each other's arms right now. As it is am going to have to content self with seasonal edition of *Holby City*.

## Saturday 3

Have been to Waitrose car park, i.e. trolley herding arena, to tell Ed the devastating news. He is, yet again, undeterred, and says he is being philosophical about the situation, i.e. it is better that she is disbelieving of the potential of his pants-based area. If we insist it was him, she may reject him for good, and claim drink addled her judgement. This way, she will slowly come to her senses, realize her fate, and fall into his manly arms (he got an Abs-buster for Christmas).

I miss the old, deterred Ed. It was always comforting to know someone was more suicidal than you. I blame Reuben

Tull (fellow trolley herder, part-time philosopher, full-time drug enthusiast). He has been filling Sad Ed's head with mumbo jumbo about Aristotelian halves. And possibly filling the back pocket of his XL combat trousers with 'herbal' remedies.

## Sunday 4

Mum has asked to see progress on my university applications as I am already perilously close to the deadline (two weeks today) and I do not want to risk mine being lost at the bottom of the pile in the ether (she still does not understand the workings of the internet) and losing out to timely applicants who lack my life experience (a Saturday job in lentil-smelling health food outlet Nuts in May). I said, 'What application?' She said, 'Ha ha.' (She has resolved to try to appreciate jokes, and see the funny side of life more, instead of foretelling doom and panicking over stains and bacteria. I could tell she was faking it though. Her lips were almost non-existent.)

She is right to be suspicious. I have not even written a personal statement. Mostly because I forgot due to the Mr Pringle trauma at the end of last year, and the Jack trauma at the beginning of this one. Though I shall say it is a stand against societal norms, and also because there is no point in me even trying because I will only be rejected by real

universities and end up doing accounting at Essex College of Further Education.

James for once is on my side. He says in any two-child family there is always an alpha sibling and a beta sibling and it is clear he is the alpha one as he is superior physically, intellectually and morally. He then went back to trying to persuade the dog to track down a packet of Junior Disprin he had hidden in his display of Middleworld crap. Mum will go mental when she finds out he has disobeyed her veto. Dad is already in trouble for trying to get out of de-clogging the drain by claiming it is his right to a day of reading newspapers and watching televised sport. She says he can go back to women's gymnastics once he has removed the persistent clot of dog/me hair from the U-bend.

On the plus side, only thought about Jack forty-seven times today. Which sounds excessive, but is down by five on yesterday. Plus am trying aversion therapy, i.e. imagining Jack snogging indigenous beauty Maya in bid to revolt self at any thought of him. So far am mostly just dissolving into tears instead.

10 p.m.
Partial success! Have been definitely revolted by thought of Jack. Though is possibly down to me giving him mullet hairstyle and bad breath for added repulsion.

## Monday 5

First day of school

*Plus ça change, plus c'est la même chose.* In other words, Mr Vaughan is back teaching drama, now that Sophie Jacobs (dad invented Microwave Muffins, likes large man nipples, now at York University) has traded him in for her professor. He says he is unbroken in the face of tragedy and is moving on with his life. I pointed out that he had not moved on, he had moved back, i.e. from York to Saffron Walden, but he says it is progress because it is in a new dynamic version, who will be unswayed by schoolgirl charms, and will be renewed in his focus on academic and theatrical attainment, i.e. we have a drama practical exam in four weeks' time and we had better get our acts together and pick a speech. Sad Ed is doing the Vicomte de Valmont from *Les Liaisons Dangereuses*. He says it embodies his newfound virility. I am going to do Juliet. It embodies my general feeling of doom. And my inability to look past the first play text on my shelf.

10 p.m.

Only thirty-six thoughts of Jack today. Including this one. And am now imagining him in giant nappy, singing a Spice Girls song and voting Conservative so it will only be a matter of time before any mention of him brings me out in heaving nausea.

## Tuesday 6

Scarlet's quest to be reunited with her mysterious Batman lover is causing ructions in Goth Corners Mark I (Tamsin Bacon's coven) and Mark II (Scarlet's coven). A fight to the death has been scheduled for Friday lunchtime. The winner gets to claim Trevor and the Throne of Magnificence (i.e. Mr Wilmott's old chair on wheels, now updated with superglued bat attachments and a velvet cushion, as opposed to the substandard Throne of Doom which is just an old plastic chair with some bats drawn on in chubby marker). I suggested, again, that the prize (Trevor, not chair) might not actually want to be claimed by Scarlet, given that she has no concrete evidence that he was the New Year's Eve kissee. She says the stirrings in his loin were all the concrete evidence she needs. Left again. For obvious reasons.

## Wednesday 7

Mathlete Corner is also in disarray. It is all down to James and Mad Harry getting confused over whose turn it is to engage in light petting with Wendy Shoebridge (Year Nine, Fifth (Baptist) Guides pack leader, bad shoes). They are clearly still persisting in their hideous love triangle. I note that Mumtaz looked on with utter disdain. I expect she is glad to be rid of them and their idiotic antics, e.g. Beastly

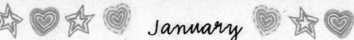
Boys (crap boy band), Beastly Investigations (the first ever wildlife detective agency, also crap), and Ghost Hustlers (not gay goth band but ghost-hunting agency involving a microwave radiation tester and the Hoover, also crap, also banned). I predict it will not be long before Wendy comes to her senses and joins Mumtaz in pursuing the more mature, more sophisticated, less-likely-to-go-out-dressed-in-furry-pants man.

## Thursday 8

Clearly my general air of gloom is having a positive effect on my acting skills. Mr Vaughan said my Juliet was utterly convincing. He says if I act like that in my auditions for drama degrees then I will be bombarded with unconditional offers, despite not having a name like Aurora or a mother who played Bianca in the RSC's legendary *Taming of the Shrew* (he is still cross at losing his place at Manchester to a minor Redgrave). Feigned excitement. Though this was apparently less convincing as he got all minty and said the youth of today expect everything to be handed to them on a platter and do not understand the meaning of hard graft. That is rich. He has spent the last four years variously stoned, snogging a sixth-former, and forgetting to come to lessons. It is hardly Dickensian grind. In contrast, Sad Ed's Vicomte de Valmont was dismissed as lacking any authenticity, i.e.

he is not the Lothario he likes to think he is. Sad Ed said, *au contraire*, his tongue skills are legend at John Major High and environs, and offered to prove it on a willing volunteer. No one came forward bar Caris Kelp (eats glue) and Sad Ed demurred on the grounds she had been licking a Pritt Stick earlier and he didn't not want to end up on YouTube in some kind of lip-welded clinch.

## Friday 9

11 a.m.
Scarlet is mad with anticipation at today's goth-off, (downgraded under official John Major High rules from 'to the death' to 'to the point where you are in sufficient pain to warrant a visit to Mrs Leech (school nurse, too much face powder, biscuit habit) for reviving bourbons and Coke'). She says by this evening she will be basking in the arms of her highly skilled lover, as they hover, bat-like, in the seventies loveswing watching *Coronation Street* (she is using it to prepare herself for the realities of living in the North next year).

Sad Ed is still being philosophical about it all. He says even if Scarlet wins the fight, she will lose the war, i.e. she will soon realize that Trevor's lips and pant area are substandard and it will be his own nether regions she will be heading to for solace. Would have left, but was wedged in the Yazoo cushion on the saggy sofa and it takes several minutes to

gain enough leverage to escape. Pointed this out to Head Boy (i.e. Sad Ed) and suggested he lobby Mr Wilmott for new soft furnishings, but he said all spending is suspended since the Criminals and Retards blew up the microwave trying to cook a shoe and it cost £89.99 for a new one, plus £47.99 for a new pair of brogues for Mr Wilmott.

1 p.m.

Scarlet won the fight by running over Tamsin's feet repeatedly in the Throne of Magnificence. She is like Davros the chief dalek, i.e. half girl, half chair. Even I was terrified. Tamsin claimed she was not defeated but Mrs Brain started waving her bean-encrusted spoon at everyone and threatened to stop stocking Ribena (ambrosial nectar to the goths) and Tamsin is more scared of her than she is of Scarlet (as is Mr Wilmott). Scarlet is going to claim her prize after school at the shuttlecock factory gates. She says it is utterly Orwellian. It is not. The factory is a prefab on the Shire Hill estate with a distinct lack of smog or gruesome packing-line deaths. I fear she will be disappointed in both setting and kiss.

6 p.m.

As predicted, Scarlet is back at the Batman drawing board. Following intense questioning, Trevor pointed out that at the time of the snog (i.e. midnight), he was back at home feeding locusts to Hedges (King Rat and superior to Benson in every way). Scarlet demanded an oral exam to back up

his statement but Trevor refused, claiming it went against the Goth Code. Scarlet claimed there wasn't a Goth Code but he said there was, i.e.:

1 Do not cheat on, steal from, or otherwise disrespect your fellow goths as they suffer ritual abuse at the hands of coloureds (i.e. people who wear anything other than black, not black people) every day.

2 Do not go out into sunlight without factor 50 on.

3 Do not experiment with fake tan.

4 Do not claim navy is the new black. It is not.

Which is why Tamsin Bacon is better suited to being Queen Goth. So Scarlet said she had proven her superiority to Tamsin with the Throne, and now the law couldn't contain her love and launched herself at him, only to stagger back in horror, hissing, 'The lips do not lie. You are not my destiny.' So then Trevor demanded to know what was wrong with his lips and Scarlet said nothing per se, just that they are not as full-bodied and tender as the mystery Batman kisser's. Did imperceptible shudder as could not actually leave due to having to help Scarlet walk home (she may have been the victor, but she is not without battle scars, i.e. an imprint of a skull ring on the forehead, minor hair loss, and a potentially fractured toe (this one not actually Tamsin's fault, she ran over her own foot at one point in her madness)).

11 p.m.
Jack thoughts down to eighteen. Is excellent result. Turning him into nappy-wearing, cack-singing Tory is genius idea.

May well patent it as post-break-up therapy. I could go on *This Morning* and help beleaguered celebrities overcome their devastation by getting them to imagine former partners as Nazis in tap shoes.

## Saturday 10

The dog is ill. It has ingested a packet of Rennies, two Dora the Explorer waterproof plasters, and a Vicks inhaler (evidence now hawked up on the landing). James is protesting innocence but Dad claims he saw him trying to get it to lick a teaspoon of Tixylix during the news. James says it is all evil lies and Dad is only trying to win points so he can watch some tedious tennis tomorrow instead of driving to the garden centre for slug pellets (a suspicious trail navigating the kitchen floor and the tinned goods cupboard appeared overnight). Mum says they are both living on borrowed time, as is the dog, who failed to actually devour the slug, yet it happily eats concrete on a regular basis.

Went out before she could menace me about my UCAS form, and to break the Batman-based news to Sad Ed at trolley herding duty. He smiled a knowing smile and said it is one down, one to go. He is irritatingly Zen-like at the moment. Not even Mark Lambert pushing Fat Kylie down the spiral exit could dent his optimism. He said she will realize her folly when she crashes into the pay and display

machine at the bottom and breaks several bones. She will not. She never learns from anything. Plus her bones are buried several kilos deep in transfats. Nothing gets past that.

11 p.m.

It is not one to go, it is five. Scarlet is still convinced the mystery kisser is the elusive 'third Batman' and has narrowed the field down to the following potential candidates:

1 Pelvis Presley (part-time crap tribute act/car mechanic, full-time moron).

2 Dean 'the dwarf' Denley (official school midget, Saturday job as meat mincer).

3 Kev Banner (Duke of York regular, works in BJ video, outwitted and outdrunk by his dog on a regular basis).

4 Stan Barret (music geek, once saw Paul Weller in John Lewis).

5 Barney Smith-Watson (blond dreads, fake Jamaican accent, on Rock Foundation at Braintree College with former object of my (and Sophie Microwave Muffins') affection, Justin Statham).

Pointed out that surely she would have noticed if it was Dean the Dwarf due to having to stoop almost a foot, but she says I underestimate the power of the kiss to befuddle her mind and lady parts. Also the power of Suzy's Flaming Mojitos to befuddle everything. She is going to track down her superhero by a process of elimination, involving a Paxman-style interrogative interview and

kiss-off. Offered to loan her Mum as she is unrelenting in her aggressive questioning techniques but Scarlet said she does not want to put interviewees off by suggesting she condones my mother's attitude, choice of clothing, or tendency to vote Lib Dem. Plus Mum does not believe in loin stirring. She believes in a steady job and neatly clipped toenails.

It is sad really. The only kissee ever to move me was Jack. Only now if I imagine him kissing me (which have only done for aversion therapy testing reasons, obviously) I feel like have just been over the humpback bridge at Audley End too fast, i.e. sick, and cross. Though not with Dad, who is usual abuser of humpback bridge rules. Although maybe adding Dad to aversion mix would be excellent idea.

11.30 p.m.
No, was step too far. Will not go into it but is never again to be mentioned.

## Sunday 11

Uncle Jim's continuing presence is causing friction at the Shreddies table. Mum says it is high time he pulled himself together and went home to sort his marriage out (she is not actually keen on him rekindling flames with Marigold, whom she has never accepted as a true Riley on the grounds she believes fairies actually exist, she is just keen on him

not being slumped on the sofa, drinking weak lager and watching cartoons all day. She says he is a bad influence on James, Dad, and the dog, who is showing signs of *Spongebob* addiction). Uncle Jim says he was born and raised a Saffron Walden boy so this *is* his home. But Mum was undeterred and trumped with a technicality, i.e. in fact his home is with Grandpa Riley, wherever he may be residing. Only James pointed out that he is residing at 19 Harvey Road, which is jam-packed with Baby Jesus (i.e. Uncle Jim's three-year-old brother) and his many accoutrements, plus it is next door to the O'Gradys' and their ever-increasing family of criminals, and surely she cannot be suggesting he subject himself to that. She said that is exactly what she is suggesting and went off to do something horrible with an oxtail (she is embracing the frugal lifestyle). I give him a week before he is begging to leave. Treena has Wagon Wheels and we are down to own-brand rich teas.

## Monday 12

School has been seized with UCAS madness. It is down to ineffectual head Mr Wilmott and his motivational assembly about application forms, i.e. if you do not get your referees to complete their bit by Friday then you are doomed to flipping burgers at ABC Barbecue. Clearly he is in a panic because so far only three people have completed theirs: Scarlet, Emily Reeve (habitual wearer of un-ironic knee-length

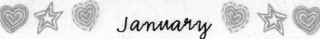

# January

socks, mother of Lola Lambert Reeve), and Ali Hassan (Lord High Ruler of the mathletes table) and he does not want to be outdone in the UCAS stakes by Burger King Sports Academy. And everyone else is in a panic because Lawrence Gavell (former trolley herder turned beet picker) works in ABC Barbecue and he has an outsized head and body odour.

Mr Vaughan has begged me to let him do my reference. It is part of his newfound dynamism and professional values. That and he is still on probation with threats of immediate dismissal if he even looks at anyone under the age of eighteen in a sexual manner. Said fine. Did not want to ruin his dream, or his job prospects.

Sad Ed, in yet another uncharacteristic Zen-like manoeuvre, has already done his, complete with reference from boss-eyed and evangelical music teacher Mr Beston. Asked where he is focusing his Theory and Practice of Popular Music sights. He said London, Humberside aka Hull, and Sheffield. Said, 'Are these not the same sights as Scarlet and her Politics and Economics next female prime minister sights?' He said obviously, as by then she will be ensconced in his manly arms, and will not be able to bear being apart from him. Plus she will probably be carrying his baby. He is more deluded than James. And he thinks the Ninja Turtles are possible.

Also had driving lesson after school. According to Mike 'Wandering Hands' Majors (forty-something Lothario, former admirer of Mum, non-admirer of me), I am showing no signs of progress. I said in which case I shall rely on being

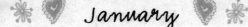

chauffeured in my future husband's Ford Mondeo. That or the Uttlesford public transport system. Mr Wandering Hands said, 'What public transport system?' He has a point. Cannot remember the last time I actually saw a bus. Plus the train station is four miles out of town. It is utterly Orwellian.

## Tuesday 13

Thin Kylie and Mark Lambert's impending nuptials have taken over the saggy sofa. They have been appointing bridesmaids on a 'who will look best in skintight gold lamé' basis. Unbelievably Fat Kylie is down to the final round. She will not look best. She will look like a Lycra saveloy. Scarlet says it is a pathetic sight, and a sad indictment of comprehensive education that they have no ambition to shrug off the shackles of their council-estate upbringing and become tomorrow's Marie Curie or Aneurin Bevan, instead of marrying the first people they slept with and becoming tomorrow's mobile beautician and all-Essex minibike champion. Sad Ed said she is wrong (a dangerous move, as Scarlet is never wrong, even when she is) because *a)* Thin Kylie had already slept with Mr Whippy but *b)* it is clear they are each other's sexual destiny, so the wedding is just acceptance of the fact that their loins and minds are utterly attuned. Maybe Thin Kylie is the key to my life satisfaction, i.e. I need to lower my sights, job-wise and

man-wise. Though I have not technically slept with anyone, and the first person I kissed was Brian Drain on the Year Seven trip to Peterborough Roller Rink, and there is no way I am repeating the incident. It was like being tongued by a conger eel. But still, Jack is clearly not my destiny. Plus he is thousands of miles away being tongued by Maya, and I bet she hasn't just eaten two bags of Nice 'n' Spicy Nik Naks.

## Wednesday 14

Went round Scarlet's after school to see how preparations for the arrival of the not-very-ethnic orphan are going. Worryingly, there was a distinct lack of any baby equipment. Suzy says she does not need modern accoutrements like a cot, or nappies and bottles as she is going to co-sleep, employ the controversial method of potty training from birth, plus she is convinced her surge of maternal love will make her 'milk come in' thus ruling out bottles, or more profits for evil Nestlé.

Scarlet is less than thrilled. This is because she was raised on SMA milk in a pair of Pampers because Suzy was too busy running her tantric sex groups to wash terry towelling, plus Bob got possessive over her breasts. Scarlet says the baby is becoming the favoured younger child already, meaning she is going to suffer from notorious middle child syndrome, i.e. she will be doomed to constant attention seeking and average attainment in life. On the plus side, she has whittled her Batman Lover List down to three on

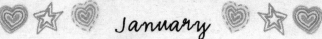

the grounds that Kev Banner never made it off the floor of the Duke (a combination of trying to drink four pints of Guinness before the dog, and Shorty's overly sticky carpet), and Pelvis Presley was in police custody after a fight with Mr Hosepipe (fireman, stripper, father of Mark Lambert) in the Siam Smile.

Think I am totally over Jack though, i.e. did not break down in wistful tears at the sight of the chair where once he ate Waitrose pain au chocolats. At one point did imagine I could hear the sound of drumming still echoing from his old bedroom, but have put this down to Edna the non-Filipina Labour-friendly cleaner trying to knock Tony and Gordon off the wardrobe. Aversion therapy is obviously a resounding success and will definitely not harbour any feelings towards him when he reappears in several months' time, having had his heart broken cruelly by Maya who has been secretly betrothed to her first cousin since the age of six.

10 p.m.
Not that I am hoping this is the case. Because am utterly over him.

*Thursday 15*

Mr Vaughan has done my UCAS statement. It compares my performance as Anne Frank to a young Elizabeth Taylor. Pointed out he had not actually seen my performance of

Anne Frank due to him being preoccupied with Sophie's Microwave Muffins, or lack of access to thereof. He said he did not need to see it, he can sense it was groundbreaking. Did not tell him it was mostly obliterated by several Criminals and Retards getting overenthusiastic with their Nazi truncheons. It is all hypothetical anyway as am not going to study drama at university. Am going to focus on a BTEC in accounting where hopefully I will meet an ambitionless but trustworthy boy, who can be the son Mum never had (the one she has is forever downgraded by association with Mad Harry and Keanu, the youngest and deadliest O'Grady boy).

Although maybe if I pretend that is what I am doing then God, if he or she or the laser-eyed dog exists, will actually deliver me a first-class drama degree, a squat in Camden, and a tortured Mercury-prizewinning musician to thwart me.

6 p.m.
James has reminded me of the foolhardiness of trying to trick God, e.g. the time he decided to hedge his bets by joining all religions in the hope that one would guarantee him everlasting salvation. It just got confusing and ended with a ban on rosary beads and Ramadan.

## Friday 16

Have witnessed yet more signs of resolution madness, i.e. Treena on a mountain bike. Actually walked into a lamp

post in shock due to the fact that Treena's usual idea of exercise is reaching across Grandpa for the TV remote. Plus she was wearing salmon-pink leggings. Demanded an explanation for this aberration. She said Grandpa Riley is showing signs of decline (i.e. he keeps forgetting where he lives on his way back from the Queen Lizzie) so she is attempting to shape up to ensure Jesus is not fatherless in the future. Plus the bike was free. Asked in what sense it was free. She said she got it for six hundred Embassy tokens. Pointed out Grandpa was not in decline, but loss of memory inversely proportional to number of alcohol units. She said, 'Don't you try to baffle me with long words,' and wobbled off into the distance like a flamingo on wheels.

6 p.m.
James has worked out the bike cost Treena £4,680, plus certain death from lung cancer.

## Saturday 17

Lacking ambition is less interesting than I thought. There is no one to commune with for a start, i.e. Sad Ed is busy trolley herding to save up for his imaginary future with Scarlet, and Scarlet is busy lurking outside the Mocha trying to gauge the fullness of Stan Barret's lips for her imaginary future with Batman. Plus James and Mad Harry have taken the dog out to sniff for heroin behind the bins at Mr Patel's. I protested

as it is my new companion of choice in general despair now that Sad Ed has finally embraced life (it is excellent at lying around looking depressed/vacant) but James said he is confident of locating one of the O'Grady's secret stashes. He will be disappointed. The only thing the O'Gradys stash anywhere in bulk is Pot Noodle and *Nuts* magazine.

Mum said if I don't have anything useful to do I can proofread my UCAS form for rogue apostrophes. (She is convinced a misplaced punctuation mark is all that stands between me and academic supremacy. And if not, it should be.) Said I'd rather Cif the bathroom. I might as well start learning the ropes, now I am resigned to life in the wretched provinces with a clone of Dad and two mildly disappointing children. Anything else would be denying the truth: that I am tragically normal. And that life will never ever be like it is in films, or books, not even one of Mum's tedious Maeve Binchys.

11.50 p.m.
Someone has thrown a giant spanner into the works of my listlessness.

It is Jack Clement Atlee Stone.

Or maybe Jack is the spanner itself. Whichever. It is still utterly spannery. Worse, he has utterly invaded my arena of gloom, i.e. he is the new assistant barman at the Duke.

Was at bar waiting to order lime and soda (belt-tightening beverage) when familiar voice said, 'Cheer up, Riley, it might never happen.' Looked up to see Jack throwing bottle of Baileys in air like idiotic cocktail shaker person. Said, 'It did.

Plus that is a complete cliché. And also very annoying.' Then had to listen to him bang on about Guatemalan temples and goatherds and how there is a whole world out there beyond North Essex and it is our duty to go out and discover it. Said I thought Columbus had already done that. Plus if that is the case, then why is here instead of in it? He said he needs to bond with the baby in the crucial early weeks. Plus his wallet got stolen by a shaman and Maya had to bail him out, so he needs to pay her back and also save up for uni next year. He is going to Cambridge. Or at least I assume he is, as it is that or Hull, and you do not have to be a mathlete with an IQ of 140 and a giant collection of Warhammer crap to work that one out.

Am stunned. Cannot believe he is back. Although he says technically he never went away, i.e. he has been holed up at Bob and Suzy's since New Year Skyping Maya (which is odd. I did not think indigenous cascading beauties had iMacs in their yurts or whatever it is they live in. Or could afford to bail out morons who give their money to medicine men), it is just that I have been so bound up in my own gloom have failed to notice evidence of his presence.

Ugh. So now not only am I doomed to obsoletion in Essex, I have to be obsolete in full view of the love of my life.

11.55 p.m.
Not that he is the love of my life. Obviously that is Ken, my accounting dream. How could I possibly be in love with an evil, nappy-wearing, girl-band-singing fascist?

26

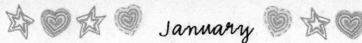 

**11.56 p.m.**
Who looks like my dad (have had to factor Dad back in to aversion equation as not even the voting Tory was repulsing me).

**11.57 p.m.**
Though maybe Jack has a point. Not about the Aztecs being role models (because if they were that tricksy, they'd have worked out a way not to get obliterated), but about there being more to life than Saffron Walden. Maybe that is my problem. It's not me that is tragically normal, and doomed to mediocrity, it is this tedious, second-rate town.

**11.59 p.m.**
That is it! It has been staring me in the face for seventeen and a bit years. I am like Kate Winslet, or Billie Piper, who were also born to averageness in Reading and Swindon, but found fame and fortune on the gritty but gold-paved streets of London.

Oh my God. I am Dick Whittington! All I need is a cat and handkerchief on a stick.

Or maybe a place at Goldsmith's College to study Film and Drama.

Oh, I have been a fool. To think I was going to settle for Ken and a semi with a through lounge on Cromwell Road. New Year's resolutions are the key to changing my hitherto pitiful existence. And so I, Rachel Riley, resolve the following:

1 To finish my UCAS form, so I may flee my lowly suburban birth and find my true place in the world, i.e. preferably a converted shoe factory with an underground bar in the basement and a friendly prostitute in the penthouse.

My ambition is renewed. I shall find real tragedy. I shall fall in love with a laudanum-addicted poet with a terminal heart problem, which he keeps secret from me until his dying moments. I shall exist on nothing but black coffee, wit, and love. In other words, I shall have the Time of My Life.

Starting tomorrow. Right after my Shreddies.

## Sunday 18

10 a.m.
And after I have persuaded the dog to stop eating tampons. It has swallowed five already and if the adverts are anything to go by its colon will be impassably plugged. Though that might be a good thing.

11 a.m.
And after a health-giving snack of Marmite on toast.

12 p.m.
And maybe lunch. It is in an hour and it would be a waste to get into form-writing mindset only to be disturbed by conversations about plumbing and golf. Plus have a full

twelve hours to go before midnight deadline and do not want to be twiddling my thumbs later on.

**12.15 p.m.**
Have changed mind. Am starting now. It is thanks to Dad who just proclaimed he has fulfilled his life's ambition by putting a practice ball down the hallway and into a cup in the downstairs toilet. How utterly depressing. I refuse to accept I am related to someone with so little imagination. Or someone who thinks finding a new way to serve minced beef is the pinnacle of achievement (Mum, not Dad. He is not allowed near the cooker for at least another six months). Will eschew all food and other small-town distractions until I am done, i.e. in two hours.

**2.15 p.m.**
Hmm. It is more complicated than I thought. Have not actually decided where I am applying yet. Have whittled it down to fifteen, including LSE (alumnus of JFK, Ed Miliband, and Cherie Blair, plus is Scarlet's first choice), and Hull (alumnus of Lord Hattersley, Anthony Minghella, and Marlon Dingle, has interesting white telephone boxes, plus it is Scarlet's reserve choice).

**4.15 p.m.**
Scarlet has been round (Suzy is attempting to demonstrate potty use and the sight is making her nauseous). She says I can't apply to LSE due to my poor choice of substandard

A levels, i.e. Drama. She has also crossed off Goldsmith's, Oxford, and the London College of Fashion.

8.15 p.m.
Under Scarlet's tutelage have narrowed choice down to following: Hull, Manchester, and Birmingham. Pointed out that this list did not contain a single London university, i.e. how I am supposed to commune with potential Peckham-based poets when I am swilling around Harvey Nichols at the Bullring. She said, realistically, Mum is never going to let me go to London on grounds of cost, crime rate, and potential to fall for a rap artist, so it is a wasted choice. Said under Mum's rules Birmingham should be ruled out (accent), but Scarlet said I will be doing Drama where affecting mad voices is de rigueur. Excellent. Now all I have to do is write a personal statement on why I am an ideal candidate, listing my many extra-curricular activities, community work, and employment experience.

10.15 p.m.
Have got Nuts in May, and playing Buckaroo with Grandpa at the Twilight Years Day Centre (it is banned at home, due to potential for overexcitement, and knocking things off the mantelpiece). This is pitiful. Will be lucky to secure a place at Stoke at this rate. Am going to wake up James. He is master of form-filling. And lying.

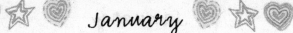

# January

11.55 p.m.

James has added political campaigning (i.e. the time I handed some leaflets out for Scarlet's Head Girl campaign), training disturbed animals (i.e. the dog), and competitive fractioning (this one is not in any way true but he says the interviewers won't have done it either so will be unable to baffle me with pertinent questions). Anyway it is too late now as he pressed send before I could have second thoughts. So hurrah! I have taken my first step out of the back of beyond and into actual beyond. All I need to do now is to sit back, and wait for the offers to come rolling in.

## Monday 19

10 a.m.

And get up on time so can pass A levels. Have already missed a vital hour of schooling. It is clear I am being thwarted by the universe, which is determined to shackle me to my small-town misery. Plus Mum forgot to wake me due to an emergency at Grandpa's (Jesus is stuck in the freezer and Grandpa is too weak to lift him out). The universe, Mum, and Jesus shall not succeed. I shall rise up more powerful and more academic than ever.

4 p.m.

Have learned that criminals, mentalists, and bishops are not allowed to sit in the House of Lords (Double Politics).

31

Am unsure this is A* material. In contrast James says he is confident he has solved string theory. He has not.

## Tuesday 20

Thin Kylie has got wedding fever. She has now decided she wants all the crèche inmates as flower girls and page boys. Unbelievably Mark Lambert is backing her. They are both mental. There are twenty of them, including Baby Jesus and Whitney Chanel Martini O'Grady. The chances of getting any of them to walk in a straight line are zero, let alone arriving at the altar without having peed, hit someone, or eaten a carnation. I shall never get married. I shall be too busy creating guerrilla theatre in Zimbabwe that will topple the oppressive regime and win me a Nobel Peace Prize and possibly an Olivier.

## Wednesday 21

If only Uncle Jim were similarly worldly ambitious. He is currently refusing to leave Saffron Walden, or, indeed, the confines of 24 Summerhill Road. I have tried to give him Jack's 'the world is waiting' pep talk, but he says the world is only full of cholera and disappointment and he would rather stay here where he is safe from disease and a broken heart. He is mad. It may be germ-free (bar the dog, although

it ate a bar of antibacterial soap this morning so it is fairly hygienic), but it is riddled with potential disappointments, from povvy pudding to limited TV access.

Had another driving lesson with marked improvement, i.e. did not reverse into kerb. Or Mrs Thorndyke (wife of Conservative MP Hugo, red-faced, makes macaroons). Mr Wandering Hands said he could tell Mum had been using her not insignificant influence on me. I said it was not that, it was my determination to escape her clutches, and the miseries of small-town Essex.

## Thursday 22

Scarlet's Batlist is down to two after a disappointing fumbling with Dean 'the dwarf' Denley behind the giant bins (aka rat corner). Though she says the fact he had to stand on an empty drum of Mazola may have detracted from her arousal. I said she is wasting her time. She will never find her true love in a medium-sized market town, she needs to focus on more worldly locations, i.e. London, or Hull. She says he could be as inbred as a Clegg if he can make *that* happen down there. Did not bother to argue. She is right: the Cleggs are complete yokels. Though did not hang around either. The thought of Grandpa or Boaz involved in arousal of any sort is more than I could stomach. At least, after Mrs Brain's meat-free pasta option (i.e. spaghetti with baked beans). Clearly I need to expand my sexual horizons as part of my new worldliness.

Scarlet is at an advantage. She has had years of Suzy's vile confessions to toughen her up. Nothing shocks her. Not even the notorious Mr Whippy sex tape.

## Friday 23

Scarlet is down to one Batman. Apparently Stan Barrett has a distinctive snaggle tooth that she would have noticed even under the influence of drink or drugs. (She trapped him on the saggy sofa at lunchtime. He has added his voice to my 'this sofa is a potential deathtrap' campaign.) So now it is down to irritating white Rasta Barney Smith-Watson, only according to David Smith (enormous quiff, pasty face, thinks he is from the fifties) he has left Braintree for stardom, i.e. he has gone on a tour of North Wales with crap neo-punk band Electric Knob, and doesn't get back until mid-February. Scarlet is undeterred. She says a few weeks is but a drop in the ocean when they will have the rest of their lives together.

Sad Ed is slightly less philosophical. It is because Barney Smith-Watson once held the official John Major High snogging record. Pointed out that his record fell to Fat Kylie, and anyone who can be outwitted, or outsnogged, by an O'Grady is no competition. He then reminded me that he had, on several occasions, been outwitted by Fat Kylie, as had I by various O'Gradys including Keanu. Said then it is a good job that we are soon to be departing from

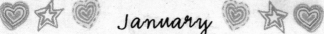
a town whose main dynasty is a family that includes a man who once blew himself up with a can of hairspray (Uncle Niall), another who choked to death on a Findus Crispy Pancake (Les), and twins called Liam. (Both of them, to avoid confusion on the part of Mrs O'Grady who cannot tell them apart so does not bother. She has a point. They are interchangeably moronic.)

## *Saturday 24*

Another tedious night in the Duke. Oh, how I wish I was elegantly wasted on absinthe in the corner of the Hawley Arms while my lover holds court with controversial novelists and installation artists. As opposed to eating endless packets of crisps and sipping lime and soda at the wobbly table while listening to Sad Ed and Reuben Tull discuss the possibility of a black hole consuming the moon, thus rendering most of Pink Floyd's back catalogue defunct, and whether monkeys will ever naturally evolve wings. It is lucky Scarlet is too busy at home preparing for the arrival of the new baby. She has a pathological fear of discussing the universe. It is Professor Brian Cox. She says his perpetual smile gives him the look of a drugged cult leader, or children's presenter.

Jack was still very much in evidence though. I do not know why he has to have a job where I will encounter him on a weekly basis. Why couldn't he go and flip burgers in

ABC Barbecue or pour overpriced coffee in Starbucks (both banned in our house for being the main source of street littering, and, in the case of ABC, for spelling cheese with a 'z'). Actually I know why. It is because he said he is not being a slave to The Man. Or corporate America. Or meat. Said he is a slave to the man, i.e. Shorty McNulty. He said Shorty puts customer satisfaction before profit so he doesn't count. Said in that case he should fix the wobbly table as it is a hazard to drink retention, and remove the graffiti in the toilet that says 'I lick arses'. Jack said the wobbly table is the only way he makes any profit at all, and the graffiti is part of the Duke's quaint charm. It is lucky Mum never comes in the pub. She would Stain Devil the charm out in seconds, along with the chubby marker diagram of a knob and the advert for Stacey O'Grady's sex services.

On the plus side, his endless wittering on about Maya and her academic prowess and taste in Beat Generation novels is proving more effective as an aversion tactic. Anyone who thinks Kerouac is gripping is clearly a moron. Nothing happens in *On the Road*. It would be much better if someone got kidnapped by a crazed lorry driver and held hostage in a gas station.

## Sunday 25

Harper Janis Obama Stone has arrived (named after a Pulitzer prize-winning author, a dead singer, and a black

president). She is in no way ethnic. Apparently even her Irish roots were overplayed as, according to Mr Lemon (formerly of Uttlesford Environmental Department, then of housing, now of social services), her birth mother was merely obsessed with Daniel O'Donnell. Suzy doesn't mind, she says it is nurture over nature and she will imbue her with her own sense of multicultural pride. I do not know how. Or why. The Stones' ethnic roots are Jersey and North Essex. Plus I am not convinced Harper is entirely nurturable. She already has her ears pierced and the distinctive bog-eyed stare of an O'Grady.

11 p.m.
Oh God. Maybe she IS an O'Grady. It is entirely feasible. Mrs O'Grady tends to pump them out at a rate of one every year. Plus she is morbidly obese, i.e. it is impossible to tell when she is pregnant or not, and there hasn't been a confirmed birth since Whitney.

## Monday 26

Scarlet is exhausted. Harper was up seven times in the night and is utterly refusing to suckle Suzy's breasts (ugh, actually did perceptible shudder as I wrote 'suckle'). Suzy says it is because she has never been able to exercise her right to breast before due to her monetarily and culturally impoverished existence, and so does not recognize them

as dispensers of nature's own ambrosia (she means metaphorical ambrosia, i.e. milk, not rice pudding or chocolate custard, I checked). Scarlet says it is because they are not actually dispensing nature's own ambrosia, or anything at all.

Suzy gave in at 2 a.m. and microwaved some emergency SMA. She is still determined to co-sleep and potty train though. Scarlet says she gives it a week. Bob already nearly squashed Harper trying to access Suzy's dispensers in his state of morning glory, plus Edna trod in a poo outside the den. Asked how she knew about the morning glory. She said there are no secrets in their house. I said there should be. For once she agreed.

Told her my O'Grady theory. She said it would only excite Suzy further to be raising the unwanted child of the working poor. Said they were neither working nor poor. (Mrs O'Grady has not had a job since she got sacked from Smeg Launderette for tipping the fruit machines, and one of the Liams is in prison again, yet they own the biggest plasma screen on the Whiteshot estate.) But Scarlet said that is not the point. The point is, Suzy will raise Harper as living proof you can overcome your humble birth and lawless tendencies if only you are given enough love and organic carrots.

Did not tell her that Mum is endlessly trying this with Jesus, yet he is still a criminal mastermind. It is Treena's dominant Bolton genes overriding nurture. He stands no chance.

## Tuesday 27

Today was the final rehearsal before Friday's drama practical exam. Mr Vaughan said my Juliet had gone off the boil slightly, i.e. she is less woeful and more manically desperate. I said it was a reflection of my changing personal circumstances, but that now I am playing her as the daughter of a family of inbred criminals and her only hope of bettering herself is by marrying the high-born Romeo, whose intellect is matched only by his enormous capabilities as a lover. Unlike the Vicomte de Valmont, whose colossal delusion is matched only by his double chin. Mr Vaughan said hopefully the external examiner will have a thing for codpieces. I doubt it.

On the plus side, Harper is not the secret offspring of Mrs O'Grady. Apparently Suzy checked because she didn't want any counterclaims once she has turned her into a socialist genius. There is some uncertainty over paternity though. Officially it is 'unknown', but on the approximate date of conception both Liams were inside, Stacey was in Benidorm, and Dane is renowned for shooting blanks (he has so far failed to impregnate any one of his forty-three 'lovers'). That just leaves Keanu, who is seven; Kyle, who is going out with Primark Donna, who is notoriously possessive; and Father Finlay, who is eighty, and unlikely to be experiencing an erection at all, let alone putting it anywhere near a twenty-two year old from Harlow.

## Wednesday 28

Grandpa rang. There has been a bike-related incident. James asked if Treena had fallen victim to cycle-unfriendly motorists refusing to allow her sufficient road space in which to perform the tricky left-turn manoeuvre. Grandpa said no, she has sold it to Ducati Mick for £50 and a pirate Stephen Segal DVD.

This is yet another sign that Suzy is doomed to failure. Even if the baby is not an O'Grady, chances are it will grow up liking the shopping channel and consuming several Wagon Wheels a day. James said in that case I am wasting my time trying to ignore my Riley/Clegg roots as it is inevitable I will end up either with a bottle of Cillit Bang welded permanently to my left hand, or Hammeriting my own face.

He is right. My bid to be the first Riley to subscribe to the *Guardian* depends entirely on Harper Janis Obama Stone. I will end my cynicism and do all I can to aid Suzy in her plight. Bar actually changing any nappies, babysitting, or watching *Waybuloo* (it scares me).

## Thursday 29

Mum is consumed with house-moving madness. (Clive and Marjory's, not hers. Her and Dad will never move. Their coffins will be wheeled along the barley-coloured carpet and down the security-gravelled drive.) They have finally got an

offer after months with no sign of interest bar Ying Brewster and the O'Gradys (put off by the neighbours, *quelle* irony). Mum has reasserted her right to veto potential buyers but Marjory says it is too late, they have already accepted the offer. But she has assured her they are model tenants, i.e. in full employment, no children under five, surname with no ideas above its station (Jones), plus the woman has a phobia of dogs so there will be no repeat of the Dog/Fiddy lovechild hoo-hah. (Not that it could as it has no testicles. Although this doesn't prevent it from trying.) Plus Marjory says she is tired of Mum trying to stand in the way of their bid to graze pastures new. Asked what far-flung reaches they were heading to. It is Clancy Court, i.e. one road away, plus they will overlook our back garden, only adding to Mum's security arsenal.

## Friday 30

Am jubilant. According to Mr Vaughan, I AM Juliet, i.e. innocent yet wise beyond her years, with slight other-worldliness about her. Did not tell him my trance-like state was down to Dog Daze, i.e. James's idiotic drug-sniffing dog training programme, which has played havoc with pill packets and what I thought was one of Mum's low-strength aspirins turned out to be prescription-only Co-codamol so spent the entire drama practical exam in a fluffy haze. It is excellent training for next year anyway. All

drama students experiment with drugs, and not just out-of-date painkillers prescribed to old men who should know better than to try to put their entire heads in the mouth of Bruce (Dog's equally moronic offspring). If only Sad Ed had made the same mistake. I fear he may be facing eternity in the Aled Jones-dedicated shrine that is 24 Loompits Road. Or at least another year of resits anyway. His Vicomte de Valmont was utterly disturbing. I think choosing to play him in a state of déshabillé could have been a mistake. Mrs Thomas's dressing gown is not capacious enough to stretch around his generous chest (i.e. moobs). At one point I definitely glimpsed unmentionables, and they will win him no prizes.

5 p.m.

Nor will Uncle Jim's. In fact I think they have sealed his fate on an early departure. He has run out of clothes (Mum is using stealth tactics to flush him out, i.e. refusing to do his washing, buy beer, or tell him the pin code to access BBC3) and has taken to wandering around the house in nothing but ill-fitting pants (he has borrowed James's) and a blanket draped around him. James said he is minded to follow suit, as he has the look of a role-play superhero. Mum said he does not, he has the look of a serial killer, and if James goes near the airing cupboard for an outfit he will be on no biscuits for the next week. I fear this is an inevitability once she discovers the existence of Dog Daze. Which is also an inevitability given the sudden disappearance of Rennies,

calcium tablets, and a tube of Bonjela, and the sudden appearance of multicoloured chalky vomit on the patio.

## *Saturday 31*

Uncle Jim has moved out. He said he cannot sleep in a room with five Glade PlugIns on full power, it is like living in a bar of soap (i.e. Mum's ultimate dream). He has taken his smelly rucksack and worry beads round to 19 Harvey Road, i.e. his new ancestral home. James has given it a week before he is back. He is being generous. There is no way Uncle Jim will be able to withstand Jesus and his destructive tendencies/ moronic questions/obsession with his own penis. Mum is victorious nonetheless. She has already Hoovered in celebration and we have been promised rhubarb crumble for pudding.

I'm RACHEL RILEY
– welcome to my so-called life.

February

Mum is unvictorious. It is because her peace, quiet, and stain-free existence is once again at peril as Scarlet has now moved in! She turned up at the Shreddies table at nine, which is proof of how low conditions at Debden Road have sunk as normally she does not get up until at least midday on a Sunday. She says she cannot be expected to excel in her A levels with all the noise, poo, and endless nakedity. The potty training must have driven her over the edge as the noise and genitals are nothing new in their house. She has played a killer hand though as Mum has been maligning Suzy as a reckless influence for years. I predict she will seize the opportunity to prove her superior child-raising skills, and secure a brace of top flight A levels under her roof.

I said I am surprised Suzy and Bob did not fling themselves down in protest to prevent her from entering a house of norm-embracing Lib-Dem voters. Scarlet said Bob drove her round in the sick-smelling Volvo. He said if it wasn't for his sexual needs he would be joining her. He is mental. Though there is no room anyway as the spare room is out of bounds until Mum has forensically cleaned it. Scarlet is on the camp bed in my room awaiting a certificate of full sanitization (actual certificate, typed and laminated by James and his arsenal of pointless stationery).

## Monday 2

Having Scarlet here is excellent. She knows everything there is to know about politics, philosophy, and penises, plus I now have access to her gothwear, tripling my own paltry wardrobe. Oh how I wish I had an older sister. She could teach me how to do sixties eyeliner, and introduce me to her brilliant and edgy university friends. Instead of trying to persuade me to become a gladiator/mesmerize my breasts into growing, which is what James and Mad Harry tend to do. Why, oh why, did Mum only have two children? All bohemian and interesting types have enormous broods e.g. the Redgraves and the Fiennes.

4 p.m.
Have asked Mum. She says two is a convenient number for entrance to a wide variety of museums, plus the Passat only had two rear seatbelts. She also pointed out that overpopulation was the province of the rich or mad. I did mention the Redgraves but she immediately invoked the O'Gradys and stalked off to the bathroom in a cloud of smugness and drain cleaner.

## Tuesday 3

James says Scarlet is like the sister he never had and has begged her to move in permanently. This is because

she has promised to procure him some of Reuben Tull's 'herbs' for Dog Daze training purposes. Plus she has a tendency to wander around in her underwear. Mum does not know about this. Or about the drugs. Or the fact that she doesn't like Delia Smith. Scarlet is skilled at appearing utterly normal. She says it is the politicians' first rule of assimilation, i.e. to be able to pretend to be sympathetic to any number of interest groups, in Mum's case, the crucial Worcester woman vote. Said Mum had never been to Worcester due to it being too near Wales, and prone to flooding.

## Wednesday 4

There is trouble afoot on the saggy sofa. Today Fat Kylie was enveloped in its stained folds in a state of Mr Whippy-related devastation. Asked if he had been at it again with Leanne Jones (sex tape shaggee, identified by her bouncing buttocks, known to do sexual favours for £2.50 and a chart CD) but apparently it is worse, i.e. he has got himself a new job driving the council's dog poo collection van. Said as the market for semi-melted Nobbly Bobblys and salmonella-laden chemical ice cream is limited to school holidays, Wimbledon week, and the occasional 'Go Crazy' Saturday in May, this is in fact economically astute in the current climate. She said, 'Don't you feckin' swear at me. He's gonna ming and I

ain't shagging someone who stinks of shite.' This is rich given that I know for a fact she has slept with 'Helmet' Higgins and he smells like a drain.

## Thursday 5

Today it is Thin Kylie's turn to be racked with economy-induced loss. The wedding has been called off as Terry (Thin Kylie's stepdad, serial cheater, purveyor of 'comedy' racist accents) says he cannot afford a sit-down lobster dinner for four hundred people, a thirteen-tier cake, or twenty crystal-studded outfits for the 'midgets' (i.e. the crèche inmates). It is a sad state of affairs when even lottery winners cannot find the money to see their daughters down the aisle. It is lucky there are so many gypsies or the bottom would fall out of the gargantuan-meringue-dress market.

## Friday 6

The wedding is back on again. Thin Kylie has agreed to a reduced number of crèche inmates, a finger buffet, and a chocolate profiterole tower. She says she is going to observe behaviour over the next few weeks and pick the most angelic toddlers for the job. She will be waiting a long time. Today seven of them, led by Jesus and Whitney,

joined forces and persuaded the sheep to join circle time. Mr Wilmott said he is astonished that neither Fat Kylie (he did not say 'Fat', though it would not be the first time if he did) nor Mark Lambert managed to see this coming. Mr Wilmott is kidding himself. Mark Lambert was cheering them on from the sidelines and Fat Kylie was waggling the pellets. She is deflecting her Mr Whippy depression into her work, i.e. making it more menacing and idiotic than ever.

### Saturday 7

Suzy has been round to beg Scarlet to return to the (non-dispensing) bosom of her family. Scarlet said she was amazed she had even realized she was gone. Suzy had to admit that she hadn't, it was Edna (non-Filipina Labour-friendly cleaner) who noticed the supply of Waitrose hummus was suspiciously undepleted. Scarlet gave her a withering look and said, 'Point proven.' (She has got that from Mum, who was also giving Suzy several withering looks on grounds of eyeliner, level of cleavage reveal, and the fact that Harper was dribbling on her hygienically clean Shreddies table.) Suzy then tried several tactics, including threats (you will end up wearing sensible shoes and working as a civil servant in Leighton Buzzard), sobbing (Edna is also threatening to leave as Suzy has banned her from smoking Rothmans within a ten metre exclusion zone of the house

so now she has to go and sit in the peace garden every time she wants a cigarette, which is every ten minutes), and her usual trump card, i.e. batting eyelashes in mad Nigella fashion. Scarlet said she was immune to such sneakiness, and the only thing that will lure her back is if Harper is annexed, preferably to the Isle of Man, or if not to the basement. Suzy said she can't as the basement is still being used to host climax classes for the over-sixties and it could contaminate Harper's innocent mind. Scarlet pointed out that this had never stopped Suzy before (Scarlet had seen an astonishing number of naked geriatrics by the age of ten). And Mum said Harper did not come across as entirely innocent. (It is the O'Grady stare again. She has the guilty look of someone who has just joyridden a Datsun or robbed a post office.) Suzy left in a fury. Albeit a weary one.

## Sunday 8

It is Mum's turn to be weary. She has foolishly agreed to stage an all-Riley Sunday lunch, i.e. us, Grandpa, Treena, Uncle Jim, and Jesus Harvey Nichols. James said this capitulation was clearly a sign of early-onset Alzheimer's and made her recite all the kings and queens starting from Ethelred (she scored one hundred per cent, though there was some disagreement over whether or not the Prince Regent counted). She says it is not Alzheimer's, it

is that Grandpa said he is feeling permanently peaky and he may be on the way out. He is not. He is just suffering malnutrition from permanently living on a diet of toast and microwave noodles. Treena has yet to master turning on the oven to the correct temperature, let alone actually cooking anything in it. Scarlet is the only person who is looking forward to it. She says it will be a joy to see the intergenerational interaction of a family that cares for all its children. She will be disappointed. There is bound to be a row about *Casualty*, and several people will have been banished to their rooms before pudding is served.

4 p.m.
Result: one spilling (me), one argument (Treena and Mum: are elves the same as leprechauns? Answer: no. Victor: Mum), and three banishings:

1 Grandpa (for giving his broccoli to the dog).
2 James (for giving his Sanatogen tablet to the dog).
3 Scarlet for using the word 'labia'.

Scarlet is jubilant. She says it is a breath of fresh air to actually be punished for once, instead of being subjected to Bob and Suzy's laissez-faire attitude to everything. I give her a week before she is begging to be allowed to drink wine and name genitals.

I note that Treena is remarkably rejuvenated despite having given up her mountain biking dream. It must be having Uncle Jim, i.e. someone vaguely her own age, around. They can discuss the music and fashions of their youths, as opposed to her rolling her eyes when Grandpa witters on about Vera Lynn.

### Monday 9

James has fallen prey to the perils of fashion. He came home begging for a pair of skinny jeans (only several years too late). Mad Harry has finally procured a pair and James fears he will be left behind in the Wendy Shoebridge stakes. Have told Mum that she cannot give in under any circumstances. I had to wait two years for a pair of Converse and anything less would be favouritism of the kind displayed by Suzy. (This is an excellent ploy as Mum will do anything not to appear like Suzy. Not that this is difficult. In fact trying to be anything like her would be a task of epic proportions.)

### Tuesday 10

I fear Scarlet will soon be the object of James's affections over Wendy Shoebridge. Not only has she got bigger breasts and a history of believing in mythical creatures, but she is backing him in his skinny jeans campaign. She has told Mum that denying him this one small item could send him spiralling into all sorts of anti-social behaviour or teen torpor. Mum looked visibly shaken. She is anti-anti-social

behaviour of all kinds. Particularly if it involves dressing like a goth.

## Wednesday 11

A travesty has occurred. James has procured his holy grail, i.e. he has got a pair of skinny jeans. He was proudly displaying them at the mathlete table at lunch. There were audible gasps and nods of approval. It is pathetic. I said I would be voicing my outrage to Mum the minute I got home but James said it will be a wasted breath as she did not purchase them. He swapped them with Kyle O'Grady for his science GCSE homework, after positive intervention from his old gang leader Keanu. Said this kind of geeksploitation was the beginning of a slippery slope, and he will be being forced to write A level coursework with menaces if he is not careful. But James said, *au contraire*, he welcomes using his intellect for monetary gain and hobbled off in the direction of the toilets to get changed back into his uniform. He managed ten steps before tripping over. He is a moron. Kyle is at least a foot taller than him. Though on that subject, there is no way Kyle would wear skinny jeans. He is more an 'enormous trousers halfway down your bum and reverse baseball cap' kind of boy/idiot. I fear James may in fact be sporting goods that are stolen, as well as laughable.

The skinny jeans are quarantined pending further investigation. Mum says he can have them back when, and only when, he can prove they are not the result of opportunistic looting or shady black-market dealings. James said this attitude was throwing his entire love life into jeopardy. He is more of a moron than I thought. Surely he knows by now that this sort of comment will only fuel Mum's determination to curtail his activities.

Plus ewwwww. He is only eleven for God's sake. I didn't even know what love was at that age. I blame Scarlet for contaminating my innocence. And James's. Her presence is only fuelling his interest in all matters pants-based.

*Friday 13*

Last day of school
Scarlet is mad with anticipation. According to fifties throwback David Smith, Electric Knob are back off tour (result: no record deal and a large dent in the van where they crashed into some marauding heavy metal fans), which means Barney Smith-Watson is back on Peaslands Road in his not-at-all Rastafarian three-bed semi. Asked her how she planned to persuade him of his destiny and she said, 'In traditional Stone manner,' i.e. by throwing an ironic anti-Valentine's Day party, and getting him drunk on love,

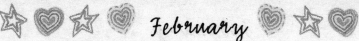 

and Waitrose vodka. Said the chances of any of this being allowed in the House of Riley were nil, as well she knows, but Scarlet said she has already paved the way with a few rudimentary enquiries, and it turns out that Mum and Dad will be next door at Clive and Marjory's for their Leaving Summerdale Road Farewell Jenga Party, and James can be won over with a flash of her pants so it is all set for eight o'clock.

## Saturday 14
*Valentine's Day*

No cards. *Quelle* surprise. I do not care though; I eschew tokens of love from anyone within the confines of the CB11 postcode. Unlike James, who is welcoming unprecedented levels of local interest. He got twelve cards, including one from Paris-Marie O'Grady (telltale use of hearts dotting 'i's, i.e. banned in this house) and one from Mumtaz (no hearts, but unmistakeable use of a Pilot G2, the pen of choice for mathletes). He said the ladies are obviously swayed by his skinny-jeaned sensuality, and used the fact that Paris-Marie's was addressed to 'Mr Lover Lover' as evidence. I said it was only proof that Paris-Marie is a moron, and Mumtaz has not learned from her past mistakes, besides which the jeans are still in the airing cupboard pending proof of purchase from Kyle. But James said in fact, under Scarlet's guidance, he liberated the jeans for his spelling bee last night, so who

is laughing now? I said no one, particularly given that that sentence involved the words 'spelling bee', but that he was playing with fire, as was Scarlet, and it was only fair of me to give him sisterly warning of this. He said he fears nothing, and in fact has invited Mumtaz round later to 'sample his wares', and he will be wearing the skinny jeans for the sampling.

This is unbearable. I am caught in the middle of James's web of lies, plus am fast becoming the hopelessly neglected middle child. This is typical. As if my life was not tedious enough.

At least Sad Ed is back to being depressed. It is the pressure of tonight's snog-off. He is convinced that Scarlet will be so determined to win Barney that she will overlook any evidence that he is not her Batman destiny. I said there is always a chance that Barney will rebuff Scarlet's advances, but Sad Ed said this is an impossibility as any man would be lucky to have her. James agreed. He says she is a goddess amongst women (clearly he has seen the bra, if not more). Left before I could work out the weirdness of being cross that your eleven-year-old brother finds your best friend more alluring than you.

12 p.m.

I take everything back. Tonight's party has been a resounding success. If you judge success by lack of stains/breakages/ playing of anything resembling R'n'B (which in my current precarious position I do). Or if you are Sad Ed, by finally proving to Scarlet once and for all that he is the loin-stirring mystery Batman. He was right that Barney did not counter

Scarlet's offer of an experimental snog, but it would seem that her pelvis is more prescient than I had credited it for, as she immediately recoiled and dispatched him and his idiotic entourage back down to Electric Knob headquarters, i.e. his garage. Sad Ed then actually did some *carpe diem*ing, which is also utterly out of character as the only thing he usually seizes is the last Malteser, and demanded that she test the glass slipper on his humble foot (he is reviving his quest to be poetic in everyday situations). Then there was some confusion over slippers and toe sucking, which I will not go into, but suffice it to say that the eventual snog was a resounding success.

James is also jubilant, as he has touched Mumtaz's right buttock (over seven layers of clothing and admittedly by accident). I said Wendy would not be best pleased with this progression but he said, 'When the cat's away (i.e. in Porthelli for a week), the dog will play.' Which is wrong on so many levels, but could not get cross because it turns out he is a more useful presence at parties than I imagined. Not only is he lightning-like in his slipping of coasters under drinks, but he can remove Diet Coke stains with absolutely no trace of spillage. Mum did not even question the fact that he was wearing no trousers when her and Dad got back from next door (skinny jeans took so long to remove he had no time to locate sensible replacements). Though this was possibly aided by the fact that she had gone crazy and consumed a small sherry to toast Clive and Marjory's new life (round the corner).

On the downside, her new caution-to-the-wind attitude has extended to letting Sad Ed sleep over, which under normal circumstances is fairly irritating due to his snoring/ tendency to get up at 2 a.m. for a 'snack', i.e. ten slices of toast, but now I have to listen to him and Scarlet feeling each other's buttocks (under all layers) and telling each other they are the loves of their lives. As if. They will have split up by Tuesday and Scarlet will be back mooning over Trevor and his bat cape.

Their pathetic union only reinforces my belief in the futility of high-school sweethearts. Which is why I am never snogging someone from Saffron Walden again. My sights are set on a higher prize, i.e. London, and its superior literary and edgy youth.

## Sunday 15

There is a new boy next door. He is approximately eighteen, and is wearing a faux fur jacket, tight pink Levi's, and limited edition Converse. More importantly, according to the goods being carried in/fought by removal men, he owns a cat (essential disdainful pet of choice for all intellectuals), a guitar, and a book of Marilyn Monroe prints. I think I might love him. Scarlet says I do not. She saw me eyeing him through the curtains and says she knows exactly what I am thinking and no he is not poetic and quite possibly misunderstood. He is, I can tell. Plus he has moved from London, i.e. he is worldly, so is

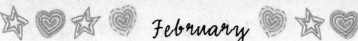 

not even out of bounds. Which is something Scarlet should be considering instead of groping Sad Ed on every available soft furnishing. He has still not gone home. It is only lucky Mum and Dad have gone to the garden centre to buy creosote and a slug drowner or she would be having a word about potential stain issues/teen pregnancy (in that order). As it is, the dog is very put out. It cannot watch *Hollyoaks* in peace without the sound of Sad Ed's exertions. (He is very unfit. He has to come up for air after ten seconds of snogging.)

## Monday 16

The new cat is sitting on the fence eyeing our patio with utter disdain. I do not blame it. It is depressingly suburban. Though by rights it should also be giving its own new garden some withering glances (crimes: hydrangeas, crazy paving, and ornamental pond).

I wish I had a cat. They are clever, and slightly evil. Unlike dogs, who are entirely unliterary.

I bet Sylvia Plath had a cat. Am going to ask Mum if I can get one.

## Tuesday 17

Mum says under no circumstances are James or I allowed any more pets. It is after the ninja frog hoo-hah (i.e. when

they kept escaping and then got smuggled to France and eaten by the death chicken. Which we then ate. Which still bothers me.) She said if and when the dog dies then she may consider a clean caged animal, e.g. a gerbil. I can tell she is hoping this is soon as the dog has now clocked up three shoutings and a banishment to the shed in the space of twenty-four hours. It is another one who does not learn from its past mistakes, i.e. do NOT eat carpet or you will live to regret it.

On the plus side, Sad Ed has gone home for clean pants and some sleep. (He has only managed five hours in the last three days, partly due to Scarlet's demands, partly due to the fact that his head is wedged under a chest of drawers. He is not the only one. I am being forced to wear earplugs and an eye mask, and it is not even a glamorous *Breakfast at Tiffanys* one, it is a standard-issue British Airways one, which was my present when the Cleggs unadvisedly went to Florida.) Scarlet claims she is not minded as she is her own woman, and does not need affirmation of her existence from a man, not even her ONE.

She is faking it though, I can tell. She has already eaten two Wispas and agreed to watch a Jennifer Aniston film, which is utterly transparent. Even militant feminists are powerless in the grip of true love. Even if the grip is the bingo-winged grasp of a gloom-mongering Bontempi organ player.

I bet the boy next door has shapely upper arms. He is too busy thinking about Yeats to bother with food.

The cat has pooed on our patio. I was watching the boy next door have a cigarette out of his bedroom window (yet another sign he is edgy, i.e. he is going against authority, medical advice, and all common sense), and witnessed the travesty in all its glory. It did not even bother to cover it up. Obviously it does not know Mum, or her arsenal of cat-countering weaponry (hose/squeegee bottles/shrieking). That or it is made of sterner stuff. It is a London cat after all. It is probably used to getting kicked by lawless youth. Though I suspect even they might balk at Mum.

Have scooped poo up with the smelly Bob the Builder spade to save the cat a shouting. Plus I do not want her ruining my reputation as edgy and urban by her confronting the Joneses with her five-point anti-poo plan. Luckily she is out anyway. She is ferrying James, Mumtaz, and the dog to Wandlebury woods. She thinks they are going to identify fungi. They are not, they are going to sniff for heroin near the A11. I do not envy James if Mr Mumtaz finds out. He was less than tolerant the time she got a bikini-clad Barbie, so he is hardly going to embrace drug-hunting. I suspect Wendy and Mad Harry will have something to say as well. James says there is no chance of either of them finding out as Wales is notoriously tricky when it comes to mobile communications plus Mad Harry is grounded for a week for applying to *Masterchef* under a false name.

What Mumtaz or Wendy sees in either of them is a mystery, but it is definitely not raw animal allure.

## Thursday 19

James has been found out. Wendy called him from a phone box this morning (how very retro). Apparently she got it off Douglas Pole (diabetic), who got it off Archie Knox (son of hairy librarian), who got it off Kyle O'Grady, who got it off Stacey O'Grady, who was busy 'burying something' in the woods. (Possibly another O'Grady. Though if it is one of the Liams I suspect this will just ease complications.) She has issued an ultimatum: he must choose between her and Mumtaz once and for all. I said this was utterly devastating. James said it is not, because the loser goes to Mad Harry so it is win-win all round. I suggested Mad Harry might like a say in this, but James says he will not mind getting the spoils. He knows his place.

Also Sad Ed is back and is fully revived, loins-wise, so am vacating the bedroom area for at least four hours. Was going to do some casual lurking next door but according to James they boarded the Toyota Prius at 8.43 a.m., in the midst of a row about whether inglenooks are ironic or criminal (I fear he may also be reviving Beastly Investigations, his crap wildlife-related detective agency. That or he is auditioning to join Mum in Neighbourhood Watch (aka The Paranoid

Army). Asked if the boy was also involved in said inglenook row (would not blame him if he was, they are hideous things, even Mum agrees), but James said no, he was slumped in the back seat looking bored. Which is just further confirmation of his worldliness and suitability.

Am going round to Scarlet's instead. She has dispatched me to fetch her biography of Maynard Keynes and her best black pants.

**5 p.m.**
Have procured items, but it was not as simple a mission as had thought. Suzy is in revenge mode and tried to persuade me to move in to replace Scarlet. Said it is a kind offer (it is not), and I would really love to (I would not), it is just that I am needed at home for dog-minding duties. (I am not, as James has taken it round to Mumtaz's as part of his suitability testing, though what this might involve is frankly terrifying, but it is all I could think of as at that point Jack came into the kitchen dressed only in his boxer shorts. Apparently he had a late night 'jamming'. He is thinking of getting the band back together, i.e. the Jack Stone Five, only with a new name and line-up. I just nodded and smiled idiotically as was temporarily mesmerized by his nipples.) Then left before could say anything idiotic. Or witness anything idiotic, e.g. Suzy and her potty-training mania, of which evidence was everywhere, and none of it in the potty.

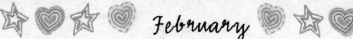 

10 p.m.

Am worried about this afternoon's nipple transfixion, i.e. am I still attracted to Jack's shapely, if not at all worldly chest? Or would I have been equally stupefied by the nipples of Pelvis Presley, i.e. it is nipples in general, rather than their owner, that I am interested in. Though not sure which is worse.

11 p.m.

I wonder what the boy next door's nipples are like?

## *Friday 20*

11 a.m.

Right. Cannot stand it any longer. Am going next door. It is my duty as a neighbour to introduce myself and welcome all occupants, particularly poetic ones, to the community. (Mum has singularly failed to do so. She is suspicious of the fact that there is a *Guardian* on the front seat of the Prius and thinks Marjory may have been exaggerating their suitability.) Plus I can bear Scarlet and Sad Ed's couplings no longer. I cannot even read Hamlet without being subjected to giggling/heavy breathing/hawking up of Smints. (The last one is the dog. James has been stepping up Dog Daze as it is the school holidays. He is hoping to have located his first major drugs haul by the end of the week.)

12.30 p.m.

Have gleaned the following information:

1 His name is Oscar Jones (i.e. he too has grown up with the pain of a run-of-the-mill name, i.e. Jones. Although to be fair Oscar is not that normal, and anyway he goes by the name 'Wilde').

2 His parents are both called Dr Jones and they are psychotherapists (i.e. utterly edgy and potential parents-in-law material).

3 His cat is called Nietzsche (i.e. he shares my philosophical leanings, which are still present despite being banned from AS by hairy Mr Knox).

4 He is not going to John Major High (disappointingly), he is going to a crammer in Cambridge to do his resits (i.e. he was too busy writing tortured Haikus to concentrate on history).

So Scarlet was wrong and he is completely poetic and utterly misunderstood. Hurrah! I am utterly renewed in my lust for life (all kinds) and predict that Wilde and I will soon be united in our torment as outcasts and misfits, in a brain- and pants-based way. Though not until at least next week as he is going back to London this afternoon to see someone called Olaf and he won't be back until Sunday night. It is clear I would make an excellent prosecution barrister/ hard-nosed journalist/interrogator at an internment camp. I have inherited Mum's Paxman-like interview technique (hopefully that is all I have inherited as I do not want her thighs, nose, or obsession with cleaning).

In other news, James has made his choice and Mumtaz wins in all categories (did not ask what the categories were for fear of brain being irreparably sullied, but am pretty sure one of them involved ability to suck Rice Krispies up with a straw). Said surely Mumtaz is horrified at being such a pawn in his giant game of love chess. He said on the contrary, she is jubilant at having beaten someone from Year Nine, who has twenty-seven guide badges, including 'Party Planner', and the notoriously tricky (and subject of a complaint letter from Mum) 'Chocolate'. He is going to break the news to Wendy and Mad Harry on Monday. Said why not now. He said in case Mumtaz fails the practical in which case he will exercise his right to switch. Did not ask what the practical was either. It is bound to be more hideous than anything I can imagine. And I am already imagining some fairly repulsive scenarios, including the involvement of the dog, and use of pugil sticks.

### Saturday 21

Jack is definitely reviving the Jack Stone Five. The Duke was awash with excitement. Reuben Tull says it is like when 'The Zep' got back together. It is not. They did not have someone on bass purely on the grounds their dad drives a fish delivery van. Reuben is thinking of auditioning (Theremin), as is Sad Ed (Bontempi and triangle). I asked Jack if he had anyone for lead vocals yet and he said he

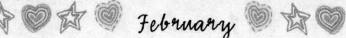
may have to do it himself and get Dean 'the dwarf' Denley on drums. I said I might know someone, i.e. Wilde the new boy next door (do not know if he can definitely sing but he owns a guitar and looks a bit like a young David Bowie and that is the important bit). Jack said, 'Are you up to your old tricks, Riley?' Said no. He said, 'Fine. Send him round Friday after school then.' I said he is not at school, he is at crammer, i.e. utterly more musician-like. Jack rolled his eyes and whatevered me. He is so suburban. Unlike Wilde, who is so hip I actually think I might faint when I look at him.

10 p.m.

What does he mean 'old tricks'? If he is implying that I am falling for someone purely by dint of them having excellent hair and mental clothes, then he is sorely mistaken. There is more between me and Wilde than that, for example our appreciation of Maybelline Ultra-Lash mascara, and I shall completely prove it to him by being even more utterly in love than he is with Maya. Although Scarlet says anyone who calls themself 'Wilde' is harbouring a serious identity crisis. Said this is impossible as both his parents are psychotherapists and would have identified and cured it by now. Besides, she is just sulking because there is no way Sad Ed could get away with leopard-print leggings and diamante-studded fly sunglasses.

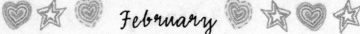

## Sunday 22

There has been disturbing news from Cornwall. Granny Clegg is getting a mobility scooter. Apparently her hip (not the replacement for the allegedly fortune-predicting hip of doom, but the other one) is a bit gyppy and she is having trouble traipsing up to the Spar to get her supply of processed foods. Said couldn't Grandpa Clegg just go instead but apparently Maureen Penrice is still not speaking to him since he, Pig, and Denzil boycotted the olives display at the peak of their Cornish independence mania. Mum said it cannot end well as the last vehicle she 'drove' was a bumper car at Newquay and she managed to escape from the arena in that. Dad says she will be arrested or dead within a week. Though I am not sure he thinks this is necessarily a bad thing.

## Monday 23

The news of James and Mumtaz's renewed alliance has rocked the mathletes table. Mad Harry has not been as gracious as predicted and is threatening to defect to Asian Entrepreneurs, taking Douglas Pole and Hugh Potts-Willets with him. James says it is a hollow threat as Ali Hassan (head mathlete) is also head Asian and will not admit anyone who has dissed a 'woman of colour', i.e. Mumtaz.

Sad Ed and Scarlet's union is not going down as joyously as hoped either. Goth Corner is up in arms about admitting someone who once bought an Adele CD. Scarlet has allayed fears by signing an agreement that he will not try to sit in the Throne of Magnificence, unless Scarlet is on his lap, and that at no point will he zoom around in it, not even to get a chip. There is no chance of this anyway; if he did try to zoom anywhere the wheels would fall off. As it is, it is looking perilous with both of them jammed into it.

Mr Wilmott is not looking best pleased either. He thought he had stymied her political ambition by appointing Sad Ed and Thin Kylie as Head Boy and Girl but now she has snuck in by the back door.

Thin Kylie said Scarlet had better not use her new position to try to usurp any of her powers (she did not say 'usurp', she said 'obliminate', which is not even a word). Scarlet said if by 'powers' she meant deciding which object to microwave next in the hope of a minor explosion then she had better things to do. Thin Kylie then immediately tried to assert herself by decreeing a ban on anyone with purple highlights sitting on the saggy sofa. Sad Ed retaliated with a ban on anyone with skin darker than pale pine on the Cuprinol scale (exceptions for actual 'women of colour', as opposed to women of St Tropez and Fake Bake) from standing on the carpet. Which then elicited a ban on anyone with moobs talking unless it is to sing classic R'n'B. Which resulted in a chorus of 'I Wanna Dance with Somebody' from Sad Ed and ended with a ban on banning from Mr

Wilmott because the noise was putting Mrs Leech off her custard creams, plus none of the Retards and Criminals had bothered to turn up to the crèche to supervise the inmates and several of them were wandering up C corridor armed with squeezy paint bottles.

I predict this is not the end of it though. Scarlet and Sad Ed's love has opened up the whole common room conflict again, and I fear the blue carpet could once again become the Gaza Strip, under constant shelling from green Skittles (inferior flavour) and orange Revels (again, inferior, though annoyingly hard to detect).

Am glad Wilde was not here to witness this shameful turn of events. This would never happen at a crammer. They are all too busy drinking black coffee and arguing about existentialism. I will prove my worldliness by refusing to partake in such pathetically small-town disagreements.

## Tuesday 24
*Shrove Tuesday*

Have been sent to Mr Wilmott. It is for hitting Fat Kylie on the forehead with a Flump. I pointed out that the very nature of Flumps mean they are mere symbolic weapons, as opposed to the Bountys being hurled by Mark Lambert and his idiotic minions, but Mr Wilmott said symbolic or not, I should be ashamed of myself. I said I was, and it was all Scarlet's fault for brainwashing me into fighting by claiming

she heard Fat Kylie say I had 'gay hair'. She is totally evil-dictatorish. Mr Wilmott agreed.

I was a fool for aiming at Fat Kylie though. She was already imbued with anger at the Mr Whippy poo-monitor debacle, and now she has an oblong pale patch where the Flump adhered to her orange foundation. I fear this is only the beginning of a long and arduous war.

## Wednesday 25

Fat Kylie has revealed her weapon of choice. It is Baby Jesus. He called me a 'mentalist' when I went to pick him up from the crèche (Grandpa and Treena were taking Uncle Jim on a day trip to Beckton Alps dry ski slope—the closest thing East Anglia has to a Himalaya). I used Mum's well-practised tactic of 'sticks and stones might break my bones but words will never hurt me'. Only he then hit me on the shin with a hobby horse.

Also, Mr Wandering Hands has put me in for my theory test. I said I hoped that trying to learn the tricky flying motorbike sign would not compromise my A levels and future shining academic career, but he said the revision will be good practice, plus he thought I was doing Drama anyway. Did not deign to reply. He is a heathen. He owns a Phil Collins CD for God's sake.

So far today I have been sprayed with Vimto (Fat Kylie) and weed on (Jesus). Have begged Scarlet to end this horror by conceding that a fake tan does not limit your IQ in any way, but she said their childish reactions only go to prove her point. She is resolute in wresting power from the mahoganied masses. Sad Ed is no help either. He says the sight of Scarlet in battle mode is completely invigorating and he is happy to play Prince Philip to her Queen. He is a moron. There is nothing good about being Prince Philip.

Am going to rise above it by going next door to tell Wilde about the jamming session at Jack's tomorrow. And hopefully get myself flung against the black painted walls of his bedroom in a fit of highbrow Byronic passion.

7 p.m.

Have not been flung anywhere. It is Marjory's fault. The bedroom is still a pale lavender sprig print, which is less than inspiring. Plus Saffron Walden and its repressive tendencies are hampering Wilde's creative juices as well as his sexual ones. He said the Jack Stone Five sounds a bit 'backwoods' and he was hoping for something more ambitious, preferably with a touch of *Torch Song* about it. I said he is right, it is all completely suburban, but he must think of it as a diversion from the 'rents' (note use of slang gleaned from Channel 4) until we can get back

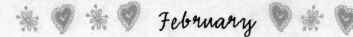 

to the mean streets of Whitechapel. He said, 'Have you ever been to Whitechapel, doll face?' Said no, but I have watched *Eastenders* so it is almost the same. Or would have, if had not been rendered partially speechless by fact he called me doll face. It is clear he has me in his enormous fly-sunglassed sights.

Think have persuaded him though, as promised him an extensive drinks cabinet, with no restrictions due to Suzy's preoccupation with Harper (though she was never that bothered before the baby anyway), potential drugs (Reuben is going), plus remembered that Jack does do a song about a broken Maglite.

## Friday 27

Hurrah, it is audition day! Not that I am auditioning, but rather am like David Bailey, pimping out my discovery to *Vogue*. Wilde is my Twiggy.

7 p.m.
Jack says Wilde is not Twiggy and I am not David Bailey. But that he can have the job given that he can hit a top C, plus the only other auditionee was fifties throwback David Smith and he has a lisp and a 9 p.m. curfew. Can tell that Jack was secretly impressed though. And so he should be. Wilde has a voice like Mariah Carey (which is odd given that he is a boy). Am jubilant.

The Drs Jones are similarly pleased, albeit in a scarily technical way. The female one (red lipstick, intimidating bob, media glasses) said, 'Integration in a very real sense is the first step in assimilation into community norms and values.' The male one (complicated facial hair arrangement) nodded and said, 'Riiiiight, riiiiight.' Wilde was unimpressed. He just said, 'Insightful analysis, Gloria, dear,' and stalked upstairs with a bottle of Chablis from the Smeg fridge. He is even more rebellious than I thought. Hurrah!

Was tempted to follow him, but do not want to arouse Mum's suspicions yet by coming home drunk and debauched. Plus had promised Scarlet I would cover for her and Sad Ed by offering to play Mum and Dad at Jenga. Will see him tomorrow night at the Duke anyway. He has agreed to test out the wobbly table for size and suitability.

11 p.m.

This deception cannot go on much longer. Have developed Jenga 'claw' and a slightly mad stare from trying to look gripped by *Casualty* despite audible panting from my bedroom. Told Mum Sad Ed has taken up Pilates. Is totally plausible as he tried yoga for half an hour once, only it caused excess wind release and he was banned from the Bernard Evans Youth Centre and any of Barbara Marsh's classes (Weightwatchers, Zumba for the Over-forties, Flower Arranging for Beginners).

## Saturday 28

Dad's birthday. Got him a set of golf balls and a card featuring Jeremy Clarkson and a rude joke. He is easily pleased, unlike Mum, for whom present and card shopping comes with a hefty list of proscribed items and shops, and a severe stare for anyone who breaks them by buying a new and untested variety of chocolate/substandard cleaning items/anything displaying a whimsical kitten. He and Mum are having a celebratory family dinner tonight. James is attending with Mumtaz. Have declined invitation on the grounds that I have community work to do (i.e. am introducing Wilde to the eclectic regulars at the Duke) plus cannot feasibly consume claggy vegetarian mince whilst James is whispering geek nothings to Mumtaz. It is bad enough that Goth Corner and the mathletes table are in such close proximity at school. Weirdly, Scarlet and Ed have accepted. Mum says she is delighted to have two additions to the table who appreciate good home cooking and stimulating conversation. This is overegging it. Sad Ed just appreciates food, and Scarlet just appreciates Sad Ed. Though on the plus side, if they are busy arguing about traffic bollards, they are not doing anything untoward.

11.30 p.m.

I was wrong. They used the post-dinner community session of watching *Doctor Who* whilst eating a monitored number of Elizabeth Shaw mints to sneak upstairs for some heavy

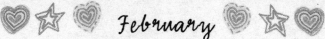 

petting. The alarm was raised when James noticed that the dog had consumed, and then regurgitated, Sad Ed's allocation of three. Mum burst in on them in the middle of an act that no one will now discuss. In their defence, I said it must be true love if Sad Ed would rather grope Scarlet than eat chocolate. But Mum is unmoved. Sad Ed has been sent home and Scarlet is in the dining room reflecting on her ways (i.e. sexting Sad Ed).

On the plus side, I had an excellent evening at the Duke. Though Jack spoilt the atmosphere slightly by refusing to serve Wilde a ninth cosmopolitan. Wilde pointed out that all musicians were renowned alcoholics, and as a fellow band member he should be encouraging his vices. Jack said, *au contraire*, it was perfectly possible to be a musical genius and remain sober. Plus he is not fellow band member, he is main band member.

He is so small-town. Cannot believe I was ever in love with him. Wilde is far more my type. When he was sick and a bit of it went on my trainers, I felt like Nancy Spungen to his Sid Vicious. We are made for each other. Or at least we will be when I am eighteen and Jack actually lets me purchase alcohol.

I'm RACHEL RILEY
– welcome to my so-called life.

*March*

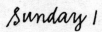 *March*

## Sunday 1

Scarlet has moved back to Bob and Suzy's. She was utterly philosophical about it, i.e. she said all golden epochs must come to an end, but that the forced separation and return to the baby-infested hell of Debden Road will only fan the flames of their ardour. Plus as Head Boy, Sad Ed gets first dibs on the saggy sofa so they will be making full use of that during free periods.

Mum was not so philosophical. She said Scarlet is living proof that a left-wing laissez-faire upbringing only leads to teen pregnancy and venereal disease. James said in which case it is an excellent job creation scheme, given Suzy's employment as a sex therapist and Bob's as an abortionist. At which point he got sent to his room to reflect on the perils of underage sex/ his idiocy. I fear he may be just going to reflect on Mumtaz.

## Monday 2

There has been a brief suspension of the ongoing common room conflict. Partly due to Mrs Leech's failure to restock the vending machine with missiles over the weekend, but mainly due to all troops being distracted by the spectacle that is Scarlet and Sad Ed's saggy sofa snogging. Scarlet (still being philosophical) says it is like the Christmas Day armistice in the trenches, with love instead of football bringing the factions together in no-man's land. It is not, it is pure horror at their

ability to lock lips for thirty-five minutes without coming up for air. Not even Fat Kylie can go that long. Though her breaks are more usually for a Screwball or a 99.

## Tuesday 3

4 p.m.
There has been distressing/moronic mobility-scooter-related news from Cornwall. Granny Clegg has somehow lost control of the vehicle (though whether she was fully in control in the first place has not been established) and was last seen heading towards the Redruth trading estate screaming, 'Save me, Norman, save me!' Grandpa Clegg is demanding that Dad drives down immediately to assist in the search and rescue party (i.e. him, Pig, and Denzil). Mum said can't he just call PC Penrice (brother of Maureen), but apparently he is refusing to answer any more 'emergency' calls from Belleview (previously Pasty Manor) after two callouts last week, one when Bruce got jammed in the front gate, and one when Grandpa couldn't work out how to turn off the radio. Mum said if Granny is still missing by the start of *The One Show* (current favourite viewing at Belleview) then she will dispatch back-up, i.e. Dad and the dog.

5.30 p.m.
Dad says there is no way he is driving to Cornwall to rescue a joyriding moron from her own inability to use a brake lever.

(He actually said moron. Interestingly, Mum did not correct him.) James got a bit upset and said what if she careers off a cliff and plummets to her death on the rocks. Dad says the chances of her navigating within a mile of the coast are nil and he gives it an hour before her battery runs out.

6.30 p.m.

Granny Clegg has been found alive and well. She was not speared on the rocks at Chapel Porth, but circling a mini roundabout outside Pengoon Plastics (for all your hygienic cladding needs). Mr Pengoon called Grandpa who rode to the rescue on Pig's tractor. I asked if Grandpa had heroically jumped in front of the runaway scooter. He said no, he waited until the battery ran out. I said this was hardly knight-in-shining-armour material, but Grandpa said his back is giving him right gyp, and anyway, it was only twenty minutes and Chips McArdle's mobile burger van was there so they just had a cup of tea and a bacon sandwich while they waited. Granny had one too. Apparently they took it in turns aiming it at her. (Sandwich, not cup of tea. Even Pig is not that mental.) But Granny Clegg's brush with driving is at an end. She says it is all too new-fangled for her, and the mobility scooter is being sent back whence it came (Truro). Asked how they will shop for essentials (Spam, Instant Whip, cling peaches) now their vehicle-owning days are at an end. Grandpa said, *au contraire* (actually he didn't, as he doesn't speak, or believe in French, he said 'aaackshully'), the whole episode has revived not only his love for Granny Clegg (ick), but his determination to get

behind the wheel once more (aagh). Apparently Denzil has had an unsellable motorhome sat on the forecourt of the Crazy Car Warehouse for eighteen months and he has offered it to them for the cut-price deal of £1,000 and a rent-free stay in Belleview while they are living their dream of freedom on the open highway. Asked which open highway they had in mind, and for how long. Grandpa said the A303, for at least a month. Mum immediately commandeered the phone to dissuade them of this insane plan, citing age, inability to drive, and tendency to get lost anywhere outside a five-mile radius of St Slaughter. (It is not that, it is that Grandpa is notoriously racist, and she fears there will be some kind of lynching as soon as he gets near London.) Grandpa said she need not worry as he has found his driving licence (issued 1951, not used since 1953), and, besides, he will be heading straight to Saffron Walden to park up at Summerdale Road and she need not worry about a spare room as they can bed down in the van and use the chemical toilet. Needless to say Mum is now filling our own downstairs toilet with chemicals in a bid to block out the horror. I am minded to join her. Their idiotic inbred ways will do nothing to persuade Wilde of my worldly credentials.

## Wednesday 4

Why do I not have the kind of grandparents who live in penthouse apartments in Kensington and foist expensive first editions of

Proust on me, before taking me out to dinner with Bill Nighy? In fact, why am I not related to Bill Nighy? Instead am cursed with the kind of morons who get bested by an electric tricycle, or marry their Benson & Hedges-addicted care worker.

Got an emergency text at school to collect Jesus from crèche (today's Fat Kylie-induced insult: 'You is weird and got man hands.') and deliver him back to 19 Harvey Road as Grandpa Riley is 'incapacitated'. Feared this might mean some hideous sex-related injury, or contortion (it would not be the first time), but it turns out he is lying on the sofa sipping home-made blackberry cordial, feeling weak and peaky. I said it is probably the flu, which is going through John Major High staff like wildfire (Mr Vaughan and Miss Mustard—lab assistant, not Cluedo card—both off for three days now), but Grandpa says it is not a virus, it is hemlock, because Treena is poisoning him so she can marry a younger model, i.e. Uncle Jim. I said he had been watching too much *Doctors* again (last month he thought he might have contracted sleeping sickness from a weekend in Benidorm in the eighties) but he insists she has been acting suspiciously for weeks. Asked where she, and indeed Uncle Jim, were. He said they were out buying Wotsits and Carlsberg at the Spar.

## Thursday 5

If it is not one relative it is another. Today it is the dog's turn to lie on the sofa looking weak and peaky (though it

is not sipping blackberry cordial, home-made or otherwise, due to ongoing ban on grounds of stain issues). Grandpa says it is in sympathy with his own plight, like a phantom pregnancy (phenomena also discovered on *Doctors*, his source of medical and most other information). It is not, it is cat-related, i.e. it is being menaced by Nietzsche. It stalks up and down the fence with a superior air, then watches with a look of definite gloating when the dog knocks itself out on the concrete gatepost every time it hurls itself in Nietzsche's general direction. James said this is shameful and the equivalent of being beaten up by a girl. Pointed out his inherent sexism, and also that this had happened to him on no less than two occasions in the past. He said exactly, so he knows the dog's pain.

## *Friday 6*

The common room war is very much back on. It is Scarlet and Sad Ed's fault. Their endless (and weighty) couplings have finally broken the saggy sofa. Thin Kylie actually welled up as Mr Wilmott and Lou (caretaker, former Criminal and Retard, once ate the school rabbit) carried it out ceremoniously (after extracting Scarlet from its inner folds). It is the Yazoo stain, caused during one of her own illicit liaisons during a lower school disco. Her husband-to-be was not so moved. It is because he knows full well that the Yazoo drinker was not himself (he favours Mars Milk).

Thin Kylie is right though, it is utterly the end of an era. Now all we have to fight over are four plastic chairs, one of which now has 'Riley is a twat' written on it. (Fat Kylie. She is upping her campaign against me. I am anticipating death threats by Monday.)

Got home from one war zone to find the Summerdale Road Conflict (i.e. the dog versus Nietzsche) also very much in evidence, i.e. the dog throwing up green water on the kitchen floor. It finally managed to breach the barricades (i.e. the fence) only to trip over itself and fall into Clive and Marjory's ornamental pond. Mum says she is minded to go next door and have words with the Drs Jones about their provocative cat, and their failure to secure or eliminate a health and safety hazard. Have pointed out the cat is not so much provocative as the dog is an idiot, but Mum said it deliberately whipped the dog up into a frenzy by showing its bottom. Have said I will raise the matter with Wilde tomorrow at the Duke. I do not want Mum wading into their intellectual household, shaming me with her easy-wear Marks & Spencer trousers or theories on cats' bottoms.

## Saturday 7

11.30 p.m.
Wilde has apologized for Nietzsche's behaviour. Apparently this is not the first time it has been in trouble for taunting lesser beings; it has already had extensive therapy in a bid

to counteract its bullying tendencies. Suggested maybe it might need a refresher course, but Wilde said it would be a waste of time as you cannot control a creature's base urges, it would be like trying to stop him reading Joe Orton or worshipping Elizabeth Taylor. Said I hope the Drs Jones do not know he is dissing their profession. He said of course they do, they have offered him therapy to help him overcome his denial.

Scarlet and Sad Ed were not in attendance. They were busy babysitting while Bob and Suzy went to a Labour Party Beer and Hotdogs do at someone called Jocasta's. I said I was impressed Suzy has been able to wrench herself away from Harper. Jack said it is the fourth time this week. He fears she may be regretting listening to her menopausal ovaries begging her for another stab at motherhood before they wither up altogether. Said I thought they already had, hence the need to adopt. Jack said it turns out it is not Suzy's eggs, it is Bob's immotile sperm that is the problem after all. Said frankly it was all too much, including the thought of whatever Sad Ed and Scarlet are actually doing as opposed to babysitting. Jack said green was not an attractive colour on me. I said I was wearing black, duh. He rolled his eyes and said, 'Tell Tallulah the band's meeting at mine tomorrow.' Said if he meant Wilde, then I'd probably just bring him. He said no, because it is for band members, which I am not.

I do not know why he is being so minty. Maybe Skype is down so he is sexually frustrated. Not that I care.

11.45 p.m.
Cannot stop thinking about Jack being sexually frustrated. It is utterly frustrating.

11.50 p.m.
Task achieved. Though not through aversion tactics, but by intervention of dog, who just fell out of my wardrobe.

## Sunday 8

The house has been infested by never before seen levels of idiocy, i.e. James and Mad Harry are having a double date with Mumtaz and Wendy in the dining room, i.e. they are timing each other on old *Times* sudoku puzzles. Mad Harry stands no chance. I know for a fact James has memorized an entire month's in preparation so he can dazzle with his superior puzzling skills. I refuse to bear witness to this madness. Am defying Jack and attending band practice. Will say am just visiting Scarlet, and then, when she and Sad Ed start to get jiggy, which is inevitable, will lurk around outside den looking like Marianne Faithful, i.e. definite groupie material.

5 p.m.
Jack and Wilde are in agreement on something. It is that I am not Marianne Faithful. The reasons are too manifold and depressing to list here. On the plus side, they have an

88

excellent shortlist of band names: Sons of Scargill, I Eat Bees (Reuben Tull's suggestion. Is possibly actually true), Hitler's Pants, and Blind Monkey Fernando. My suggestion of Blair's Babies utterly rejected on grounds that it is too close to Justin Statham's band Thatcher's Grandchildren. I said maybe Jack should invite Justin Statham back to form a supergroup, and perform hits from the glory days of Certain Death, but Jack said he'd rather chew tinfoil, and my pleas were utterly transparent. I demanded to know what he meant, and he said obviously I am still not over my string of ill-advised liaisons with the Cut Price Cobain. I said he was utterly wrong, and I had my sights on a higher prize (i.e. Wilde, but made it deliberately obtuse so that it could mean academic glory or an Oscar), but it is obvious that he is not over my science experiment snog with Justin during our own ill-advised liaison. He said the only one who was ill-advised round here was him and it is lucky he has Maya who understands the meaning of loyalty, and a Heathcliff complex. I said she speaks remarkable English for a Guatemalan, at which point he appeared to start choking on a Pringle. At which point I left before he could badmouth me any more in front of Wilde. Plus the jam session was about to commence and apparently it is against jam law to allow bystanders, and according to Jack a half empty Pringles tube does not count as percussion.

Got home to discover James with a black eye and a broken Pilot. He is more upset about the pen. Asked him

how it happened but he said he cannot bring himself to divulge details, but suffice to say he and Mad Harry will not be double dating any time soon.

## Monday 9

Oh joy. Another Monday, another day of substandard education, and being pelted with fizz bombs.

4 p.m.
I have been reprieved. Fat Kylie was off school! It is the fifth anniversary of the day her dad Les choked to death on a Findus Crispy Pancake. She has gone to join the many other O'Gradys for a mourning vigil outside HMP Norwich where one of the Liams is incarcerated.

## Tuesday 10

Fat Kylie is back in school with a new spray tan rather than a mask of grief. Gave her my condolences anyway. Am rising above our differences (which are many, and mostly relating to whether or not 'spazallist' is offensive and actually a word) in a bid to broker peace. Am considering a career in the UN. It would not be the first time a celebrated actor had gone into politics. Look at Arnold Schwarzenegger.

Found a Flump with my name on it (literally) taped to my locker. Clearly the Kylies are not ready to lay down arms. It is disappointing, but I will continue to rise above it. Fat Kylie is merely taking out her other frustrations on me (she is still refusing to do it with Mr Whippy until ice cream season begins). Oooh, I am completely psychiatric. Maybe the Drs Jones will spot my potential as a future analyst and beg me to give up my drama/UN dream and train under their tutelage as the next Freud or Jung.

6 p.m.
The dream is over. Dr Jones (woman) said I need four A levels in science at A*, and what I am talking about is not psychiatry, it is psychology, which is entirely different. I do not know how, they are both about mentalism and dreams about teeth.

Had gone round to report more Nietzsche activity (and ogle Wilde). It has taken to dangling off the fence then clawing the dog on the nose when it jumps up. The dog stands to lose an eye at this rate and it is mental enough without adding half blindness to its misery. Dr Jones (man) said this is Darwinism in action and it is survival of the fittest and to intervene would be to play God, who does not exist. Said surely trying to fix mentalists was playing God, but apparently I am wrong. And also 'mentalist' is neither appropriate nor a real word. Who knew? Asked

where Wilde was. Dr Jones (woman) said she did not know. Am sure I spotted a dark look pass between her and Dr Jones (man). Maybe they are covering for him because he is seeing someone at crammer! Ooh, maybe I would make an excellent private detective instead. Maybe my destiny is to be Jessica Fletcher. Only younger, and without the slacks.

**7 p.m.**

James said that with my pathological obsession with creating drama where there is none, my destiny is to be a C-list actress, or reporter for the *Walden Chronicle*, and that Wilde is not seeing another girl at crammer. (This accompanied by withering look, as gleaned from Mum.) How and what does he know? This is all very suspicious. He also said that, on the plus side, if the dog loses an eye it will be no bad thing as it will only heighten its sense of smell, thus raising the chances of Dog Daze getting off the ground. I asked how far it had actually got so far. He said it is not even hovering due to the dog's consistent inability to tell the difference between a Tic Tac and an aspirin.

## Thursday 12

There is more suspicious activity afoot (ha-ha). Grandpa Riley rang in rage to say he had caught Treena doing Uncle Jim's toenails, which is a private activity, and only between a man and his wife. He says it is further evidence of poisoning

(he is still constantly nauseous and dizzy) and has booked himself in with Dr Braithwaite (huge hands, lazy eye, bottle of whisky in desk drawer) on an emergency appointment first thing in the morning, and packed a bag to move back in with us, should the tests prove positive.

### Friday 13

Despite the portent of doom date, it transpires that Treena is not poisoning Grandpa for her inheritance. He was doing it all by himself. It was Elsie Stain's home-made blackberry cordial, which was not cordial at all but potent liqueur. He has been perpetually drunk for nearly a month. It is incredible, and worrying, how little change there was in his behaviour. Mum is visibly relieved. She had only just got rid of Scarlet and the thought of someone else clogging up the house with their hideous tendencies was clearly a concern.

### Saturday 14

Hurrah, Scarlet has invited me for a sleepover. Bob and Suzy are taking Harper to an Irish music festival for the weekend to immerse her in her native culture, so she and Jack are making the most of the poo- and noise-free time. He has invited the band for an extra-long jamming session and all-night viewing of seventies prog rock DVDs, so they can get some

new influences for their sound. Am taking James's leftover camping sleeping bag, which is both soiled and broken, so Wilde will have to invite me into his. Obviously I cannot be expected to sleep in Scarlet's room as Sad Ed is bound to be in attendance with his gargantuan upper arms and needs.

Mum is jubilant for once. She says what with Dad and his endless work woes (they have lost out on a crucial paperclip contract to Sutcliffe Stationery Supplies), James and his Mumtaz woes, and the dog and its Nietzsche woes (and general idiocy), one less Riley to deal with will be a blessing. Hurrah! By this time tomorrow I will be Mrs Oscar Wilde in the making, or at least his mistress. He is bound to get overcome by desire and snog me on the hovery loveswing.

## Sunday 15

Did not get snogged in the love swing. Or invited into his sleeping bag (ironic Barbie print). But I do not care. Something better and more worldly has occurred, i.e. Wilde told me I am a female version of him, i.e. his soulmate! (He did not say this part, I am inferring. And the first part was a bit slurred as well, due to Suzy's Christmas Amaretto, but just because he was under the influence of mind-altering substances does not mean it was not true.) Oh it was seminal. We talked all night, and he told me his Desert Island Discs (including 'Lola' by the Kinks and 'Defying Gravity' from *Wicked*) and did his Oscar-winning speech. He says he knows

he is destined for infamy so it is best to be well-prepared, hence the fly sunglasses at all times, even when they are an impediment to actually walking without crashing into stuff. He is so utterly eccentric and me-like. This is why he is not making a move. He knows we are going to spend the rest of our lives together, so there is no hurry to sully our cerebral connection with matters of the flesh.

Scarlet is not in agreement. She says I am nothing if not predictable. Jack also unimpressed. He says I am barking up the wrong tree. I said I am barking nowhere (unlike Sad Ed last night), and it is a purely intellectual relationship. Did not say I hope to raise it above the intellectual level to the pants-based at some point in the very near future.

Got home to find that Uncle Jim has moved back in. He says he cannot be expected to cope with recent activity at 19 Harvey Road. Apparently the near-poisoning has, Clegg-like, reminded Treena of her love for Grandpa and they are renewing their vows on a daily basis. Plus Jesus pooed in his rucksack. Mum has gone to bed early, as has Dad. Though this is nothing to do with vow renewing. Dad is reading a Dick Francis novel and Mum is staring blankly at the ceiling.

## Monday 16

Scarlet has got her first university offer. It is from Hull and is three Bs. I said this is setting a low standard but she said no,

it shows they want her anyway, even if she is compromised exam-wise by an ill-timed period or bout of hay fever.

### Tuesday 17

Scarlet has another offer. This time it is an A and two Bs, but is from Sheffield, her back-up choice (she says due to obvious reasons, though not sure how it differs from Hull. They are both industrial and poor), so she has rejected it outright, due to their self-important inclusion of an A when they should recognize their own shortcomings, realize she is an asset, and beg her to come with three Ds. Unbelievably Sad Ed has got an offer too. It is from Humberside to do Music Industry Studies. This is outrageous. He can barely strum 'House of the Rising Sun' on guitar and he has a place, yet I am legend in these parts for my seminal Anne Frank and I am being pointedly ignored. Plus my driving is less then luminary according to Mike Wandering Hands. He is right. I am doomed. How can I expect to escape my pitiless existence if I am beholden to the 799 bus?

### Wednesday 18

Have been rejected by Manchester. This is a bitter blow as living in a grim northern city is second only to living in London in the edginess stakes. Plus to add insult to injury,

Carrots McGoogan (ginger, six foot four, penis like a button mushroom according to Leanne Jones) has an offer from Coventry to do business studies, and he has barely two GCSEs to rub together.

Went to see Wilde after school to mutually share our rejection but it turns out Manchester have not recognized our soulmate status as they have offered him three Bs. He already has a place in a house on Canal Street and his final year dissertation planned. It is 'Chameleons? The Changing Gay Stereotype in BBC Daytime Drama'. I admire his embracing of the gay canon. It is unusual in us lesser heterosexuals, and to be applauded. Which I said. He said, 'You're so cute, sugar tits.' Then we put on some vintage Madonna and listened to that until the Drs Jones said it was time for 'supper' (banned in our house for having ideas above its station). I was hoping for an invite to dine on poached sea bass in their stimulating (in every sense) company, but they had only set three places so had to eat Bird's Eye fishcakes and talk about verrucas with my own decidedly unstimulating family.

## Thursday 19

My life is Shakespearean once more, i.e. Mum has decreed the Drs Jones are not 'of our kind' and to be scorned. It is because Nietzsche had finally gone too far and managed to get the dog trapped in the gate so she went round to complain, only

to be given the Darwinian/God spiel. She says they definitely do have ideas above their station. And also she does not like the cut of Wilde's jib (he was wearing hot pants) and I should think twice about spending too much time with him.

James shook his head wearily and said she had played the wrong hand. If she had told me that Wilde was a charming young man, and that I should invite him for a Riley High Tea (slightly above station, but redeemed by also being Cornish, therefore inbred), then I would have left well alone. As it is, she has only stoked my loins.

He is revolting. If right. Though the likelihood of me ever inviting him to a Riley High Tea is nil. There is nothing edgy about Marmite sandwiches. Not even cut into fingers.

## Friday 20

On the plus side, I have finally been offered a place at university, i.e. Birmingham. On the downside it is highly conditional, i.e. three A*s. I do not stand a chance. Only Scarlet, the mathletes, and Emily Reeve are going to manage that. Though the latter is a miracle given that Lola Lambert is going through the terrible twos (she is fast threatening Whitney's position as chief menace in the Camilla Parker Bowles Memorial Crèche). Went to see Wilde to share my partially joyous news but Dr Jones (woman) said he had gone to see Olaf again. I am not sure I like this mysterious Olaf. I hope he is not trying to usurp me as Wilde's soulmate.

## Saturday 21

The band has a name. It is Blind Monkey Fernando, which won a popular vote in the Duke by eleven votes to two. (Kev Banner and his dog both voted for Hitler's Pants. I said this was a shameful indication of latent right-wing tendencies, but Scarlet says it is more a shameful indication of finding the word 'pants' funny in any context. It is better than Wizard Weeks though who voted for Venn Diagram, which was not even on the list.) Wilde says he might change his name to Fernando, as he is the metaphorical blind man, i.e. he stumbles around in this cruel world, but is sheltered from the ugliness by his sunglasses. He then tripped over Reuben as if to prove a point. Jack has banned him though, as he says it will give the wrong impression that Wilde is the Jagger of the band, when in fact it is him. And then everyone got into an argument about whether Jagger was better than Ronnie Wood, and who could do the best Keith Richards impression.

Walked home with Wilde. I said I was surprised he did not argue his case with Jack more about being the metaphorical Fernando, but Wilde said he did not want to burst his bubble, but it will be clear that, as lead singer, he is Fernando, whereas Jack is the drumming monkey. I said I had thought the exact same thing at the exact same time. Was hoping he would then take the opportunity to confirm my soulmate status with a moonlight or at least orange-sulphuric-street-lamp-light kiss, but he was too busy being

sick in Thin Kylie's front garden. He probably has an alcohol intolerance. It is his sensitive nature. He is like me. We are united in our inability to consume cheap liquor without our bodies rejecting it (though in my case, also involving me doing something catastrophically stupid). Oh, is there nothing we do not share?

## Sunday 22

Besides relatives he is not mortally ashamed of.

The Cleggs are one step closer to their dream of world (or at least south of England, avoiding all motorways, major conurbations, and ports with high levels of immigration) domination, i.e. they have taken possession of the motorhome, i.e. Denzil has towed it over with the pickup truck and deposited it on the front garden. Asked why he hadn't actually driven it over. Grandpa says the engine is undergoing fine tuning. Asked how fine. He said it is in two bits on Denzil's kitchen table, but it is not relevant as Granny has to do the decorating first (women's work, along with all cooking, cleaning, and unblocking toilets). This does not bode well. I predict intolerable colour schemes and china knick-knacks stuck on every available surface. Bruce has moved in already. Grandpa says it appeals to his sense of adventure. I suspect it rather more appeals to his idiocy/ sense of smell as Denzil was keeping chickens in there until the Cleggs were foolish enough to buy it.

Mum is visibly relieved. She says the longer they are engineless the better, as it is bad enough having Uncle Jim malingering on her sofa. James says he needs a woman to relight his fire, because now that he has Mumtaz, he cannot wait to leap out of bed in the morning, and he has an extra spring in his step. Mum said the extra spring is down to vitamin C tablets, Clarks shoes, and excellent career prospects (he is top of the class in everything bar PE, but he is putting this down to inheriting Mum's short legs and Dad's short body. Though being top at John Major High is not the pinnacle of academic excellence. Half the school cannot use an apostrophe, including the teachers), and what Uncle Jim actually needs is a job. She is driving him to the job centre in Bishop's Stortford tomorrow to find him gainful employment, and is confidently expecting him to be installed in Moore and Moore Family Solicitors by the end of the week.

## Monday 23

Mum has begrudgingly scaled down her ambitions for Uncle Jim. There were only three jobs on offer: head of the Camilla Parker Bowles Memorial Crèche, meat shaver at Capital Kebab, and barman at an 'up-and-coming gastropub'. James suggested the crèche as then he can spend extra time bonding with Jesus, but he said he would rather shave meat. He has an interview for that and for the barman job,

though is keeping his expectations low. The last time he was a barman he got sacked for inventing a new cocktail: the Double Jimmer (two parts Jim Beam, two parts Jameson). I said surely invention should be rewarded, but he said not when you taste-test eleven during your shift.

James says the lack of openings is a sign that the economic crisis is biting in every corner of Britain, even the sacred home counties, and that Dad could be next in line for the chop. Dad said right now that might be a blessing as office tensions are high due to Mr Wainwright being the subject of a divorce suit from Mrs Wainwright Mark II. (It is over a rogue lipstick mark. Oh, the cliché!) Dad has paid for his careless remark with a burnt sausage and meagre mash ration for tea.

## Tuesday 24

8 a.m.

James is jubilant as, for once, he has been given exactly what he asked for from Mum for his birthday, i.e. a telescope. I said this bodes well, and maybe I will ask for a car and actually get one, instead of the predictable substandard gifts. Dad said this was utterly unfair as he asked for a new sat nav and got an AA map of Great Britain. Mum said that's because there was nothing wrong with the current sat nav (there is, it keeps directing you to Scotsdales Garden Centre, regardless of where you actually want to

go. Mum has not noticed this as she only ever drives to Scotsdales Garden Centre) and anyway, the telescope was second-hand from Marjory's nephew Louis. James is not minded, he says it is yet another step along the road to love and career success. I said being a star-spotting nerd does not instantly bestow him with hero status, in fact, quite the opposite. But he gave me a withering look and said Professor Brian Cox 'gets more' than Justin Bieber, at which point he got dispatched to school. The horror is not over though, as Mum has foolishly allowed him to have a party after school, and agreed to pop over to Marjory's for the duration. She is leaving Uncle Jim in charge, to give him a sense of responsibility ahead of his meat-shaving interview tomorrow. I said this was a catalogue of lapses on her part, but she says James has signed an agreement promising that things will not get out of hand (i.e. no stain-inducing drinks, or overly crumb-making crisps), plus it is a 'bromance' party, i.e. is boys-only, so no one can get pregnant or attempt to. Will go over to Scarlet's as I do not think I can bear witness to the inevitable festival of sensible shoes and faux street talk.

6 p.m.

James has been banned from having parties until he is sixteen. Mum came home to find Ali Hassan with his trousers off. She accused James of hosting an orgy, but it turns out it was a game of strip Warhammer. Though not sure which is more alarming. Uncle Jim (wearing only

Y-fronts and socks) has also been barred from positions of responsibility/childcare for the foreseeable future. I said it is sad how easily he is swayed into crime but Mum said her interrogations revealed that it was his idea in the first place. Asked how long he took to crack. She said four seconds. It is her best yet. Also asked what Mad Harry was doing sat on Thin Kylie's wall looking morose. James said it is because he was not invited due to the love-square black-eye-injury debacle, and it is his pathetic attempt to get 'back in the gang'. Apparently he has been doing surreptitious walk-pasts since four o'clock. I said it was like Beastly Boys all over again and James might as well save himself time and bother by making up now as it is inevitable. They are the ultimate bromance and are destined to be together, like me and Wilde. James said *a)* me and Wilde are not destined to be together, unless I am planning on growing a penis and *b)* Mad Harry is not being allowed back into Dog Daze or his affections until he has learned his lesson. Asked what the lesson is. James said it involves camels and eyes of needles.

He is mad. Plus he is wrong about Wilde. Even though his demeanour and dress sense would indicate gayness, he told me in no uncertain terms that I reminded him of his first love, a girl called Marlene, so it is clear I do not need a penis to fulfil our destiny.

Though possibly some enormous sunglasses and a feather boa would not go amiss.

Uncle Jim has failed to secure a position as Saffron Walden's premier slicer of elephant leg. He says his refusal to sample the wares may have hampered his chances. Which is worrying, given that he has willingly eaten lamb's brains and fried crickets on his various travels.

In other news, Fat Kylie has been reunited with Mr Whippy and his cone of contentment. The unseasonably clement conditions and approaching Easter holidays mean he has given up his dog poo position in anticipation of a flood of orders for semi-melted Cornettos. Normally I would be less than enthusiastic about the perils of someone with a tendency to morbid obesity going out with a supplier of transfats (and chlamydia), but her snogging/strawberry Mivvi satisfaction means she has failed to pelt me with any perishables today so I will hold my tongue.

Have not told Mum about the vacancy. She would leap at the chance to have a member of the family in charge of clearing up the menace that is dog poo. Instead she is busy trying to persuade Dad to get Uncle Jim a job at Wainwright and Beacham. Dad does not seem keen. He says it is the only time he gets away from Riley family demands and disasters. I know how he feels. Sometimes school is my only solace.

## Thursday 26

Though not today. The common room is awash with potential university entrants. Even Mark Lambert has been offered a place at Anglia Ruskin to study midwifery. He says that way he can safely deliver all of Thin Kylie's horde of children in the comfort of their own living room. I said I was not aware that he and Kylie had found a house (they are not allowed on the housing list yet, despite attempted fake pregnancy, and Lambo claiming he is 'a homeless' (he is not, he got sent to his Nan's for a night for tampering with Mr Hosepipe's fire engine)). He said as soon as they are married he is moving in with Kylie at her mum and Terry's. He is mistaken if he thinks Cherie is going to let Kylie bear down in the front room. There is no way she is going to allow placenta anywhere near the cream shagpile or L-shaped corner suite.

## Friday 27

Uncle Jim has got a job. He is going to be a commis chef at the Fighting Cocks on the A11 starting Monday. James is mental with Gordon Ramsey anticipation. He says it is the first step to an appearance on *Masterchef: The Professionals* and his own contemporary fusion restaurant. Asked what being a commis actually involved. He says he is in charge of the boil-in-the-bag cod in parsley sauce.

Maybe I take after Uncle Jim and could be a Masterchef. Maybe the lack of letter from Hull is a sign that I should be eschewing academic ambition and looking to my hitherto undiscovered culinary skills on which to hang my fortune.

6 p.m.

So far have burnt an omelette, exploded some soup, and lost one of the twiddly knob things. Mum has now banned me from the kitchen (actually a re-enforcement of an earlier ban). I said she could be stymieing the next Jamie Oliver, but she said I am more like the next Granny Clegg. Even Dad admitted this was harsh. She cannot make toast without potentially burning the house down or claiming to have found Jesus's face in it.

## Saturday 28

My cooking dreams are over, because my true destiny (academic, not pants-based) has arrived, i.e. I have a letter from Hull inviting me to an audition weekend in two weeks. Will be sharing this joyous news with my other destiny (pants-based), i.e. Wilde at the Duke later, particularly that the distance from there to Manchester is only 98.1 miles (according the AA website). James said it is substantially longer by train, including a change at Doncaster, but I said I will have passed my test with flying

colours by then so he is barking up the wrong tree (as is the dog who is convinced Nietzsche is hiding in the Leylandii. It is not. It is in our kitchen on the window sill. Mum does not know this or she would be mental with cat/ Jones contamination issues.)

4 p.m.

Have told Sad Ed about the audition. He says this is indeed excellent as then I can lodge with him and Scarlet, thus cutting their household bills considerably. I said I was unsure Scarlet had definitely picked Hull, and also unsure I wanted to share with them, given their tendency to conjugate at every available moment, but he said, *au contraire*, she is definitely going to Hull as then she can claim to have experienced extreme poverty when she stands for MP selection, plus the honeymoon period is over. They have only done 'it' four times in the last week, and he is already looking at ways to spice up their 'bedroom time'. Left him to herd some trolleys at that point. He is deluded. Four times is above average, according to James (and his trusty companion Google), plus they barely ever bother with using the bedroom. I know for a fact last week they managed it in Edna's cleaning cupboard. Have texted Scarlet anyway. (She is being Bob's plus one at genito-urinary medical conference in Coventry. Suzy is too busy with Harper to make small talk about pelvic inflammatory disease.)

**5 p.m.**

Scarlet says yes she is definitely going to Hull, and yes the honeymoon period is over, though one of the off days was down to cystitis.

Am now doubly worried that *a)* I will not pass my audition and will be cast aside by her and Sad Ed in their house of (albeit slightly diminished) love and *b)* that I need to step up fitness levels before Wilde finally throws me onto the ironic Barbie sleeping bag. I cannot even run up the stairs without breaking a sweat. Sad Ed has a stored up body fat advantage. He could feasibly keep going for days as long as the pace was slow enough, and he could stop every hour to ingest a Snickers.

**11.59 p.m.**

Wilde (but of course, he) has come up with a solution to both mine and Sad Ed's problems. He says we need to channel a dead celebrity, and their brilliance and genius will shine through in everything we do. Apparently he has been channelling Elizabeth Taylor all week. Sad Ed is inspired. He is going to channel a Miliband in the hope it will revive Scarlet's flagging interest in his nether regions. I am going to be Sylvia Plath. Jack said this is hardly going to help with my fantasist tendencies, but Wilde said my fantasist tendencies are exactly what he likes about me and they should be embraced. Jack stormed off to restock the Cheese Moments (Sad Ed had eaten twelve packets to stem his pants-based depression).

I have been a fool for too long, thinking Jack understands me. How wrong I was. It is Wilde who knows the very essence of me, i.e. I *am* Sylvia. Starting tomorrow morning.

## Sunday 29
*Mothering Sunday*

Sylvia is already causing controversy at the Shreddies table. It is because she decided to eat my Mother's Day present (Green & Black's Miniatures) at one this morning whilst listening to obscure fifties swing beat. It is not so much the lack of gift as abundance of cocoa solids on my duvet that is causing the mintiness. I (i.e. Sylvia) am not minded. It will take more than thin lips to deter us.

4 p.m.
Mum has banned Sylvia from the house. Along with Galileo (who James has been channelling, i.e. telescoping everything, including Dad in the bath), and Nietzsche (cat not dead philosopher). It is because I persuaded it into my bedroom so I could stroke it elegantly while sighing and looking wistfully out of the window, and the dog chewed some wall in its anger. I said not allowing me a cat was possibly thwarting my chances of gaining entry to a top university and a glittering career as an actress/presenter of the *South Bank Show*. She said getting a cat would thwart the chances of the house actually staying in one piece, plus

James pointed out that Hull is ranked sixty-second in the *Times* university tables.

## Monday 30

Am feeling utterly Sylvia-like (i.e. am dressed in housecoat from fancy dress box, with ankle socks and Birkenstocks) and will be taking her to school using her preferred method of transport, i.e. a bicycle (admittedly she did not ride a Raleigh mountain bike, but it is that or Mad Harry's BMX which has been languishing next to the lawnmower for four months and I do not think Sylvia would do a barspin). Mum's lips went a bit thin at the Shreddies table but she knows she is powerless to restrict my channelling activity outside the environs of 24 Summerdale Road, and her usual failsafe eye-rolling no longer works on me. I am a woman of the world. Albeit a dead depressive one. James is still utterly in her sway though. He came to breakfast in a hideous collarless jacket (fashioned by himself, using an old school blazer and Mum's sewing machine. He is remarkably, and worryingly, handy on a Bernina.), but fled upstairs to change at the first sign of lip reduction. Plus Mum pointed out the lack of lapel could warrant a detention and blemish his untainted record, thus costing him his £1 end-of-year bonus.

Have suggested Uncle Jim try a similar tactic for his first day as a gastrochef, i.e. channelling legendary cook Elizabeth David or legendary drunk cook Keith Floyd. But

Dad says he has enough to think about remembering which side is right and to wash his hands without trying to flambé oranges whilst swigging brandy.

4 p.m.
My Sylvia look did not go down as well as anticipated. Fat Kylie said I smelled like her nan and Thin Kylie said it is no wonder I am a virgin. Plus Sylvia is not as brilliant at English as she should be, e.g. instead of concentrating on *The Tempest*, she preferred to stare mournfully out of the window. Mr Camden (history, English, metalwork) said if I do not buck my ideas up I will be lucky to scrape a C, at which point I would normally have apologized, and blamed lack of sleep due to reading Thomas Hardy into the small hours, only Sylvia decided to weep delicately, and write a poem about death. Think I may leave channelling to Drama. Mr Vaughan is more open-minded when it comes to experiments. He has smoked drugs and only narrowly avoided the sex offenders register.

I hope Uncle Jim has had more success than me. Mum has made special tea (Waitrose salmon fishcakes, on 2 for 1) to celebrate his return to 'normality'. She is hoping he will be moving out into his own bachelor pad by the end of the week, or at least one of the rooms above the Fighting Cocks.

6 p.m.
Uncle Jim is on a warning. It is for over-buttering the par-baked baguettes. His boss (Gary Brains: limp, permanent

sweat, no sign of living up to surname) says all ingredients are monitored and if he goes over his butter quota it will come out of his wage packet. Plus he rejected his special tea. He said he had a boil-in-the-bag lamb shank at work. Mum said this was hypocritical given Gary's stinginess over butter but Uncle Jim said it was past its use-by.

## Tuesday 31

Thin Kylie has put a spanner in Lambo's one-man-baby-factory plans. She says she is thinking of concentrating on her career first, i.e. opening a baby beauty salon. She is going to do hair and piercing and Fat Kylie is going to do fake tan. Lambo is outraged and says she is questioning his virility (he did not say 'virility' he said 'power of the knob') and it is her duty to get 'up the duff'. She said it is his duty to support her in her quest to open 'Ugly Ducklings'.

Scarlet is jubilant. She says it proves that even chavs can find their feminist ideals and allow them to flourish. I fear it is more her obsession with painting the O'Grady children an unnatural shade of orange (except Whitney, who is already brown, and whose paternity is still undocumented).

Also, Uncle Jim has been sacked. It is not for over-buttering baguettes, it is for differences of opinion over Ipswich Football Club, which led to Gary Brains getting knocked out by a frozen sausage. Uncle Jim says it is for the best as he cannot remain in a position that toys with

his commitment to serenity and inner peace. It is more likely his commitment to daytime TV and comics. Mum is livid. Especially as he had to forfeit all his wages to pay for partially melted pork products.

I'm RACHEL RILEY
– welcome to my so-called life.

April

# Wednesday 1

The Kylies are in trouble with Mr Wilmott. It is for testing out 'Ugly Ducklings' with the crèche inmates. Lola Lambert Reeve has cornrows and Jesus looks as if he has been dipped in creosote. It was utterly embarrassing walking him home. There is no way Sylvia Plath would have been seen in public with an Oompa Loompa. Luckily Grandpa Riley was out on his birthday treat with Treena (playing the slots at Magic City in Harlow) so Mum scrubbed him with some Swarfega to tone it down a bit. I cannot be certain, but it is possible she also sprayed him with Vanish Stain Remover. Though compared to the chemicals he ingests on a daily basis under Treena's microwave regime, it cannot do much harm.

# Thursday 2

There has been devastating news from Cornwall. Apparently Denzil has fixed the motor home engine (banging and a lot of superglue) and the Cleggs are planning to hit the open road on their inaugural marriage-cementing road trip tomorrow. Mum quickly said the Lake District is particularly beautiful at this time of year, plus they are not too adventurous with food up there, but her words fell on deaf (or possibly just stupid) ears. They are heading up the A303 and are due to arrive in time for tea and Battenburg

cake on Sunday afternoon. James said on the plus side, they do not need beds or a toilet as they have both on board the dream machine. But Mum said knowing Grandpa Clegg he will clog it within a day and also not to call it the dream machine as it very likely isn't. She is just terrified of the fall in social standing that comes with having an overambitious camper van parked on the gravel. Mrs Dyer (unconvincing dye job, fat feet, smells of Yardley) has never fully recovered her ranking on coffee morning rota after Mr Dyer persuaded her to get a caravan.

10 p.m.
Have just had horrifying thought. Wilde is bound to notice the Cleggs and will realize I am of inferior, unworldly stock. It is bad enough that we have magnolia paint and real carpet, but being closely related to someone who says 'proper job' (Granny) or who thinks Russia is in China (Grandpa) could be the end of our soulmateism. Oh God. It is terrible news. And Sylvia is no help. She would definitely stick her head in the oven at this one, only ours is electric and totally unsuitable for suicide (Sad Ed checked at the peak of his untimely death ambition).

## Friday 3

Hurrah, hurrah! Wilde and the Drs Jones are going back to London for two weeks so they will not bear witness to

the freak show that is the Cleggs *en vacances*. I said this was terrible news, soulmatewise, but that we can text (and also telepathically send each other messages down the M11, obviously). He said, 'Cute idea, Sylvia, baby, but the ringer's out of bounds.' Obviously he is doing extra cramming and cannot be disturbed. On the plus side, I am in charge of feeding Nietzsche. Which means not only will I ingratiate myself as a definite cat person, and potential daughter-in-law, but I get to look in his bedroom!

5 p.m.
Obviously will not look in his diary. Or pants drawer. But just absorb the essential Wildeness from his vast collection of Man Ray postcards and back copies of *Vogue*, which will aid me in my final coursework drafting and exam preparation.

### Saturday 4

James and Mad Harry have made up. I asked if Mad Harry had learned his lesson. James said yes (though is still unclear how) but more importantly, he has four tickets to see the Scott exhibition on Wednesday and they are taking 'their bitches'. Luckily Mum was busy arguing with Dad over whether reading the newspaper counted as pleasure (Mum) or important business (Dad), or he would be spending the day in his room reflecting on his use of sexist and abusive

language, and decision to wear a backwards baseball cap (almost as bad as tattoos or heroin in her book (actual book)). Have not told her I am feeding Nietzsche. She would see it as the ultimate betrayal. As would the dog. And I am already in its bad books for eating the last piece of toast and Marmite this morning. Have told her I am popping to Mr Patel's for essential Tippex for coursework, i.e. am using my notorious inability to spell Shakespearean characters to my advantage.

12 p.m.
Mum has demanded to know why it has taken me two and a half hours to purchase Tippex from the corner shop. Said Mr Patel has stopped stocking it to make room for more crisps (feasible) so had to traipse into town to WHSmith. She then asked to see said Tippex so had to add another lie to my tissue of deceit and say they had sold out, citing the treacherous run-up to exams as the culprit. She looked unconvinced. On the plus side, have spent several hours absorbing worldly bohemian glamour at 26 Summerdale Road, i.e. the Jones residence (ignoring the unbohemian vestiges of Clive and Marjory). According to the evidence on Dr Jones (male) side of the bed, they subscribe to the *Economist, Time*, and *Private Eye*, while Dr Jones (female) is reading several Daphne du Mauriers. This is even better than Bob and Suzy, hitherto my beacons of *Guardian*-reading intellectualism, whose bookshelves mostly consist of sex manuals.

6 p.m.

Mum says according to her investigations (i.e. dispatching her loyal minions James and the dog on the pretext of emergency envelopes) WHSmith has a replete display of correction fluids. Said they must have moved them then. She said, *au contraire*, they are where they have always been, underneath the Bics and next to the Post-its. Said maybe exam fever is addling my brain in which case I need a relaxing Diet Coke at my hostelry of choice, i.e. the Duke, i.e. out of her and James's interrogation zone. (He thinks I am secretly hoarding Tippex in a bid to get high. He has twice sent the dog into my room to sniff for that and Copydex. It found an old chocolate button so was pleased with itself, unlike James.) It does not matter that Wilde will not be there. Or Scarlet and Sad Ed (trying to recapture the halcyon days of three weeks ago and the legendary twice-in-one-nighter). I will have stimulating academic arguments with other regulars. It is time I widened my social circle now that I am soon to wrest off the straitjacket that is suburban small-town living and become northern and fascinating.

10.30 p.m.

Or alternatively spend two hours discussing whether aliens are real with Kev Banner and someone called Fish. The only vaguely interesting person there was Jack and he was too busy wittering on about Maya to Reuben Tull. Apparently she is coming to visit soon. No doubt she will be dazzled

by the high-tech inventions like electricity, power showers, and mini-roundabouts. I almost envy her her naivety and innocence. For true cosmopolitans like me, Saffron Walden will never be enough.

## Sunday 5

6 a.m.

As if to reinforce the misery of my genetic inheritance and upbringing, the Cleggs are here, infesting the front room with their racist tendencies and perpetual smell of Fray Bentos. Mum did point out that the Cleggmobile (now official title) had adequate tea-making facilities, but apparently the kettle only works when you are going above thirty miles an hour, so they have not had a cup of tea since they left St Slaughter (fourteen hours ago, including two spent driving round the M25 when Grandpa Clegg got momentarily mesmerized by a lorry and missed his turn-off). Mum asked them how long they were planning on being away (normally Grandpa Clegg comes down with gyppy stomach and overbearing misanthropy if he is away from the 'homeland' for longer than a few days) but Granny said they are never going back. They have rented Belleview aka Pasty Manor out to Pig, who is having marital difficulties with Mrs Pig (unsurprisingly given his face (pig-like), smell (pig-like), and attitude towards women (male chauvinist pig-like)). Mum's lips virtually disappeared and she had

121

to be made a reviving cup of coffee (emergency only, due to fear the caffeine will deplete her calcium reserves and she will shrivel to three feet tall), but apparently they are only planning on staying here for a week and then they are going to see the 'wonders of the world' (i.e. Norfolk, similarly weird and cut off, so a home from home). James is jubilant as he claims it means he now has gypsy heritage, which he says gives him an air of Romany mystery. I said it gives him an air of frightening hairdos and inbreeding. For once Grandpa Clegg was in loud and slightly bug-eyed agreement. He said he is 'no pikey' (he is) and in fact he is more like Columbus on his expedition to discover America (he is not).

## Monday 6

**9 a.m.**
Came downstairs to find the Cleggs asleep on the sofa with Bruce nestled revoltingly between them. Apparently they were kept awake by the howl of a wild animal in the night. Grandpa thinks the Beast of Bodmin tracked them from Cornwall and is intent on terrorizing them wherever they roam. James immediately rang Mad Harry to revive Beastly Investigations but Dad pointed out that if the Beast of Bodmin really had it in for the Cleggs it would have been able to outwit them months ago and it is far more likely to be Nietzsche. James is getting Mad Harry over anyway.

They are going to take it in turns to pretend they are gypsy prize fighters. Morons.

11 a.m.
The madness has started. It is Bruce and the dog, who are attempting to use the advantage of sheer numbers to get Nietzsche. I do not rate their chances. Alone they are idiots. Together, they are one colossal force of mentalism. It is like watching the Chuckle Brothers try to take on a T-rex. Luckily I do not have to witness the hoo-hah any longer. Sad Ed has called with an emergency. He is handcuffed to Scarlet's bed only she went downstairs for a glass of elderflower cordial and the next thing he heard was the front door slam and the sick-smelling Volvo depart at speed. Am going to release him. (Spare keys to both house and handcuffs kept under doormat—Mum would weep if she knew this. Or more likely go round with a list of security improvements.) Have also texted Scarlet to demand an explanation.

11.15 a.m.
Scarlet is in Cambridge buying bras with Suzy. She says she got distracted by croissants and the next thing she knew she was in Topshop. He is right, it is all but over.

4 p.m.
Sad Ed is free, but utterly despondent. He is blaming his moobs. I said it was not the moobs. It was the irresistible

smell of Waitrose patisserie products. This is a lie. It is the moobs. And the muffin top. Though luckily he had managed to wriggle under a sheet so could not get full view. Asked him how he managed to call me, given his lack of digits with which to dial digits. He said I do not want to know. He is right.

## Tuesday 7

2 p.m.
Sad Ed is not the only one for whom the bell has tolled on the honeymoon period. James and Mad Harry have been on match.com all morning. The evidence was visible for all in the internet history, which happened to pop up when I was Googling Wilde (one photo of him with Florence, of Machine fame, which I found under his bed this morning anyway, and one page about someone with the same name who once burned down a public toilet).

It is pathetic. They will never get away with it. The profile claims James Riley is six feet tall, thirty-eight, and 'free-living'. Dates are going to get a shock when a four-foot eleven schoolboy shows up with his Clarks shoes and less then free-living curfew. Though Mum is bound to catch him before that. It is only the distraction of the Cleggs that has prevented her thus far. As predicted, the Cleggmobile toilet is blocked and they are in and out of the house on an almost hourly basis, as are Bruce and the dog. Mum has dispatched them to

B&Q for the afternoon to sightsee modern furnishings so she can get some peace, and disinfect all surfaces.

3 p.m.
The Cleggs and their moronic canine assistants are back. Assumed they had been banned (it would not be the first time) but apparently Grandpa Clegg did not like the smell of the carpet section so they bought some Ginsters at the Spar and are now on the sofa watching *Columbo*. If Mum had any sense she would keep them there. At least that way they cannot get arrested.

## Wednesday 8

9 a.m.
Mum is babysitting Jesus for the day while Grandpa and Treena 'decorate' (aka do 'it'). I predict more Clegg-related trouble ahead. They are still not talking to each other after the infamous Terry Wogan row of 1985, plus they are less than complimentary about Grandpa's 'Jezebel bride' aka Treena (she is from Bolton, barely thirty, and wears leggings, though even I admit the last one is criminal). At least James and Mad Harry are unable to add their twopence worth of idiocy to the mix. They are at the Scott exhibition with Mumtaz and Wendy (i.e. the 'bitches'). Maybe the atmosphere of dedication and sacrifice will revive their love, and they will renounce the internet dating madness.

**5 p.m.**

As predicted the Terry Wogan row has reared its ugly head. I blame Mum for letting them watch Alan Titchmarsh (their new favourite TV presenter). It was only a matter of time before the conversation segued into 'who is the best chat show host of all time'. This time it was Uncle Jim who dared question their authority (he favours Graham Norton). On the plus side, Jesus is very taken with Granny Clegg. It is because she is happy to play snap for hours. Plus her pockets are a mecca of boiled sweets and dog biscuits.

**7 p.m.**

The Cleggs have demanded a sleeping arrangements swap, with Uncle Jim getting the inferior sofa while they enjoy the luxury of the spare bedroom. (Compared to the Cleggmobile, or even Pasty Manor, it is luxurious. It does not have Pig in it for a start.) Mum has agreed on a compromise. Uncle Jim will sleep in the bottom bunk in James's room. He then demanded top bunk as he is the oldest but Mum said the struts are weakened from the time James and Mad Harry tried to teach the dog to fly, plus Uncle Jim has developed a paunch so she is unsure it will take the excess weight. These are harsh words for a man who is jobless and facing divorce. Though true. He is following the Sad Ed depression diet, i.e. carbs before and after 6 p.m. and as little green matter as is feasibly possible when Mum is involved.

## Thursday 9

Mum is already regretting her rash decision of allowing James to share with his notoriously wayward uncle. He caused a stir at the Shreddies table by asking for jam to add to his peanut butter (American and therefore banned). Plus his match.com madness shows no sign of ending. He is now also conversing with someone from Harlow called SexySal. It is pathetic. And disturbing. He will end up on *Jeremy Kyle* if he carries on.

## Friday 10
*Good Friday*

9 a.m.
Hurrah! A day of relative peace. The Cleggs are off to Cambridge to visit its wealth of international standard tourist attractions, i.e. dreaming spires, punts, and Hilary Aneurin Bevan Nuamah, i.e. former home help to the Cleggs, and ongoing son of St Slaughter's first-ever black dentist. Was tempted to join them (to absorb heady atmosphere of academia, not to ogle Hilary, am over that now as his worldliness pales in comparison with Wilde's, despite the advantage of being black and a member of the Labour Party), but Bruce and the dog are going, plus James begged to part of the gypsy entourage, and the inevitable shame could adversely affect my exam results.

11 a.m.

I spoke too soon. Mum has discovered my illicit Nietzsche feeding activity by her preferred method of subterfuge, i.e. lurking at the landing window with James's binoculars. I am now limited to a five minute 'in-and-out' visit once a day, or she will be allowing James to take over the duty. Have agreed to all terms and conditions. There is no way I am letting James into the Jones's. Or Mum for that matter. They would be there for hours cataloguing all the various transgressions of acceptability (failure to adequately separate meat and fish products in the freezer, more than one bottle of wine open at once, Vegemite (banned for being a pale imitation of the only true yeast extract, and for being Australian)).

3 p.m.

As predicted, the Cleggs have yet again brought shame on the House of Riley with their idiocy, backwoods ways, and inability to read 'keep off the grass' notices. They are barred from ever setting foot within a Cambridge college, as is James. He is inconsolable, as he had been planning on following in the wheelmarks of Stephen Hawking and becoming a world-class theoretical physicist, and he is now having to bank on his various back-up plans, i.e. taking over as CEO of Apple, being the world's first merboy, or inventing gold. He is back on the computer, no doubt pouring his soul out to SexySal. (Mumtaz is not allowed to indulge in social networking, email, or other computer-based 'chat' for fear of contaminating her innocence and intellectualism.

Though why Mr Mumtaz allows her to consort with James at all is a matter of constant wonder.)

## Saturday 11

It could not last. James's secret internet life has been revealed.

Unbelievably it was Granny Clegg who unmasked him as a potential pervert. Mum was trying to teach her how to check the opening hours of Spar by the wonder that is the interweb, when she accidentally back-clicked and brought up the evidence for all to see. Granny Clegg accused him of being an internet pornographer and Mum threatened immediate withdrawal of all privileges. I said witheringly (and poetically I thought) that I had begged him to cease, but my pleas fell on deaf ears. Only Mum did not see the poetic or withering side as she immediately revoked all my privileges too. I said I didn't have any, unless she meant first choice of yoghurt at tea.

But, before she could list any, and in an unexpected twist, James revealed that he was not the chief pervert, but merely the pervert's lackey, i.e. he was using his superior internet and chat-up skills to secure a brace of dates for the other James Riley, i.e. Uncle Jim. Frankly, this is an immense relief, though it did nothing to appease Granny Clegg who said in her day the singles of the village just lined up at the annual Tinners' dance and got picked on grounds

of wideness of hip and straightness of eye. Unbelievably Mum is siding with the Cleggs. She says Uncle Jim will end up being fleeced out of his life savings or identity by a gold-digging hussy. I pointed out that his only life savings were the foreign coins he was keeping in an old Strepsils tin, and it was unlikely that any gold-digger would want to masquerade as a twice-divorced dental hygienist, albeit a sexy one. At which point Uncle Jim was about to say something only Granny Clegg hit him with a copy of the *Daily Mail* (anti-pervert weapon of choice) and Mum noticed that she hadn't sent me to my room for my earlier misdemeanour of withholding information so took the opportunity to enforce it immediately.

Thank God I will not be party to any of this hoo-hah next year. I intend to stay in Hull, returning only for Christmas and emergencies.

### Sunday 12
*Easter Sunday*

9 a.m.
The Cleggs are leaving early. Grandpa says they cannot be expected to enjoy Sunday lunch in a house of ill repute, and will picnic on the hard shoulder instead. They have gone to Spar to stock up on essentials for the journey (Ginsters, milk, Murray Mints).

I note Mum did not bother to plead for clemency. I

suspect she is relieved at their departure. It is the caravan tarnishing her reputation as middle class. Apparently Mrs Noakes (formerly of WHSmith, bad perm, calls trousers 'slacks') gave her a funny look over the olive dispenser thing in Waitrose yesterday. Though Mum says she is in no position to cast stones given that she has Austrian blinds.

The only person who is sad to see them go is the dog. It is losing its son, heir, and accomplice in mentalism (i.e. Bruce) and is pining inconsolably at the front door.

10 a.m.
Dog was not pining at Cleggs. Nietzsche was on the doorstep licking its genitals.

11.05 a.m.
The Cleggs have finally departed in a cloud of exhaust fumes and ill-founded disgust. Grandpa says he will not be darkening the driveway again until all perverts (i.e. Uncle Jim) have been extracted. He will be waiting a long time.

In a fit of remorse, and madness, James made a last-minute plea to join them on their 'wagon train adventure'. Mum sent him to count his Easter eggs before he could attempt to infiltrate the Cleggmobile. This was a cunning move as he is determined to hit an all-time high this year, though there is some discrepancy over whether a tube of Mini Eggs counts as one or forty-seven.

3 p.m.

James has had his count of seventeen (Mini Eggs judged to be one) verified by an independent adjudicator (i.e. Mad Harry). Though his jubilance was short-lived as Mad Harry got twenty-one thanks to Wendy's gift of six Creme Eggs, as opposed to Mumtaz's ill-thought-out single Kit Kat egg.

## Monday 13
*Easter Monday*

Hurrah. It is now officially the week of the BIG AUDITION, i.e. on Friday I shall be winging my way to Hull for two days of intensive workshopping and character investigation at my first-choice university. Am not at all nervous as, according to John Major High's ineffectual headmaster Mr Wilmott, my Anne Frank last year was 'like nothing he has ever seen'.

4 p.m.

James says, *au contraire*, I should be nervous, as these days it is mostly about having a deprived family background and I am points down due to John Lewis duvet covers and Duchy Originals biscuits, etc. He says he will be running an X Factor-style bootcamp in the dining room tomorrow to put me through my paces, as my only hope is to uncover a Leona Lewis-style hidden talent.

# Tuesday 14

9 a.m.

James was suspiciously absent from the Shreddies table this morning. I said he is shirking responsibility as he is supposed to be running an all-day dining room X Factor-style bootcamp thing. Mum said he is not as *a)* the dining room has been declared a boot/shoe free zone following the fox-poo-on-sage-green-shagpile incident (perpetrator still unknown but widely believed to be Dad) and *b)* she is commandeering it this morning for internet purposes. Asked what purposes these were. Only now I wish I had not. It is horrifying news, i.e. instead of me getting the train to Hull on Friday in a worldly and grown-up manner, she is planning a Riley family Yorkshire-based minibreak and they will be dropping me off in the Passat and picking me up again on Sunday. I have begged her to change her mind, or at least drop me several miles from the Gulbenkian Theatre, but she says she has already Googled crime stats and Hull is rife with murders and mobile phone muggings so she will be walking me to the doors in an armlock. This is utterly unfair. Am now praying that all cottages are fully booked or fail to meet strict fixtures and fittings standards (i.e. cotton sheets, Waitrose within ten-mile radius, and absolutely no whimsical figurines).

1 p.m.

James is back from Mad Harry's, still unvictorious egg-wise, but not alone. He said there is no point doing bootcamp half-

heartedly as it is a complete misnomer, so he has secured the services of Mad Harry (annoying judge) and Wendy (pretty but stupid judge), and he will be Simon Cowell, overlord of them all. I said surely James should be annoying judge due to his pedantry and impish aura, but James has pulled his jeans up very high and is refusing to change places. I said it was all hypothetical anyway given that the dining room is out of bounds for Mum's minibreak research.

2 p.m.

It is like the nun person says in *The Sound of Music*, as God opens a door, he slams a window shut, possibly shattering the glass in process, i.e. all cottages are utterly booked up due to staycation madness, which I was utterly jubilant about, until James took over the Googling and found a clean and comfortable eight-berth caravan in Scarborough. Mum was initially and joyously unconvinced, due to an excess of whimsical everything and the camp shop being not Waitrose but Spar, but James says it will be an historical educational visit and they can learn all about the 1950s. And then he demanded that Mum vacate area immediately as bootcamp is about to commence. He is definitely Simon Cowell, i.e. demonic and irritating. With helmet hair.

5 p.m.

Bootcamp is over due to judges' failure to agree on anything, plus annoying judge tried to snog pretty-but-stupid judge during biscuit break and the dog got

overexcited by rich teas and did wee on carpet. Mum has cordoned off area while she tackles the urine stain, and also a scuff mark where Simon Cowell tried to demonstrate breakdancing.

## Wednesday 15

Caravan minibreak horror has just gone postal, i.e. Grandpa Riley has invited himself, Treena, and Baby Jesus along. Mum uninvited him but Grandpa claimed he is on his last legs and could be dead by summer so it would be a last hurrah, and Dad caved in. He is now descaling the toilet as punishment. Mum says at least Dog is going into kennels so will be one less mess-maker to worry about.

## Thursday 16

Sad Ed and Scarlet have been over for pre-audition talks. Sad Ed said I have nothing to worry about and that I should just be myself. That is easy for him to say. He has notched up a suicide attempt and had sex with a lesbian. Scarlet is in disagreement though. She says under no circumstances should I be myself and instead I should be her, i.e. semi-emo with TV sexpert mother and an adopted sister called Harper. It is so unfair. Life

would be so much better if I had an adopted sibling, even a possible former O'Grady with a genetic tendency to covet Peperami and QVC.

## Friday 17

9 a.m.
It is D-Day, i.e. audition and Riley family minibreak. Hurrah! Dad and James have taken the dog to kennels and Mum is making final adjustments to her car seating chart.

10.30 a.m.
Dad and James are back from kennels. But so is the dog. Mrs Gemmell (red face, tweed, overlord of Catmere End Canines) has refused him a place. Asked why. James said it is because she is a dog racist, i.e. she only wants pedigree inmates, despite genetic inbreeding causing behavioural problems and squished faces. Dad said is not dog racism, it is down to the fact that the dog had bitten a Yorkshire terrier called Katinka and soiled itself within five minutes of arrival. It has thrown Mum into mess-making/seating arrangement panic. Apparently Grandpa and Jesus do not want to be in the same car. And Jesus and Dog cannot be in same car due to maximizing spillage/soiling issues. Plus Dad is refusing to have Jesus in car due to tendency to sing Bob the Builder/Pussycat Dolls endlessly.

**12 p.m.**

Crisis solved. Grandpa is going with Mum, Dad, James, and the dog, and I am going with Treena and Jesus. On the downside I have to put up with 'Jai Ho'ing but on plus side we have Wagon Wheels, Um Bongo, and Tangfastics. Hurrah! In four hours (allowing for predictable hold-ups on the A1(M), one Marmite sandwich stop and two wee stops) will be delivered by loving step-grandmother (albeit she is only thirty-one, and lifetime ambition is to be on *Jeremy Kyle*) onto doorstep of dreaming spires of university life. It is utterly *Brideshead Revisited*.

**10 p.m.**

Is not completely *Brideshead*, i.e. dreaming spires actually more concrete chimneys. Plus halls of residence room is not oak-panelled suite overlooking quad but is magnolia-painted box with wood-effect chest of drawers and overlooks car park. But is still utterly inspiring nonetheless. And will not be in halls anyway, will move into rat-infested student house and live in utter squalor. Hurrah! Plus have already met potential squat room-mate, i.e. Harriet, who was waving goodbye to immaculate Audi A6 at same time as I was ejected by Treena from the smelly Datsun. She was also wearing edgy black vintage despite having tedious parents in beige Marks & Spencer linen. Plus she has totally unmanageable hair. She is utterly me!

Although think she may think she is utterly not me. As is possible may have accidentally given her slightly

misleading impression of Riley family circumstances, i.e. due to variety of coinciding events, i.e. floor of Datsun rattling with empty Bacardi Breezer bottles, plus Jesus escaping and me having to chase him round car park while Treena swore at him through fug of Embassy smoke. Plus when she asked me, 'Is that your kid?' did not say no immediately. In fact did not say anything because could not get word in as she was blabbering, 'Oh my God, that is so cool. I wish I was pregnant, it would be utterly *Juno*.' And then we both got excited about *Juno* and started saying forshizz a lot and I forgot about having not told truth about dull reality of Rileys. Is not important. Will make all clear tomorrow. Must sleep now as need to be fresh for workshop in morning. Although am quite buzzy. It is because I was late due to woeful under-calculation of wee stops (thirteen, not four, due to excess consumption of Um Bongo) so missed dinner and have had to eat Doritos and Skittles in room.

## Saturday 18

8 a.m.

Have had possibly only two hours sleep and look like heroin addict. But it does not matter. This weekend is about talent, not beauty. Am interested only in mind and spirit of fellow auditionees, and they likewise.

**10 a.m.**

There is an utterly beautiful boy in workshop group. Admittedly he does not have Wilde's unique dress sense (Elizabeth Taylor circa 1950), but even so, he is definitely worldly. According to Harriet he is called Milo and is a former ACTUAL drug addict and ex-boyfriend of a pop star, and also has a cut on his arm which could possibly be a cat scratch but also potential self-harm! Hurrah! Also, have not yet revealed Riley reality. In fact have elaborated slightly on teenage mum thing. It is not all my fault: Harriet asked about Jesus's father and I said he is a much older man (i.e. Grandpa Riley, i.e. not a lie at all) and then she asked if he ever hit me and I said yes (because last week he thwacked me with electric fly swat). So am now potentially embroiled in incestuous relationship with my own grandpa. Which is vile. But utterly groundbreaking. And I think Milo is definitely sort to be only interested in groundbreaking girls. Not ones who used to wear days of week pants.

**1 p.m.**

Think fabricated family thing possibly just a little bit out of hand, i.e. during 'introduction session', Call-Me-Bill, aka head of first year (long hair, knee-length leather boots, no eyelashes) asked us to reveal secret about ourselves. So in Milo-sympathetic mood, I said I had a 'bit of a drugs problem' (did not say had actually thought was herbal headache thing but turned out to be psychedelic

mushrooms. Also did not say was a one-off and have not done anything else ever, unless you count the time Sad Ed made me sniff a whiteboard marker.) But then Harriet said, 'Tell them about the baby,' i.e. Jesus. So I did. But I also said that the woman who dropped me off, i.e. Treena, was my care worker (not an utter lie as Treena is a care worker in Twilight Years Day Centre, which is almost the same, i.e. arguing over TV remote and drinking too much cherry brandy), as my parents had kicked me out (of car, but did not say that bit). Anyway, if you think about it, this weekend is all about acting, and am clearly very convincing actress. So convincing, in fact, workshop piece is going to be based on my life story. Hurrah!

7 p.m.

My life story now also involves a drug overdose, attempted suicide, and custody battle. But is all gritty realism and very Donmar Warehousey, according to Milo. He is playing part of Grandpa Riley, and of inspirational care worker who gets stabbed to death by Grandpa Riley (is interesting test of acting skills), hence being replaced by Treena, who is being played by Harriet (complete with random shouty Geordie accent and cross eyes) who is also playing Janet Riley, i.e. Mum (no Geordie accent, but very convincing thin lips).

Milo very sympathetic with my tragedy due to own 'drug hell' story. Is like we are made for each other. OMG. Maybe he is my ONE after all and not Wilde.

11 p.m.

It is SOOOO unfair. My life is finally riddled with tragedy and it turns out I am TOO tragic. Milo says he thinks it is best if we do not get too close as I may drag him down and compromise his drug-free recovery. He says he is looking for a more normal sort of girl, i.e. Harriet. This is utterly typical. Have texted Scarlet for advice but she says it is too late to change tack now and I will have to effect miraculous change of circumstances come September, IF I get a place.

Said there was no need for capitals on IF. Scarlet said yes there is as she has seen my Anne Frank. She is wrong. Will be so convincing tomorrow as myself (version 2.0) that they will give me unconditional place and full grant too.

## Sunday 19

9 a.m.

It is performance day. Am in costume already, i.e. regulation drama student black T-shirt and leggings (sixties muse sort, not saggy mauve Treena ones), with Baby Jesus in position, i.e. have put Harriet's toy kangaroo Elton (no idea) up T-shirt. Is brilliant. Nothing can go wrong. In just three hours' time will be star of new intake of drama department and potentially get signed up for *Hollyoaks* by talent scout who has wandered into workshop in hope of spotting next Carey Mulligan. Hurrah!

**10 p.m.**

Hurroo. Have not been spotted by *Hollyoaks* talent scout, am not star of drama department, and instead am back in John Lewis-decorated bedroom as Rachel Riley (version 1.0), i.e. no drug habit, no baby, and no tragic care home. Plus reinvention not undergone surreptitiously within confines of Treena's Datsun on A1(M), but on stage in front of Milo, Harriet, and Call-Me-Bill. Events unfolded as follows:

**9.45 a.m.**

Cast and crew assemble backstage for voice exercises and group hug. Rachel Riley gives Milo extra special 'I feel your pain' hug. Milo feels actual pain and has to take two of Call-Me-Bill's prescription painkillers.

**9.55 a.m.**

Milo still in pain from hug and demands two more painkillers.

**10.00 a.m.**

Cast assemble onstage. Rachel notes absence of Jesus's father (fake) and suspects potential heroin overdose. Production postponed whilst cast forensically search theatre for body.

**10.02 a.m.**

Body located in sound booth, but is not dead, is asleep, clutching packet of Propain. Harriet aka Mrs Riley throws

bottle of Evian over body. Body does not respond so Mrs Riley (fake) kicks body in genital area. Body swears violently but is suitably revived, though limping. Rachel notes is more in character, given Grandpa Riley's alleged war injury in left knee (not sustained in war, but in ill-advised badminton phase).

10.05 a.m.
Cast reassemble onstage, including limping Grandpa Riley (fake).

10.06 a.m.
Rachel Riley looks up from fake pregnancy test to note presence of limping Grandpa Riley (real) on front row. Also accompanied by full cast of Rileys, i.e. Janet Riley (evil drunken mother of Rachel), Colin Riley (distant, former film-star father of Rachel), James Riley (autistic *Rain Man* type), Treena Nichols-Riley (care worker), and Baby Jesus Harvey Nichols-Riley (son of Rachel) (presence later disclosed to be due to catalogue of caravan-related hoo-hah including lack of hot water, abundance of people from Birmingham, and consumption of whimsical decor by dog). Rachel feels surge of nausea, but decides to channel feeling for convincing morning sickness scene, plus notes that at least Dog Riley absent, so is not all bad. Possibly he is locked safely in Passat. Or potentially has fallen off precarious cliff railway to his death in swirling Scarborough sea.

**10.07 a.m.**

Dog Riley makes surprise appearance on stage having apparently escaped Passat confinement/railway death. Dog Riley eats Baby Jesus (fake). Mrs Riley (fake) breaks down and has to be given emergency oatcake by James Riley (real).

**10.10 a.m.**

Production postponed indefinitely due to complete confusion of boundaries between real and imaginary Rileys. Rachel says it is groundbreaking destruction of fourth wall and is utterly Brechtian. Call-Me-Bill's assistant, Call-Me-Jools, says is not, is complete chaos.

**10.15 a.m.**

Grandpa Riley (fake) notes that Mrs Riley (real) does not appear to be evil ex-drunk as described by Rachel Riley but is more kind-hearted, if fastidious, motherly type. Plus care worker has just snogged father of Baby Jesus which, while utterly *Jeremy Kyle*, does not fit in with version of events described in play. Rachel says how would Grandpa Riley (fake) know, he is on drugs. Grandpa Riley (fake) says paracetamol not mind-altering, is just dulling pain of cider hangover. Rachel offers to soothe hungover brow. Grandpa Riley (fake) declines.

**10.20 a.m.**

Mrs Riley (fake) revived by oatcake and carton of apple juice and decides to take stand against oppressors of Rachel Riley

(version 2.0) by telling Mrs Riley (real) that she is neglectful mother. Mrs Riley (real) makes lips go very thin and tells Mrs Riley (fake, also thin-lipped) that she has been duped by compulsive liar Rachel Riley. Rachel (no idea which version) tells Harriet is utter proof Mrs Riley is psychopath.

### 10.22 a.m.

Call-Me-Jools gets minty and demands that all Rileys, real and fake, decamp to staffroom with Call-Me-Bill to separate fact from fiction, and also locate wet wipes as Baby Jesus (real) has got Wotsit residue on her ballet pumps.

### 10.30 a.m.

Mrs Riley (real) engages in well-practised Paxman-style quick-fire questioning. Rachel Riley (all versions) attempts to utilise well-practised avoidance tactics (cough, feign death, blame it on dog) but Mrs Riley (real) throws in trick question about the mung bean cultivator and Rachel Riley breaks down and admits truth, i.e. that she is not edgy Junoesque teen mother, but is tragically normal product of depressingly unbroken home. And Mrs Riley not evil ex-drunk but sober, if irritating, Marks & Spencer-wearing former accountant with Cillit Bang obsession.

### 10.35 a.m.

Grandpa Riley (fake), i.e. Milo, says Rachel should be ashamed of self, and that there is nothing edgy or fun about being pregnant at age of fifteen, or having drunk mother

or living in care home. Rachel points out that it is easy for him to say as he is ex drug addict. But on plus side it means she is ideal girl for him as she is completely middle class and dull. Milo says does not know who real Rachel is any more. Rachel says he wouldn't want to. Milo tells Rachel is about time she took long look in mirror and tried to see who real Rachel is because she might actually like what she sees. Said is unlikely as she has Clegg dark circles inherited from Mum's inbred Cornish relatives, plus hair is mental.

10.40 a.m.

James Riley says whole episode has brought shame to House of Riley. Call-Me-Bill says possibly, but also was very convincing acting. Rachel sees opportunity and says was all on purpose, i.e. utter experiment in guerrilla theatre (not gorilla, know that now). James Riley says no it was not, was typical Rachel trying to pretend she is someone she is not, e.g. Anne Frank. Or Amy Winehouse. Rachel tells James to cease and desist before she tells everyone about time he wore fake furry pants and tried to be a gladiator. James tells Rachel to cease and desist or he will reveal details of time she weed in Pringles tube at Glastonbury. Mrs Riley (real) tells Rachel and James to cease and desist, before exiling them to Passat to think about behaviour.

10.50 a.m.

Harriet comes to Passat to say goodbye. Rachel apologizes for possibly misleading details of life. Harriet says she totally

understands as her mum has coasters permanently welded to hands to swoop in case anyone tries to put drink down on wooden surface. Rachel asks how Milo is taking it. Harriet says he is reading Sartre in darkened room. Rachel sobs at injustice of it all. Plus because dog has just jumped on back seat and banged head on her nose.

**10.51 a.m.**
Rachel takes long last look at drama department, confident in knowledge she will never see it again and will spend college career at University of Stoke-on-Trent (formerly Stafford Adult Education Unit).

**10.52 a.m.**
Passat departs for 24 Summerdale Road, Saffron Walden, stopping only for a Marmite sandwich break, four wee stops (two dog, two James), and one emergency calming down (Dad).

**10.30 p.m.**
Oh, the shame. Is like *The Metamorphosis* in reverse, i.e. instead of being edgy cockroach am back to being utterly tedious Gregor Samsor person. It is so unfair. Why was I not born to rock-star parents? Then I would be drinking vodka with them in the Hawley Arms, instead of being shut in room with penitent's supper of cheese and crackers (no butter).

10.35 p.m.
Or maybe Milo is right. Maybe I should take long hard look in mirror and will like what I see. Yes, will be revelation. Will see real Rachel beneath shroud of invention.

10.40 p.m.
Except real Rachel still has Clegg dark circles and hair is unfeasibly big. Although could be due to polar-bear-friendly low-energy light bulb. Maybe will sleep on it. Maybe will wake up tomorrow and will love self completely.

10.45 p.m.
Or if not will go and see Sad Ed. He is bound to be more depressed than me.

# Monday 20

8 a.m.
Having looked in mirror and ascertained enormity of hair, still do not love self entirely, but distracted from gloom by fact that Shreddies table is playing host to an unusual presence, i.e. Uncle Jim, who is rarely up before the clarion call of *This Morning*. Under extensive questioning, it transpires that during the Rileys' northern exposure he has secured a position at an 'establishment of some reputation'. It is as acting manager at lentil-smelling health food outlet Nuts in May, i.e. my former employer

(until they cruelly turned me out onto the streets in the ongoing financial crisis)! Mr Goldstein (hunchback) is semi-retiring and needs someone to restock chickpeas and operate the Till of Confusion. James (revived by the prospect of free Buzz Gum and Carob bars (like chocolate, only really not)) says this is excellent news, match-wise, as an unusual job is like sexual honey to the bees that are desperate housewives. He got dispatched to school immediately for every part of that proclamation. He is right though. This is an utter new beginning for Uncle Jim, and he can cast off the shame of joblessness and enforced celibacy, and embrace love and life once more. Mum is just pleased because now he can start paying rent or get his own flat. She is immune to the possibility of romance. It is being married to habitual vest-wearer Colin Riley.

4 p.m.

There has been another groundbreaking event in our absence, i.e. the ATC hut (youth group for the criminally weapons-obsessed) has been razed to the ground, i.e. burned down (I had to check as razed is misleading). According to Lambo (high in the ranks of the ATC thanks to his shaven head and ownership of nine knives), it was the Scouts who have had it in for them for months. Scarlet says it is more likely CND and anyway, it is a good thing as it shows an intolerance for aggression. As if to prove a point, Lambo then threw a plastic spoon at her. But it missed and hit Sad

Ed (this is easy, given Scarlet's catlike reflexes, and Sad Ed's gargantuan midriff).

Went to see Wilde after school to share this fascinating and worldly news, but Dr Jones said he is grounded and she will not tell me why. This is typical. I leave the hitherto uneventful Saffron Walden for a matter of days and immediately a whole host of brilliant and worldly things happens. Knowing my luck, by the time I return from Hull, the town will have been taken over by Muslim insurgents.

Also Nietzsche is missing. Felt racked with remorse as I realized I had not fed it for an entire week due to audition madness. Plus, come to think of it, I have not seen it since the genital licking incident last Sunday. But cats are utterly independent, and walk by themselves according to brilliant if possibly racist poet Rudyard Kipling.

7 p.m.
Ooh, maybe it has been kidnapped by a suburban witch for a feline sacrifice. Nothing would surprise me in this newly interesting environ. I bet it is Mrs Housden (moustache, bulk buyer of Waitrose own-brand cat food according to Sad Ed). She goes through cats like socks.

### Tuesday 21

I fear my highly fictionalized family history saga may have jeopardized my worldly, Wilde-seducing ambitions, i.e. have not received an offer from Hull yet. James says no news is good news, but Mum says, *au contraire*, no news is a portent of failure.

Also, Nietzsche is still missing, presumed dead (or being strung out on a sacrificial altar on Audley Road). Dr Jones (male) was putting up a poster at Mr Patel's on my way home from school. He is wasting his time. No one reads those things. There is a still an advert there for a PS1.

## Wednesday 22

It is official. The Britcher/Lambert union is off. Fat Kylie says it is like Wills and Kate divorcing. It is not. Given their failure to actually reach the aisle in the first place and the fact that Thin Kylie is orange and says 'arse' and 'shitsticks' on a regular basis. None of which the Duchess of Cambridge does (at least I hope not, or the monarchy is doomed faster than even Scarlet had hoped for).

## Thursday 23

According to the *Walden Chronicle*, bastion of uninvestigative journalism, the police (i.e. PC Doone and his obese Alsatian) are no closer to solving the mystery of the ATC inferno. They are blaming disenfranchised youths, failing to note

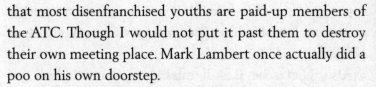

*April*

that most disenfranchised youths are paid-up members of the ATC. Though I would not put it past them to destroy their own meeting place. Mark Lambert once actually did a poo on his own doorstep.

In other news, notorious town madman Barry the Blade has been barred from the Siam Smile (formerly the Dog and Duck, run by Les Brewster and his Thai bride Ying, who met in a sex bar) for taking their new all-you-can-eat promotion literally. He ate seventeen nasi gorengs and was sick on the table. He is claiming compensation as a no-vomit clause was never mentioned.

## *Friday 24*

Nietzsche is alive! Though possibly not well, as it turns out it had stowed away in the Cleggmobile! Apparently it made a surprise appearance at the Peterborough services, leaping out of the toilet (quarantined) in which it had become wedged. Asked how Granny had failed to notice the howling. She said it is hard to tell what is cat, what is engine noise, and what is Grandpa Clegg and Bruce singing sea shanties. Granny Clegg says Dad can collect it from Cromer, their next stop-off. Asked when they would be arriving there. Granny said it is fifty miles so probably Sunday.

Clearly cats are not as intelligent as I had previously imagined, as a foray into the confines of their meat-scented mobile home was bound to end in death and/or idiocy. Have not told the Drs Jones. Or Mum. Will just get Dad to collect it and sneak it back through the cat flap. There is nothing to be gained from admitting my failure as a guardian, or, in the case of the Joneses, the fact that I have relatives who own a motorhome.

7 p.m.

Dad has reluctantly agreed to fetch Nietzsche. Had to bribe him with two leftover Easter eggs (Mum still has him on her low cholesterol, low sugar, low fun diet). Ooh, maybe will not sneak Nietzsche back in, but will pretend have found him emaciated (he is bound to be if he is living with the Cleggs and their poor dietary choices. Unless he eats Bruce. Which is a possibility) and then will gain reputation as a cat-sympathizing Samaritan type, which may counteract my failure to get into northern university establishment, i.e. there is still no word from Hull. James, in an uncharacteristic fit of optimism, says it is probably just held up by Royal Mail, which loses 332,000 letters a year according to Google. I fear he is clutching at straws though, and I am doomed to an NVQ in typing at Harlow College of Further Education.

## Saturday 25

Hurrah. I take back my Plathesque/Sad Edesque pessimism, as dependable postie Beefy Clarke has delivered joyous

news (as well as a gas bill postmarked a month ago and something for Marjory) in the form of an offer of three Bs from Hull. So, as long as I do not forget to turn up, then I am guaranteed a glittering future, as James says anyone can get a B now in today's devalued exam regime. This good fortune bodes well for Uncle Jim's date tonight with SexySal. They are going to the romantic idyll that is Luigi's Pizza (owned by Dave, from Sible Hedingham, not Napoli). James has instructed him to stick to subjects like eighties music, never to mention Marigold, and avoid the salad bar as it is a salmonella-breeding deathtrap. Would have argued that he is falling for Mum's paranoia, but she is right about the salad. It is a wonder it has not been shut down. Actually it is not. Dave is married to Shelley Lemon, who is sister of Mr Lemon, who is head of environmental health.

11.30 p.m.

Have had excellent evening at the Duke, declaring that university letter heralds the end of an era, etc. etc. Scarlet said eras do not officially end until August when we actually get our results, if there is a still a university system left by then, given the swingeing cuts to higher education in the budget. She is just taking out her frustration. She and Sad Ed have not done it in six days. I give them a month before she is single and stalking main Batboy Trevor again. Uncle Jim is suffering similar gloom, pants-wise. SexySal turned out not to be. James has emailed match.com to complain. But, in ongoing optimism (or obsession), has also arranged a

rendezvous with CrazyJulie. He is the one who is crazy. She is bound to be a midget with no breasts and a mental health disorder. Granny was right. The internet is a playground for perverts and the facially afflicted.

## Sunday 26

10 a.m.
Dad has gone to fetch Nietzsche, though is, fittingly, quite philosophical about the prospect. He said it is either that, or disinfect the kitchen cupboards with Mum, or play eighteen holes with Mr Wainwright, who is taking out his financially crippling divorce trauma on his Pings, so a five-minute rendezvous with the inbreds (he actually said this) is welcome relief. He has taken his clubs as cover though. If Mum rumbles the subterfuge she will have him in her power for months.

2 p.m.
Dad is back with Nietzsche. But all is not well, i.e. it is not the emaciated creature I had hoped for. Instead it has managed to develop morbid obesity and a drooling habit. It is the Cleggs and their poor dietary habits and ability to stare into the middle distance for hours without moving. They have probably been feeding it cheese sandwiches and Spam. Changed my mind about playing the heroine and instead Dad has delivered the stray cat via the method of

throwing it over the fence. On the plus side, have realized that it is lucky Wilde is grounded, as our status as soulmates would mean he would see through my transparent charade and know that I had been harbouring a dark guilty secret. Whereas this way, they will just assume it has been locked in Mr Patel's storeroom for a week.

## Monday 27

It transpires that Dad and I are not the only Rileys who are enveloped in a web of deceit. On my lunchtime aimless wander around the sheep field with Sad Ed (attempting to think up news ways to keep Scarlet interested), we found, hidden in the long jump pit, aka cat toilet, none other than James and Wendy Shoebridge. James claimed they were discussing pi, but as Sad Ed pointed out, pi is not to be found in the vicinity of tonsils (though where and what it actually is I am still unclear). He then attempted to appeal to my worldly sympathies and asked if it was so wrong to love two women? I said yes, given that his mother is Janet Riley, lover of only one man in entire existence, bar a brief slow dance with someone called Beets Trelawney at a Young Farmers' disco in Redruth. He has begged me to keep his secret until he can work out a mathematical way of satisfying all parties, including Mad Harry. Said he has until Friday or I am fessing all, and the solution had better not include adding a third woman to the equation.

He is a moron. There is no way Mad Harry will let him off this time. It explains his perpetual state of glee though.

## Tuesday 28

6 p.m.
There has been grave news from the cut-throat world of office supplies, i.e. Wainwright and Beacham may be downsizing, i.e. Dad might be sacked! Mum is mental with poverty-line anticipation. Dad says it is not his fault, it is the declining market for treasury tags and hole punches, but Mum says it is more likely Dad's declining focus on the prize and has demanded evidence of any recent failures to ingratiate himself with his superiors. He has so far fended off interrogation by eating a chewy date, but I fear the whole missed golf match/obese Nietzsche rescue mission will soon be blurted out like Pernod sick from an O'Grady.

6.10 p.m.
That is quite poetic. In a bleak and Byronesque way. Maybe I should revive my career as a semi-suicidal poet.

6.15 p.m.
Have been sent to my room. As has Dad. As predicted he lasted only minutes before crumbling and confessing all. I did point out that given Mum's aversion to the Joneses

and Nietzsche she should be thanking us, but she retaliated by removing one of my crackers (penitent's tea) so shut up before I lost my slice of cheddar. On the plus side, this exile will give me ample opportunity to write more vomit-/ alcohol-based poems.

7 p.m.
Or read an old *Famous Five*.

## Wednesday 29

Hurrah. Soon I will not have to rely on Dad to ferry me to Scarlet's/Cambridge/rescue my animal charges from the Cleggs. It is because Mr Wandering Hands has put me in for my driving theory test. It is a week on Friday, and if I pass, I can do the practical bit after my exams. Hurrah. My worldliness is almost guaranteed. Maybe I can persuade Jack to lend me the non-sick-smelling Car of the People and I can spend my summer driving around the A1, acclimatizing myself to the north!

## Thursday 30

Sad Ed is experiencing similar car-based jubilance. He is also taking his theory test next Friday, and, in a bold and possibly ill-thought-out move, is basing his entire relationship with

Scarlet on a pass. He says that way he can drive her to exotic locations for conjugation, e.g. the coast, or Hadstock aerodrome, for that element of danger and excitement. I said Hadstock is hardly exotic, Barry the Blade has been known to 'satisfy' Mrs Stimpson (female tramp, wears white flares, smells of wee) there. He said nothing can dampen his enthusiasm. His fat hands will. They are an impediment to speedy gear changes. He will never pass the practical.

I'm RACHEL RILEY

– welcome to my so-called life.

# May

*Friday 1*

7 p.m.

It is D-Day for Uncle Jim, i.e. it is just half an hour until his date with potential mouth-breather CrazyJulie. He is buoyed with enthusiasm. Unlike Mum, who says he is gambling with his own, and possibly our, lives. And James, who says he smells of beanburger and 'hippies' and needs to freshen up if he intends to be 'doing the do' later. They have both been sent upstairs to wash their respective orifices.

8.30 p.m.

Uncle Jim is back and he has definitely not been doing any doing. He is refusing to talk about it and has shut himself in his room. James has been sent in to minister sympathy and glean information (he is more wily than Mum in these matters as he has the added quality of knowing more words for genitals).

8.45 p.m.

James is out. He says there was an undercalculation of age (by about fifteen years) and an overcalculation of attractiveness (by at least seven on a scale of ten to Fat Kylie). Plus she had a tattoo of Brian May on her left buttock. Asked if this was conveyed by word of mouth. James said no, it was conveyed by pulling her tights down and showing him, and Clive and Marjory who were sat at

the next table. Mum is now mental with internet-dating-induced shame. She says it is worse than the caravan and Marjory is bound to tell Mrs Noakes who will tell the entire town. Said on the plus side, this time it was a Riley who brought about the shame, i.e. she can blame Dad. She was marginally cheered, but not enough to prevent an immediate though random ban on hot chocolate. (Ill-timed advert during break in *Morse* repeat, i.e. the first thing she saw. Or actually second as first advert was for Mr Muscle Sink Unblocker but this is unbannable due to superior declogging ability.)

## Saturday 2

Hurrah! Wilde has texted. He is ungrounded and is coming over after band practice to escort me to the pub. Suggested maybe a quiet night round mine instead (Mum and Dad are out at Clive and Marjory's doing post-tattoo-incident damage limitation) but he says he needs to see a man about a dog. Said which man. He said Reuben. Which is odd as I know for a fact Reuben does not have a dog. Asked how Nietzsche was. He says it is still utterly traumatized and incapable of doing anything but lying on sofa watching daytime telly. It is not traumatized. It is Clegged.

 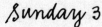 

## Sunday 3

**8 a.m.**

Have woken up with Ronan Keating on ceiling. For a minute I thought I was still trapped in a nightmare, or had somehow ended up staying the night at Thin Kylie's (Cherie has posters of Ronan and Gary Barlow above the water bed. She says they 'inspire her'. She has not said how, though I have my suspicions), but then noted presence of copy of *Of Mice and Men*, and a plate of Marmite on granary toast, which are non-Britcher friendly items (along with most novels and anything wholegrain). Plus remembered that Wilde came back last night after the pub, and encouraged poster arrangement during session of celebrity channelling. Said that I was unconvinced that Sylvia Plath would see Ronan as a muse, given his relentlessly cheery face, and less than academic career choice. And nor for that matter would Elizabeth Taylor. But he said he is done with Elizabeth and is now channelling Amy Winehouse, and she was capable of anything. This is true. And would also explain his wild eyes and silver shoes. In fact he is excellent impersonator of drug- and drink-addled songstress. Though do not think that will placate Mum. Nor will fact that he adhered to the ongoing ban on Blu Tack by using superglue. She is going to go mental. Am banking on her tendency to keep eyes on the ground at all times looking for stray fluff to hoover up while I formulate cunning plan.

11 a.m.
It is all over. Mum has seen the ceiling. It is the dog's fault. It came in demanding to sit on the window sill (it is annoyed at the newly unprovocative Nietzsche and has taken to trying to see into their living room via my bedroom window) but it fell off just as Mum walked in offering health-giving snack of raisins, knocking them flying, which sent her eyeline upwards. Have been issued with predictable shouting and a week's grounding. Have texted Wilde. He said it's like *Footloose* and I am Ariel (i.e. the preacher's daughter, not substandard washing powder (Persil only in this house)) and Mum is conspiring to keep us apart. Which is exactly what I thought. Which is yet further evidence that we are destined to be together. He is my Ren and my Romeo (Baz Luhrman version).

### Monday 4
*Bank holiday*

Ha. Mum has been semi-thwarted, as being grounded on a bank holiday will make no difference to my enjoyment of my environs as there is nothing to do anyway bar wander around Mole Hall in the unseasonal drizzle looking at otters and a marmoset. Will study *Highway Code* instead.

11 a.m.
I was wrong. A damp marmoset is infinitely preferable to trying to remember how fast you can go on a motorway or

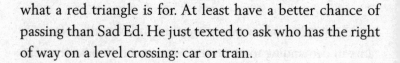

what a red triangle is for. At least have a better chance of passing than Sad Ed. He just texted to ask who has the right of way on a level crossing: car or train.

## Tuesday 5

James's infernal love square conundrum has been solved for him by one of the right angles being aggressively lopped off, i.e. Wendy Shoebridge is moving to Bury St Edmunds (inferior market town, due to unambitious pargetting (Mum) and distance from London (me)). James and Mad Harry (and most of the mathletes) are now mired in despair. I said he for one should be jubilant as now he is not likely to get maimed by Mad Harry when he finds out about the illicit cat toilet gropings but James said it is not that, it is that they are only moving because Mr Shoebridge is jumping off a sinking ship, work-wise. Asked what the sinking ship might be. He said it is Wainwright and Beacham, office suppliers to the east of England, and employer of Colin Riley, i.e. Dad! Had to lie down on Saggy Sofa Mark II (criminal brown leatherette, allegedly stain-repellent, but already sporting one sticky patch and one 'Kylie is a slag' (weight unspecified, but feasibly either)) in shock while Scarlet administered claggy Cow & Gate apricot puree and Sad Ed administered philosophical musings, i.e. Mr Shoebridge is probably a shirker, with a stationery thieving habit, so now that he has left, the ship will be lighter and less sinky, and

Dad will be reprieved. Said his words are kind, if utterly misguided. I know for a fact Dad spends several hours a day playing solitaire and our sideboard is full of pilfered Post-its.

5 p.m.

I was right. Dad has been given until end of May, and then it is the scrapheap for him. He said it is not the scrapheap, it is the jobs market. James said it is the scrapheap as the chances of him gaining employment of equal calibre, given his age, qualifications, and lack of ambition are about four per cent (he Googled it). Mum has not said anything. But her decision to dust the curtain rails speaks volumes.

## Wednesday 6

It is Mark Lambert's turn to feel the force of rejection, i.e. Thin Kylie has replaced him, love-wise. Worse, it is with an O'Grady (Liam 2). She said he is more supportive of Ugly Ducklings, plus he has a Subaru (won off Stacey in a bet about rats). Lambo is devastated. I said at least it is not Liam 1, who is still incarcerated (which I would not put past her; it is always happening in *Chat* magazine) but Lambo said at least that way he would know her virtue was intact (he did not say this, he said 'chuff was knob-free'). Personally I think it is a miracle that this is the first time the two mighty chav dynasties have been united in more than mere fondness for Peperami/gang membership,

given the sheer quantity of O'Gradys, and lack of quality control regarding Thin Kylie's previous choice of mates. The potential offspring do not bear thinking about though. They will be born knowing how to jemmy a window and drink eleven Bacardi Breezers without puking.

## Thursday 7

Mum has been scouring the *Walden Chronicle* for suitable jobs for Dad (results none, unless he wants to sell pies or empty dustbins, which he does not, according to Mum). Dad says she is overworrying as he gets hefty redundancy package and so we can continue to live comfortably for at least a year. Mum is not in agreement. She is worried he will get a taste for an idle life and will render himself unemployable by wearing his pyjamas all day and becoming addicted to *Deal or No Deal*.

## Friday 8

The mathlete table is still stuck in a quagmire of gloom. It is the impending loss of Wendy Shoebridge, thrice mental arithmetic champion of North West Essex. They have a crunch meet against Burger King Sports Academy next month and are facing annihilation by the Wily Whoppers. Scarlet is jubilant. Their loss of focus means she has been

able to surreptitiously increase Goth Corner by several metres, allowing the investiture of two Year Sevens with bat pretensions. Sad Ed is hoping her expanded empire, and his impending licence to stall his mum's Renault Clio unsupervised will renew her vigour love-wise. Judging by his performances in Lambo's first break *Highway Code* pop quiz (he learned to drive aged seven) this is unlikely. Though am not sure 'Can a Suzuki Bandit do one hundred and thirty-seven miles an hour or is Davey McDonald lying?' (answer still unresolved) will actually be included in today's exam. The flying motorbike sign had better come up though. Mum has been drumming that one into me for days, along with 'Man opening an enormous umbrella', 'Stereotypical bent old people', and 'Improbable leaning tower of cars'.

6 p.m.

Hurrah. I am now officially clever enough to drive a car, despite not recognizing the 'Migratory toad crossing' sign and opting for 'accelerate hard' when faced with an amber traffic light. Predictably Sad Ed is still without prospect of ever gaining wheels. Unless he straps some to his feet, roller-derby style. He has begged Mrs Thomas to let him enter again next week but she says she spent her last thirty pounds on a signed triptych of Aled Jones and is limiting him to one entry per month. He is going to focus on his trolley herding skills in the hope of wooing Scarlet with a never-before attempted sixty-seven trolley dash. He will get

sacked. Lawrence Gavell once tried fifty-eight and he was officially special needs.

## Saturday 9

Ugh, am still grounded. Begged Mum to allow me time off for good behaviour (passing test, cleaning teeth without being reminded, not spilling Shreddies milk from precariously overloaded jug) but she says she is not falling for that one. Am not even allowed to sit in the trolley herding arena watching Sad Ed ram VWs as Mum says it will be too enjoyable. It will not. It will be noisy, cold, and end in dented metal and egos.

4 p.m.
Unsurprisingly, Sad Ed has been moved off trolleys and on to pet food for a month. Though this is folly on the part of Waitrose, as it elevates Reuben Tull to chief trolley herder and he thinks a laser-eyed dog rules the universe.

7 p.m.
Am so bored am going to bed. Tomorrow cannot come soon enough.

8 p.m.
Ooh. Someone has thrown a stone at window. It is probably Sad Ed come to share his unemployed trolley hands/

penis gloom. Will tell him to go away as do not want to compromise ungrounding.

8.15 p.m.

It is not Sad Ed. It is Wilde, dressed in a blue frilled dinner shirt and tight satin trousers! He says he is my Ren, come to take me to the dance. I said, 'What dance?' (as only known event is golf club disco and do not want to do the locomotion with Margot Gyp) but he said, 'The one in my head, sugarplum.' Further interrogation revealed he means the Duke, which is less *Footloose*, but does have fewer Pringle jumpers per square metre. Said I could not, as was being held prisoner by malignant forces, i.e. Mrs Riley and her evil minion (James—Dad is at the disco, networking potential employers/doing the 'Macarena'), but he said rules are made to be broken, and anyway, he is my fairy godmother (as well as Ren, which is brilliant, though think he must have meant Prince Charming), and like Cinderella, I will be safely back in bed by midnight, via his dad's extendable ladder. Have agreed. Mum and James are engrossed in Danish crime drama (i.e. like *Heartbeat*, but with more snow) and will not even notice my absence. Plus will stuff pillows under duvet and put CD of Smiths on repeat. It worked for Ferris Bueller so is infallible!

11.59 p.m.

Am regrounded. James is claiming ultimate victory as not only has he proved his superiority as obedient sibling, but

it was the dog who sniffed out the presence of drugs in my room and so his future as head of freelance crime-solving agency Beastly Dog Daze (incorporating Beastly Investigations) is assured. Pointed out it was not drugs, was packet of Cherry Mentos, but he is undeterred. As was Mum. She has given me two weeks this time. She makes Middle East dictators look lenient. In fact may well write to government to attest abuse of human rights.

## Sunday 10

As if to add insult to injury, have had text from Jack to ask if I have seen Wilde. Said not since he tripped over an ornamental frog last night and temporarily went to sleep in the pond. (Have checked, he has definitely moved. Only visible living creature is Nietzsche, though he not really moving, more staring forlornly at back door wanting to regain access to TV.) Jack said he has failed to show up for practice and his excessive drinking is compromising the band. Said fourteen vodka and Diet Cokes is not excessive (is it?) and anyway, all great musicians were drunkards. Jack said I am deluded. Said I will take that as compliment, and that he is just jealous, at which point he whatevered me. He is utterly pathetic. Only Year Sevens and Suzy do whatevering any more. It is *complètement passé*.

Have texted Wilde to ensure he has not been fatally injured/kidnapped by O'Gradys 'for fun' though. (It would

not be the first time. Barry the Blade has never quite recovered from the time they put him in the boot.) No answer as yet.

2 p.m.
Still no answer from Wilde. Maybe he drowned in pond after all and is being autopsied at this very minute.

3 p.m.
Still no answer. If this carries on, may have to break the rules of my grounding by actually calling him.

4 p.m.
James has been in to inform me Wilde is in bed eating cream crackers and watching an Audrey Hepburn triple bill, and if I persist in breaching my confinement then he will have no choice but to report me to the fuhrer (i.e. Mum) who will like as not confiscate my phone entirely. Have agreed. My need to play Angry Birds is worth more than my need to be edgy and parent-defying right now. Asked how he knew about Wilde. He said if he told me, he'd have to kill me. Said was it using binoculars and the ladder that he left up last night. He said yes.

Wilde must be ill, judging by the crackers (patented Riley cure for weakened stomachs). It is overexposure from his near-drowning last night.

# May

## Monday 11

There is grave news from the House of Riley (chav wing). Jesus has lost his precious toy monkey 'Shane', and is inconsolable (i.e. sobbing into a packet of Wotsits). Mum asked Grandpa where he last saw it. He said in the saloon bar of the Queen Lizzie. Mum is visibly annoyed. It is not just the location of the incident, it is the fact that Treena has deliberately flouted her rule that toys must be interchanged regularly to avoid over-attachment. She has a point. When James dropped Olivia (rabbit, battery-operated 'boing' sound, prematurely silent through overuse and eventual removal of battery) out of a bus window, thanks to Mum's judicious swapping, he had four sheep and the naked Prince William to comfort him.

## Tuesday 12

Mark Lambert has been suspended. It is for an 'incident' in the crèche, i.e. throwing a Buzz Lightyear at the window after Thin Kylie came into school with four love bites and bed hair. Mr Wilmott says it sets a bad example to the inmates. (Buzz, not the love bites. They are used to that from Fat Kylie. Once Mr Whippy made her entire neck go purple. It looked like she'd been strangled.) He is deluded though. The inmates are expert in throwing Disney crap and have broken the window on no less than three occasions

174

(two with a Zac Efron mug and once with a *Camp Rock* microphone).

Scarlet says Lambo brought it on himself by refusing to support Thin Kylie's Ugly Ducklings dream, and by allowing himself to be at the mercy of his Neanderthal testosterone levels, and that it just proves how mere possession of a penis is a hindrance intellectually. I feel sorry for him though. He is lost without Kylie. Sad Ed was none too pleased either. He fears his penis may be a hindrance on all counts when it comes to Scarlet. They have only done it twice in the last fortnight, and one time Sad Ed says she was definitely watching BBC4 over his shoulder.

Also, according to Fat Kylie, Jesus is still distraught at the loss of Shane (she did not say 'distraught' she said 'having a spazz-out'). He refused his Wotsits at snack time and has not tried to block the sink for two days. James says it is a job for Beastly Dog Daze (it is not) and is going to make laminated posters. It is pure self-interest. He has been looking for a use for that laminator other than randomly preserving Waitrose receipts for years.

### Wednesday 13

Have broached the subject of Sad Ed and his seemingly unattractive penis with Scarlet, i.e. said, 'So, how is life in the romcom?' She said it is not romcom, it is more edgy Ken Loach (it is not, no one in Ken Loach films has almond

croissants for breakfast or a Cath Kidston ironing-board cover), with occasional interludes of dirty French film. Said I had heard on grapevine that dirty French film is not as dirty as she had hoped, and screenings less frequent. She said, 'Did Sad Ed say that?' I said it might not have been Sad Ed, it might have been Edna (she is notoriously unable to keep secrets). She said, 'Was it Edna?' I said no, it was Sad Ed. She then launched into lengthy and slightly incomprehensible explanation involving suffrage, the *Lysistrata*, and at one point, a documentary on Barbara Castle. But I think the gist was that, as a strong, liberal socialist woman (with militant tendencies), she needs to focus heavily on her impending A levels to secure her future as the first female Education Secretary, and Sad Ed's pants are too distracting. Plus the university years are designed specifically for sexual experimentation (not according to Mum, who says they are designed for eight hours a day in the library and learning to make a packet of lentils last a month), and she does not want to miss out because of a pathetic and outdated social norm that one should stay with their childhood sweetheart. I said absolutely, which is why Wilde and I are remaining non-pants-based, as we do not need to be connected sexually to be utter soulmates. Scarlet said I am deluded if I think that is the only reason. She is just minty because she has not been able to get access to Saggy Sofa Mark II since Thin Kylie commandeered it for Ugly Ducklings practice. She is using the impressionable lower sixth instead of crèche inmates. Mr Wilmott has no jurisdiction over their hair or

skin colour, despite Scarlet pressing Sad Ed to demand a ban.

So, on the plus side, Sad Ed's penis is not off-putting, rather it is *too* alluring (which I find hard to believe, but then, she has snogged Kev Banner), but that it may shortly be made utterly redundant until she has graduated from university, or possibly, been elected to government.

Also, the streets of Saffron Walden are now bedecked with laminated posters featuring a photo of Shane (dressed in a Barbie outfit) underneath the aggressive headline

### 'HAVE YOU SEEN JESUS'S MONKEY?'

and the promise of a 'generous reward'. Asked James what this might be. He said £5 and the joy of knowing you have made Jesus smile. Luckily the chances of anyone replying are nil anyway (it will have been binned, or burned if the finder has any sense), or I fear recriminations and trade-descriptions prosecutions.

10 p.m.
Wilde's lack of interest in the contents of my bra or pants is odd though. He is so liberated in all other ways (e.g. drinks experimental concoctions of gin and cherryade, wears tulle). What is wrong with my breasts or minky? Unless I remind him too much of the mysterious Marlene, his first love. Maybe she traumatized him and he is rendered impotent. That would be typical.

## Thursday 14

The missing monkey saga has taken a new and disturbing twist. Mum has received a text message saying 'I got Jesuseses monkey' (sic). But her reply asking for an address from which to collect said monkey was met with 'Your not in charge, I am'. She is mental with anger. Not only is Shane being held hostage against his will, the captors cannot spell or punctuate properly. James then commandeered the phone and demanded a photo to prove that their monkey was in fact Shane. They said no because picture texts cost 25p but that its distinguishing features were a missing tail and a smell of cheesy crisps. It is definitely Shane. James is now awaiting further instructions. Unlike Mum, he is beside himself with joy as he is now fully embroiled in his first criminal case. He is now training the dog with packets of Wotsits so he will be able to sniff Shane out in the criminal's lair. He is wasting his time. The dog is just eating them, bag and all.

## Friday 15

There has been further communication in the Great Saffron Walden Monkey Kidnap. It is a virtual ransom note, i.e. the captors sent a text demanding £100 in used notes. James has asked for a rendezvous time and lair location. They said they will send it tomorrow, because MTV is on and it's too loud to think. James is insistent it is a London gang with Mafia or Triad

links, but it has the classic hallmarks of the involvement of an O'Grady. He is going to be sorely disappointed when the lair does not turn out to be a disused volcano, or underground cavern, but is a semi on the Whiteshot Estate.

## Saturday 16

The rendezvous has been set. It is tomorrow at 3 p.m. at Barry Island (i.e. the car park on the common where various morons go to rev up their crap Datsuns). James has already assembled his Beastly Dog Daze equipment (camera, water pistol, faithful if hairy assistant). Grandpa says it is too terrifying a job for a child and we have to call the police but Mum says she will go. To be fair she is more menacing than PC Doone and any of the police dogs. They make the dog look normally intelligent. Which is a feat of reckoning given that right now it is eating its own foot. James is not happy. He says he has laid all the groundwork and Mum is stealing the glory. She is not, there is nothing glorious about arguing with an O'Grady in a car park over a monkey called Shane.

## Sunday 17

2 p.m.
It is just hours to go until Shane's release from captivity. Dad is trying to be manly and protective of Mum (i.e.

has made her have a second helping of apple crumble in case she gets kidnapped too and is forced to live on ready meals and pizza). I note he has not volunteered to go in her place though. She wouldn't let him anyway. He is notoriously weak-willed when it comes to any negotiations, whereas Mum is MI5-like in her bargaining skills. Have asked where her envelope of used tenners is. She says she is not taking any money, not even the Monopoly notes that James had already counted out. This is sheer foolhardiness. She is going to get kidnapped for sure. Or at least beaten senseless. And Shane will be lost forever. Oh, the tragedy!

**3.30 p.m.**
Mum is back, with Shane, and with no visible bruising. As predicted, it was the devilment of an O'Grady though not, as I suspected, Keanu, the youngest and deadliest of them all, but was 'the one with the silly hair', i.e. Liam 2, sucker of the neck of Thin Kylie. Asked Mum if he had put up any sort of resistance. She said the use of the words 'you are heading to the scrapheap of society' seemed to confuse him (unsurprisingly, he probably thinks she is referring to town dump), and she saw her chance and gave his unmentionables a good poke with her umbrella. She is going round to Grandpa's now with Shane, and a stern lecture on the perils of lackadaisical toy monitoring.

5 p.m.

Mum is back, as is Shane. Apparently Jesus's affections are now being bestowed on a hamster (real). She says it will be dead or missing within a week. The dog has got Shane instead. It will probably eat it, so in fact it could have just been left with the O'Gradys and saved everyone some bother. As it is, I am now facing the wrath of Thin Kylie who probably had that £100 earmarked for perming solution and his unmentionables earmarked for something equally unmentionable.

## Monday 18

The inevitable has happened. Sad Ed has been dumped, a victim of feminism, and possibly his own inability to stop eating Dairy Milk. So great is his woe that Thin Kylie has allowed him exclusive use of CD corner and the Saggy Sofa Mark II so he can lie and stare vacantly at the ceiling during all free periods listening to Leonard Cohen (plus his depressive torpor means she can use him for eyebrow shaping practice (she is readying herself for Whitney O'Grady, whose monobrow is worse than Mr Knox's)).

I said this news is devastating and the end of an era, friendship-wise, as well as politically. But Scarlet said, *au contraire*, she is remaining as his political advisor until the new Head Boy is announced (odds on favourite is Max Calloway (Deputy King Mathlete, too-big trousers)) and will remain his friend for eternity, unless he transgresses goth law, in which case he will be dead to her. I fear the worst; he has always been quite keen on being dead anyway, and this will only rekindle his spate of suicide bids.

## Tuesday 19

As predicted, Sad Ed has tried to kill himself. Luckily it was by the guaranteed-to-fail method of overdosing on Wind-eze. Scarlet is unmoved. She said it lacked real ambition, and was a hollow cry for help, i.e. access to her hoo-ha, which she has made clear he will not be getting for the foreseeable future. Have told Sad Ed he must follow mine and Wilde's example, i.e. be non-pants-based soulmates (and then be best-placed for seduction when they are suitably drunk/high on Busby Berkeley musicals). He seemed slightly cheered by this idea. At least, after he had stopped choking on his Snickers. I said concept of me and Wilde in passionate embrace was not that unthinkable. He said I have more chance of bedding Edward Cullen. Ugh. As if. He is as passé as whatevering.

Also, it is Treena's birthday. Got her the thoughtful gift of a free makeover with Fat Kylie. It is beneficial for all participants, i.e. Fat Kylie needs the practice, Treena cannot look any worse than she already does, plus all it cost me was the indignity of pretending to be interested in a photo of Mr Whippy's new tattoo (it is 'carpe diem' on his neck, which

is laughable, given that the only thing he seizes with any enthusiasm is Fat Kylie). In any case, it is superior to Jesus's gift, created during 'cookery corner' at the Camilla Parker Bowles Memorial Crèche, i.e. a birthday cake consisting of two Wagon Wheels sandwiched together with squirty cream (both banned in our house since their invention for obvious reasons).

## Wednesday 20

Renovation work has finally started next door, i.e. the Drs Jones are removing all trace of unworldly Clive and Marjory (i.e. ornamental pond, avocado bathroom suite, horrible hint of lavender paint job), and creating a 'live/work area', a wet room, and a study. Mum is mental with 'ideas above their station' and potential noise pollution issues, and has dug out her anti-social-behaviour notebook in anticipation. I said I would be happy to go round to request a downing of drills during the lunchtime news, and periods of illness, but she said she is not falling for that one and grounded means no departing from the boundary of 24 Summerdale Road except during school hours or under strict family supervision (i.e. her or James, as Dad has repeatedly failed to meet her strict 'responsible adult' criteria).

# Thursday 21

Mum's anti-Jones fervour has reached new peaks. There have been four ceaseless hours of drilling at number 26, and she has definitely seen Farrow & Ball paint tins being taken in (paint with ideas above its station). Said maybe it was just Dulux (paint of choice chez Riley, with no highfalutin ideas) in a new tin design, but she said the binoculars do not lie. Plus she is minty as there are still no jobs in the paper suitable for Dad and he is being sacked tomorrow. Said it was not sacked, it was 'redundancy', which is no-fault implication, but she says there is fault, and it is firmly Colin Riley's. She is going to widen her search for suitable employment to include the entire southeast region. James pointed out that a commute from Saffron Walden to, e.g. Gravesend, could be ruinous, financial and health-wise, but Mum said if the fancy paintwork travesty continues next door, then moving might be the only option. Although Kent is a step too far.

Hurrah! Maybe Dad will get a job in London after all!

10 p.m.
James says the whole of London has also been blacked out on Mum's Colin Job Map (stuck on fridge with acceptable fixative, i.e. magnets in the shape of vegetables). She has no imagination that woman.

# Friday 22

The atmosphere at the Shreddies table is imbued with solemnity (I am SO going to get an A* in English with sentences like that). It is end of an era fever, i.e. it is Dad's last day as chief paperclip monitor person at Wainwright and Beacham, my last day as a full-time superior upper sixth form member and occupant of Saggy Sofa Mark II and Goth Corner (on occasions), and Wendy Shoebridge's last day as mathlete, member of the Hypotenuses Competition Squad, and part-time lover of Mad Harry and James. Even the dog is gloomy. Though that may be due to the fact that it is not allowed in the back garden since the renovations next door began due to its tendency to walk in wet concrete/climb inside heavy machinery/eat wallpaper paste. In fact the only cheerful consumer of wholewheat cereal this morning is Uncle Jim. (I do not know why. He is going to a concert with Hairy Rosamund later, and she is bound to spend the entire time scratching either her nits or her eczema.) It is James I fear for the most though. Wendy's departure could wreak havoc on his grade average, not to mention his loins. Whereas I am worldly and eager to move on and experience new academic frontiers, particularly ones that do not involve O'Gradys.

5 p.m.
Ugh. Am racked with nostalgia already. No more will I smell the sweet odour of rubber as Criminals and Retards melt

stuff in the microwave. No more will I wonder where the rats of Rat Corner actually live. No more will I wander the hallowed corridors of learning, avoiding crèche inmates and stray sheep. Scarlet said in fact I will do all of the above as I have to go back in for exams, and for handover-of-power day, and for the end-of-term prom. She is being deliberately unsentimental. It is all part of her focused, high-achieving, feminist, anti-pants-area stance, also including refusing to look at Sad Ed's 'come hither' eyes (which are not very hithery at all, they are more borderline serial killer). James is similarly philosophical, and spent most of last break reaffirming his commitment to Mumtaz, i.e. feeding the school locusts together. Said what about Mad Harry, who is experiencing devastating loss. James said he is thinking of setting up a John Major High internet dating agency to help cases like his. I said surely his lack of success with Uncle Jim is a deterrent but James said, *au contraire*, it has fuelled his ambition to be the King of Matchmakers (*Clueless* style, not nobbly chocolates). Dad is not depressed. He is just drunk. He will be depressed in the morning though when he realizes he has no control over his finances any more, and is under Mum's jurisdiction on a twenty-four-hour basis.

## Saturday 23

Hurrah! I am ungrounded. And it could not come at a better time as Mum has reinstigated austerity measures at 24

Summerdale Road, i.e. limited snacks, an hour of TV a day, and Wi-Fi to be turned off except for essential job searches/ emailing/bargain hunting. Luckily Dad is still asleep so he cannot even think about consuming his customary five digestives and coffee with one sugar (only allowed as a 'treat' and now banned for the foreseeable future). Am going to Scarlet's to arrange wild night of abandon before revision begins in earnest on Monday. Plus Wilde is round there for band practice, so can ask him to come along at the same time. It is utterly economical in terms of my exertion so Mum cannot complain.

3 p.m.
Ugh. Scarlet is babysitting Harper. And Wilde will be in Bishop's Stortford with Jack as Blind Monkey Fernando have their first ever gig. Begged to go with them but there is no room in the van due to the enormity of the drum kit, and of Fin Fenton (plays bass, Dad is plumber, hence van) and Dad is not allowed to drive me due to newly imposed petrol limits (Waitrose once a week, Scotsdales once a month, and golf on prior request). Plus I was wrong about Mum. She is utterly complaining on every level. Though mostly it is about the dog who escaped and ate wet cement, thus scoring a personal best on the idiocy front, and Dad who has been sick four times, thus also beating his own record. She is now refusing to fund any non-exam-related excursions. I said going to the Duke was very exam-related as we could have a groundbreaking discussion on proportional representation.

She said it is more likely to be about socks. She is right, but did not give her the satisfaction of agreeing. Instead am going for Plan Z, i.e. go with Sad Ed, who, while being utterly moany and annoying, is at least minted from stacking Kitekat so can fund my lemonade and Cheese Moments.

10 p.m.
Am home and watching Formula 1 highlights with the dog and Dad and their handy vomit bucket. Sad Ed's depression has reached new highs, or lows, i.e. he drank four pints of cider and started singing 'Desolation Row' with Reuben Tull. Plus Jack's replacement at the bar is a woman who looks exactly like nineties Geordie TV regular Jimmy Nail, i.e. mullet, broken nose, bad tattoos. It is most off-putting.

Actually wish I was grounded again, then I would have some excuse for Saturday nights being tediously suburban.

*Sunday 24*

10 a.m.
Sad Ed has texted to say he has woken up with a carrier bag of what looks like doner kebab next to his bed and do I know anything. Have said I do not. It is probably something to do with Jimmy Nail woman. Maybe it is a love token. She is probably a feeder, and is hoping to turn him into a gargantuan mass that she can keep locked in her semi on the Cromwell Road Estate.

# May

**2 p.m.**
Wilde has texted. He has been thrown out of Blind Monkey Fernando! Have demanded an immediate summit at the back fence (thus not risking any more groundings/wet concrete incidents).

**11.30 a.m.**
It is all Jack's fault. According to Wilde, the gig was a triumph, with his style being compared (but of course) to a young David Bowie, both voice- and catsuit-wise. But clearly Jack could not cope with Wilde getting all the attention and has replaced him with Fin, who does not look a young anyone, except possibly John Prescott. Said I will go to Jack's immediately to defend his honour, and right to wear skintight purple Lycra. Wilde said I am wasting my time as Jack is clearly pathetically suburban and has no clue as to real talent or taste, hence his repro Ramones T-shirt. I said actually it was an original, but that did not give him the right to throw his weight around. Am going round immediately.

**4 p.m.**
Jack has contested Wilde's version of events, *quelle* surprise. He said the only accolades were for his own ability to keep to a four-four while Wilde slurred his way through 'Metal Kettle' and fell off stage seven times. I said it sounds legendary. Jack said the only moment that will go down in legend is when Wilde was sick on the man

from the *Harlow Gazette*. I said it is probably stage fright, masked by overconfidence and bravado, and a feather boa. Jack said it is more likely Jack Daniels and shitness. He is clearly green with envy. It is like when Liam Gallagher sacked Noel Gallagher for having a better voice and less of a monkey face.

On the plus side, Scarlet is setting up a hothouse revision centre at hers for the next week. Have said we have to invite Sad Ed as he is in danger of being imprisoned by a woman who looks like a bad 1980s football player. Scarlet said I am over-imagining again. I said the next time she goes to the Duke she will see that I am not. Amazingly Jack backed me up. He said he was there when Shorty hired her, but it was her or Kev Banner, and he would drink the pub out of business in a week. Anyway, Scarlet has agreed. We start Tuesday, as tomorrow is taken up with the arrival of Maya. Suzy said I absolutely have to come as I am practically family (I am not, as Mum has pointed out on several occasions). I said I will check my revision schedule. (This is a lie as I do not have a schedule, I have yet to commission James and his arsenal of highlighter pens and reward systems, I am just not sure I need to spend an afternoon in the presence of ethnic beauty who is bound to keep mispronouncing things in an irritatingly endearing manner. Plus Edna's version of a Guatemalan feast is probably a Spanish omelette.)

## Monday 25
*Bank holiday*

**1 p.m.**
Am going to Scarlet's. There is only so much of James and Mumtaz snogging, and Dad and the dog moaning that I can take. Plus it is my duty to welcome Maya to the unfamiliar and exciting first world, albeit one that still has a shop that stocks girdles and elastic trousers.

**5 p.m.**
There has been some kind of miscommunication, i.e. Maya is not an exotic innocent, born and raised among the goats of Chichicastenango, and schooled only in the classroom that is life, she is a former Latimer girl, born and raised on Westbourne Grove, i.e. Notting Hill! So my gift of a Spanish–English phrasebook (borrowed from James) did not go down as brilliantly as I had hoped. Jack said it was 'vintage Riley' but it was with a definite smirk. This is so typical. No sooner do I acquire a worldly soulmate with piercings and parents who once went to dinner with Joanna Lumley, than Jack retaliates with someone who is related to a Rolling Stone.

## Tuesday 26

Revision at Scarlet's was not as mind-expanding as I had hoped. It is Sad Ed's fault for spending most of the time

weeping on a beanbag. He said it was because he was moved by the plight of the working men refused a vote until the reform act of 1884. It is not, it is because Scarlet was wearing a revealing black camisole and he cannot bear to look at what is no longer his. Plus I could hear the distinct sound of Maya and Jack 'revising' in his bedroom and it was not in the least bit academic. Also, Edna is now nannying as well as cleaning, now that Suzy has U-turned on being a full-time mum and is being the sexpert on *This Morning* three times a week. She says it is so she can set Harper an example, but I do not know how talking about knob malfunction on national television is an example of anything.

## Wednesday 27

Scarlet says she has had all she can take of Sad Ed's self pity (threatening to stab himself with a Bic) and that he needs to buck up as there is nothing as unattractive as an underachiever. I said in fact I am frequently attracted to people with no qualifications other than raw talent and good hair (e.g. Wilde, Justin Statham, and the man who does road sweeping on Wednesdays) but she said this is why I am doomed to failure and will end up like Grandpa Riley.

She may be right. Treena was at home when I got back (no talent, no qualifications, bad hair) to show off the results of her Fat Kylie makeover. It is less 'transformative' than I hoped, i.e. she still looks like a thirty-something from

Bolton, only one who has spent four weeks on a sunbed and grown inexplicably bushy eyebrows. She said it is the fashionable 'scouse brow'. I do not think there is anything fashionable about looking like a werewolf. Both Grandpa and Jesus are in shock. Even the dog refused to go near her, and she is usually its prime target due to her carrying of 'emergency' Cheestrings.

## Thursday 28

Unbelievably Scarlet's anti-moping speech has had an effect on Sad Ed. He is now utterly motivated and has learned Hamlet's speech to the players overnight. It is pathetically transparent though. He is just hoping his heroic acting will woo Scarlet back into his bulky arms. It will not. Plus he cannot pronounce Termagant. It is lucky his other A levels are Art and Music, i.e. involving no words whatsoever. Maya said if he is really serious about being a musician then he is wasting his time with A levels anyway and what he really needs to do is go travelling so he can 'find his sound'. She is wrong. He found his sound aged eight and it is Abba songs on the Bontempi organ. It put Jack in a tricky position though as he is completely pro further education as the basis for any career, which I pointed out. So he gave me the evils and said maybe travelling was an education in itself and that school does not suit everyone (pathetic attempt to stay true to self and Maya) but Scarlet pointed out that

travelling does not suit Sad Ed as he gets car sick and is afraid of foreign toilets. Told Scarlet afterwards that I do not trust Maya. I fear her happy-go-lucky trust-funded outlook on life may be compromising Jack's middle-class (but with working-class soul) ideals. She said Jack is big enough to fight his own battles, why do I care anyway, and isn't Wilde just another version of Maya. Said shut up, I have prime ministers to revise.

4 p.m.
Reminded Mum I have a driving lesson tomorrow. She said I do not, as austerity measures mean that from now on she will be teaching me (Dad has tried already to the dissatisfaction of all parties) and that I can start by backing the Fiesta down the drive in anticipation of the Big Shop tomorrow (still at Waitrose, but with the threat of a change to Tesco if Dad does not buck up his search).

4.05 p.m.
Mum says she will not be teaching me after all (reasons too numerous to list, but mainly featuring my failure to back down the drive, and instead narrowly avoiding hitting the garage door, and dog who was licking it at the time). Instead she is going to see Mr Wandering Hands (on foot) to come to some 'arrangement'. I hope it is not sexual. James said it could be, given Dad's recent redundancy, which can have a devastating effect on potency of penis. Oh God. The imagery.

5 p.m.

Thankfully it is not sex, it is answering the phone and filing, for which she will be paid £7.50 an hour, and get a twenty-five per cent discount on my lessons. James said Dad needs to take note from her impressive tenacity in finding a job in these dark times. Dad said that he lacks the 'accoutrements' required by such an employer. Mum said it is not down to her accoutrements at all, but her proven organizational skills, and the fact that Mrs Wandering Hands has Yogalates every morning. I fear James may be right about the potent penis thing though. Dad seemed very testy at the whole debacle. He had better buck up before Mum does swap him for someone with gainful employment and a libido.

## Friday 29

10 a.m.

Have crashed Mr Wandering Hands's Fiesta into a gatepost. It is Barry the Blade's fault. He was standing outside Mr Patel's wearing a helmet and what looked like Wilde's feather boa. I hope Wilde has not started consorting with notorious madmen. Though it is quite edgy. And maybe in fact Barry the Blade is a leading expert on Coleridge (latest channelling). In fact am going to go and find out. Capital Kebab opens in an hour and the bins are his first port of call.

11 a.m.

Barry the Blade is not an expert on Coleridge. I said, 'It was an ancient mariner . . .' only instead of 'and he stoppeth one of three', he said, 'Got twenty pence for some ketchup?' Which is not poetic. I have checked on Google. Though it is steep for ketchup (also checked on Google). Plus got a phone call from Mum. She has found out about the Fiesta damage and says any more misdemeanours and she will ban me from the driving school. Said as filer and phone answerer she did not have that authority. She said as Janet Riley she had every authority and to get back to my books immediately or I will end up like Granny Clegg, i.e. unqualified, unable to drive, and stuck in the hinterlands. Which is a point. No one has heard from the Cleggs since the Nietzsche incident. I hope they have not accidentally driven off the edge of Beachy Head. Or worse, into Peckham.

## Saturday 30

10 a.m.

The Cleggs are not dead or in Peckham. They are not even in the Cleggmobile. Predictably, they are reinstalled in the broken Parker Knoll and hideous settee at Pasty Manor. Grandpa said they had seen the world, and it was not for them. Asked what bits they had seen. He said Saffron Walden, Norfolk, and the Hangar Lane gyratory for about two hours. I said surely this hasty abortion had thrown their living

arrangements into disarray, i.e. I thought they had let Pasty Manor out to Pig during his marital issues. But apparently they are all living in perfect harmony, with Pig sleeping in the Cleggmobile but using the indoor 'privy' on request. Also he said no one had had an abortion and he is minded to report me to Mum for even mentioning the word. Said she is too busy disentangling the dog from the landing window after it spotted Nietzsche having a poo and made an attempt to fly. James is jubilant that his lessons paid off after all. Mum is less jubilant, and rightly so. It is her spying that encouraged the dog in the first place. Though I am the main victim in all this. She has banned me from going to the pub until exams are over. I said this was tantamount to grounding. She said it is not an official grounding, but is more an instillation of optimum exam conditions. I said this is the kind of distinction used by Nazis to install the ghetto (not sure if this is true but it sounds feasible) plus conditions are less than optimum given that Uncle Jim has invited ailment-riddled Rosamund over for dinner so I am likely to catch something horrible and miss my exams anyway. Mum did not have an answer for that as the dog fell out of the window at that point, though was relatively unharmed due to a soft landing on Dad who was reading a John Grisham on the patio.

10 p.m.

Why Uncle Jim chooses to spend his 'me' time with Rosamund as well as his Mr Goldstein lentil time is beyond comprehension. She has taken up crocheting her own clothes, and given up shaving her armpits. It is frightening. Even the dog opted to eat in the kitchen, which is its least favourite dining venue, due to over-cleanliness of all surfaces, i.e. nothing interesting to be licked.

## Sunday 31

10 a.m.
Revision conditions are about to hit new lows, i.e. Jesus is coming for lunch, and is bringing his new 'best friend', Lorna, i.e. the hamster. Asked if was named for the eponymous heroine of the Blackmore novel. It is not, it is named for the woman who does the ironing at Smeg launderette.

3 p.m.
A mysterious incident has occurred, i.e. the washing machine has broken, flooding the kitchen. I said it was not that mysterious, given the presence in the house of Jesus and the dog, but Mum said it was only serviced two weeks ago and Mr Fenton (father of Fin, no discernible ear-lobes) said he had never seen such a shiny drum. James is mental with excitement and is using his full Beastly Investigations toolkit to investigate.

3.30 p.m.
Cause of flooding has been identified. It is a bite-shaped hole in the rubber seal. All fingers point to the dog (habitual

198

chewer of all things non-edible), but James is insisting on a tooth identity parade, including Lorna. Grandpa pointed out Lorna had been housed in a plastic ball rolling around the downstairs toilet (all carpeted surfaces deemed too prone to wee-staining) for the last hour but James is insistent.

4 p.m.

As suspected, the dog has been found guilty. There was a tricky moment when measurements revealed Dad's mouth was in fact of similar size, but Mum pointed out that he has a full set of molars, unlike the dog who lost one biting a brick, leaving a telltale imprint on the seal. Also, as suspected, Lorna has not been rolling around the downstairs toilet, but has escaped due to either a faulty ball (Grandpa's theory) or user error (Mum's theory, who claims Grandpa didn't tighten it properly). The house, and dog, are now undergoing forensic searches.

4.30 p.m.

Lorna found alive and well inside a packet of Minstrels secreted in Treena's handbag in case she didn't like pudding (she never likes pudding unless it is Angel Delight, which it never is, due it being banned for being less than delightful). James said Jesus could keep it in his pocket and train it to sniff out snack goods but his idea has been rejected by everyone.

I'm RACHEL RILEY
— welcome to my so-called life.

June

 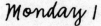
# Monday 1

**8 a.m.**

Ha! James has gone back to school. He says he is minded to lobby Mr Wilmott for exam leave for Year Sevens for their pointless progress tests but Mum says he can jolly well use his *Tracy Beaker* time for revision. I fear he will not be dissuaded though. He says it could be the cornerstone of Max Calloway's (newly crowned head mathlete now that Ali Hassan is Oxbridge-bound (not actual place, as discovered last year)) Head Boy campaign. It will not be. It will be hollow promises and free tat as usual. On the downside, Mum has banned me from going to Scarlet's. She says Dad can supervise my revision, as it will give both of us a sense of focus and purpose while she is out toiling for Mr Wandering Hands. It is not that, it is that she does not trust Dad to operate any machinery (heavy or otherwise) in her absence, or the dog not to consume something untoward. I am not minded. I will shut myself in the bedroom where I cannot be distracted by their idiocy.

**11 a.m.**

Or alternatively sit on the sofa and watch excellent morning television, i.e. *Lorraine* and *Jeremy Kyle*. Today was 'My schoolgirl daughter is engaged to a seventy year old so his inheritance can fuel her heroin habit'. I said it is a shame nothing like that ever happens in Walden as it would give people something to talk about rather than the

ongoing mini-roundabout hoo-hah and whether culottes are acceptable golf-wear. (Not. Nor are they acceptable wear during non-crap sports time.) Next up is *This Morning*. Then I will definitely focus on Drama.

**2 p.m.**
After *Doctors*. Which is very dramatic, and like a modern-day Shakespearean tragedy if you think about it.

**3 p.m.**
Is not really worth starting now as Mum and James are back any minute, and they are bound to disturb my concentration with their endless discussions over the optimum time for toast making.

## Tuesday 2

Another day, another session of 'Jeremy Club'. Dad says it has opened his eyes to the plight of Britain's disenfranchised underclass. It has not, he just likes watching fat girls fighting in velour tracksuits. *Doctors* was also excellent, i.e. a cricket-playing IT consultant with herpes infects wife of IT boss man, who is also captain of opposing team. Brilliantly implausible, yet utterly compelling.

## June

### Wednesday 3

*Jeremy Kyle* again compelling this morning, i.e. 'Has my mum had a baby with my husband?' (answer: no, was the man off the fish counter in Morrison's called Roy) and 'Who is father to our baby: me or my dad?' (answer: my dad. Horrifying thought. Especially as the dad looked like Barry the Blade. Wilde's dad looks more like Tony Blair. Also a horrifying thought). Jeremy also appalled at low morals. And the fact that conception took place in a lift at the Trafford Centre. Jeremy is like a modern-day healing person. Billy Graham. Or Jesus. But with a shinier face and bad suit. Oh, that is an excellent profound thought. Degree level even. Maybe I should have opted for Philosophy instead. I could become the next Nietzsche. (Person, not cat. Cat is still horribly overweight and unacademic.)

Also had a second profound thought (which is an unprecedented occurrence) that Jeremy Kyle and Gok Wan should join forces in a single, all-changing therapeutic television bonanza. Decent haircut and swapping yellow leggings for palazzo pants would do wonders for life chances. Plus wide-leg trousers are a complete contraceptive. It is a well-known fashion fact.

5 p.m.
James is not in agreement over Jeremy Kyle being Jesus. He says if anyone is Jesus it is Graham Norton. I said Graham is gay. He said when did I ever see Jesus with girlfriend. Which is a fair point.

## Thursday 4

Scarlet has joined Jeremy Club! She says conditions at Debden Road are unbearable again due to the endless arguing. I said I thought Bob and Suzy were enjoying a second honeymoon now that Edna had taken over some, if not all, of household responsibilities, but she says it is not them it is Jack and Maya. They cannot decide what they are doing next year. I said I thought Jack was definitely going to university, but Scarlet said Maya wants him to move to Westbourne Grove so he can hang out with minor Jaggers and infiltrate the music scene by the back door.

Dad was not too happy about the new addition. He is worried she does not understand the rules, given her track record of defending the underclass, but she promised to take the moral high ground and not to be over-sympathetic towards anyone with neck tattoos or wearing Burberry.

## Friday 5

9 a.m.
Jeremy Club is becoming unduly popular. Membership now comprises me, Dad, the dog, Scarlet, and Sad Ed, who says he has finished revision already and so is just twiddling his thumbs, which he might as well do in a house where

'Walking in the Air' is not on repeat. Dad is delighted. He says the company keeps him young, and as Mum is now gainfully employed the pressure is off for him to do anything constructive.

11 a.m.

A terrible thing has happened. Jeremy Club has been outed! It is all James's fault. Mum got called to school because he had been sick in rural studies and it was bright red so there was a panic that he had internal bleeding. (He does not. It is because he drank a bottle of red Quink in a bet with Mad Harry.) Mum demanded to know why Dad had not answered the phone when Mrs Leech rang. Dad had to admit it was due to the impending DNA results of a man called Stacey from Wigan. Mum has banned all daytime television, revision clubs, and biscuits, plus I am grounded. I said I was in the house in the first place so grounding me is not an appropriate punishment but she looked like she might actually combust at that point so I sent myself to my room before she could add that to the list.

### Saturday 6

Am shut in the dining room with a sheaf of A4 paper, Wikipedia, and James's patented revision schedule (this year featuring a stick approach as opposed to carrot,

with forfeits for any incomplete tasks, e.g. 'do "Lord of the Dance" performance, barefoot, on gravel'). I am only allowed out for toilet breaks, and other family members are only allowed in for consumption of health-giving meals/random checks to ensure I am not asleep/idly roaming around YouTube. Plus I am to show evidence of my learning by regaling her with one excellent A* grade fact per day.

4 p.m.
Fact of the day: Margaret Thatcher did not have an affair with Ronald Reagan.

## Sunday 7

Fact of the day: Neil Kinnock may have lost the 1992 election due to being Welsh and ginger. A sad indictment of prevailing prejudices in that most selfish of decades. Luckily we are all more embracing of difference today).

5 p.m.
Bar the Cleggs. Grandpa Clegg just rang to rant about Mr Nuamah's new assistant dentist Mr Smeeton. He said it is bad enough Mr Nuamah is 'one of them' (he means black, or possibly Welsh) but the assistant is from Devon.

## Monday 8

Forfeit of the day (following attempt to watch cats falling off a treadmill): take dog for a poo (it is still barred from the garden while next door's ornamental pond is filled in, lest it should get accidentally buried). Though this proves James's lack of foresight when it comes to forfeiture as being allowed out of the house was a gift in itself, even if I did have to pick up a smelly deposit.

Bumped into Thin Kylie on the way back and asked her how her plans for Ugly Ducklings were going. She said they are on hold because Liam 2's court hearing is in a week so she needs to see if she has to move closer to Dartmoor. I fear she may have been too hasty in swapping Lambo for an O'Grady. He may be a minibike-obsessed moron, whose only real talent is being able to burp pop songs, but at least he did not attempt to hijack a milk float (unproven until court hearing, but evidence suggests he is the guilty party).

## Tuesday 9

Fact of the day: William Pitt the Younger was only twenty-four when he became Prime Minister. This bodes well for Scarlet. Though not the fact that he graduated Cambridge at the age of seventeen. She was still battling Tamsin Bacon in the Throne of Magnificence at this point

and I am pretty sure parliament would frown on that kind of activity.

## Wednesday 10

Fact of the day: Fidel Castro once made a speech to the UN lasting four hours and twenty-nine minutes, which makes Mum look half-hearted (this morning's 'why one must NEVER use the butter (actually low-cholesterol-olive-oil-based spread) knife in the Marmite jar' to Dad only ranked up twenty-two minutes in comparison).

10 p.m.
Also, he did not invade the Bay of Pigs. And nor did the bay actually have any pigs in it.

## Thursday 11

Fact of the day: This is worse than my self-imposed Anne Frank confinement. At least she could read what she liked and didn't get pop quizzed on parliamentary procedure by Paxman and his idiotic sidekick (Mum and James, who is chief setter of questions, though his suitability has been called into doubt due the unlikelihood of 'What colour are the benches in the House of Lords?' actually featuring in tomorrow's Politics exam. Answer: red. Though had to Google it).

## Friday 12

8 a.m.
Thank God I have an exam. My allotted three hours out of the confines of the dining room will be liberating, even if it is all spent trying to see what Scarlet has got written on her thigh (Suzy's preferred exam-passing method).

1 p.m.
And so it is back to the coalface, insecure in the knowledge that I may have just failed A level Politics by describing the Prime Minister as an immoral dictator. Scarlet says it just shows that I am a political being, with valid opinions instead of regurgitated drivel. I fear I may have also regurgitated some drivel, including randomly asserting that red benches in the House of Lords contributes to an unjust system which favour peers over elected members because everyone knows red is better than green.

## Saturday 13

Fact of the day: Mad Harry is now going out with Charlotte Coston. According to James her mental arithmetic ability is acceptable, and she has the value-added factor of living on a farm, which as everyone knows, means she will be more open to advances what with seeing the cows at it. Pointed out the Costons' farm is arable. He says what Mad Harry does not

know will not hurt him. Plus he has bigger fish to fry, i.e. he is working on a mate for Max Calloway as everyone knows an attractive first lady is imperative in any election campaign.

## Sunday 14

Hurrah! Mum has officially decreed Sunday a day of rest. She says that too much focus on exams could lead to failure, depression, or, in extreme cases, suicide (thank you *Times* for your overly panicking and Murdoch-tainted facts).

2 p.m.
Though I think even Murdoch would have something to say about her concept of 'rest' which mostly involves Hoovering hard-to-get-to crevices. Though it is not as bad as James. He is having to clean the dog's teeth (notoriously tricky due to its unwillingness to open its mouth, and willingness to eat claggy substances). It is punishment for holding first lady try-outs in the back garden. The less said about which the better. Other than none of them is Jackie Kennedy.

## Monday 15

Apparently I have done enough to fend off potential suicide and so it is back to the dining room regime. Mum would make an excellent political dictator, despite her brevity of

speech. Dad agrees. He is sulking because he says Jeremy Club is not the same on his own (he has evaded Mum's rulings by watching it on ITV1+1, which she did not clearly prohibit in her list of regulations. Asked him what today's feast held in store. He says it is the return of Stacey for his showdown with Bryce. If only John Major High had offered progressive A levels like media studies, then watching endless shows about questionable paternity would be encouraged.

## Tuesday 16

English Literature revision surprisingly enjoyable. Am rereading *Jane Eyre*. Maybe what Wilde needs is to be actually blinded (as opposed to metaphorically being Blind Fernando, or the Blind Monkey, or whichever he was), then he would realize that he is Rochester and I am his Jane.

10 p.m.
Though I suspect he does not have an insane first wife locked in Marjory's eaves. More's the pity.

## Wednesday 17

No, he is definitely Heathcliff. Heathcliff is more poetic, slightly mental, and has better lips (Tom Hardy version, not Ralph Fiennes version).

8 p.m.

Oh God. What if I am Miss Havisham though? I will die, jilted and alone in a mansion, my wedding dress ragged, and with cobwebs in my enormous hair. Though thinking about it, it is completely edgy and gothic. Scarlet would approve.

9 p.m.

Scarlet does not approve of Miss Havisham theory. She says anyone who sets that much store by one penis that they will condemn themselves to celibacy and decrepitude deserves utmost disdain. Though she is to be commended for adopting Magwitch's daughter, thus raising a potential pickpocket to the levels of high society, and thumbing her nose at the establishment. Maybe I will raise this point in my exam tomorrow. My feminist interpretation may win me crucial points.

## Thursday 18

Or at least it would have had it been English today. Luckily Drama does not need real revision.

Plus have had revelation that I am not Miss Havisham. Obviously, Wilde is John Keats and I am his Fanny (Brawne, not minky, though admittedly name is unfortunate). All I need now is for him to contract TB so I can lovingly tend to him while he writes heartbreaking poetry that will remain unrecognized in his own brief lifetime.

## Friday 19

Hurrah, my excessive English revision has paid off as spent three hours proving Dickens's unquestionable misogyny and suggesting improvements to *Great Expectations*, including a possible age gap coupling of Miss Havisham and Pip.

## Saturday 20

Mum has allowed me a bonus day of rest. Mainly because James and Mad Harry are composing a theme tune for the Head Boy election campaign in the front room and it is impossible to concentrate when someone is singing about fractions to the tune of 'Ooh Aah . . . Just a Little Bit'. Am going into town to purchase obligatory Father's Day present from preordained austerity list:

1 Golf ball (singular).
2 Bar of Fruit & Nut.
3 Shave stick (he is using his unemployed status as an opportunity to grow facial hair, which is banned for being unhygienic and suspicious. Mum hopes this will discourage the unsavoury activity).

James and I are under orders to make our own cards. Mum says it will be a test of our imagination, and ability to find interesting and appropriate pictures in a copy of *Woman's Realm*.

# Sunday 21
*Father's Day*

Dad pleased with shave stick, and says he will save it for when he next has an interview. Mum did not look too pleased about this, but luckily James had 'gone rogue' and got a four-pack of Carlsberg so her first priority was dealing with his defiance, and getting to bottom of exactly how he had managed to purchase alcohol given his entire lack of body hair bar on his head, and below average height.

2 p.m.
There is yet more Father's Day hoo-hah. This time it is over the placement of the apostrophe. James's card (some ducks and a Magimix) has it after the 's' whereas mine (Maureen Lipman) is in the traditional before 's' position. James claims it is a day for all fathers, not just ours, therefore he is in the right and deserves to be reinstated as number-one child. Mum has rung Marjory (fellow pedant) to check (she does not trust Google ever since it proved fallible on the subject of the Oxford comma (though I am still unclear as to what this is, why it exists, and why only Oxford has one)).

2.10 p.m.
Marjory was inconclusive. But in any case, we are both more right than Jesus (i.e. Fat Kylie) who wrote 'Happy Farthers Day' in Grandpa Riley's card. Though I am not sure the one from Dad was much better (leftover Christmas card with

inappropriate message Tippexed out). And Uncle Jim forgot due to an appointment to churn butter with Rosamund.

## Monday 22

There are now five days until my final exam (Politics), and Mum has been in to give her well-practised 'Final Countdown' lecture, i.e. this is your last chance to prove yourself at rigorous academic activity, as even if you do get into Hull to do Drama, the exams will only be pretending to be toasters or prostitutes (no idea) etc., and if you fail, then it is a lifetime of microwaving pasties in Gregg's for you. I said technically, if I fail, it is resits, but she threatened to remove my upstairs bathroom privileges, meaning all toilet breaks must be accompanied by the dog. (Who is quarantined after eating an unattended bowl of bran flakes. Mum is waiting for them to come back out as quickly as they went in.) Have capitulated anyway as I do not want to *a)* pee in front of the dog, who has more than once tried to intercept a urine stream *b)* work with Pie Shop Pearce or *c)* do resits, as this will mean another year of living in the wretched provinces, where every day is like Sunday (only not Sunday in London, which is obviously full of brunch, vintage markets, and gigs on Clapham Common, just Sunday in Saffron Walden, where brunch is banned for being new-fangled and American, and the only entertainment to be had is watching Morris Men). From now on I am immersing myself in my studies. Am not

even going to write in my diary as I do not want to waste vital joules of energy on tittle-tattle.

**11 a.m.**
Except to note that Nietzsche has been locked out of the house. It is probably in a bid to force exercise on him. Mum tried this tactic on Dad once. He walked round Clive and Marjory's, borrowed a golf club, and broke in, thus doubly annoying her for outwitting not just her but her security measures.

## Tuesday 23

And that Mrs Pledger (married to East Anglian media tycoon Jethro, has 'downstairs' problem) has had an ill-advised haircut. It is clearly an attempt to make her look several decades younger, yet has succeeded only in rendering her the spit of Noel Edmonds.

## Wednesday 24

And that Mr Whippy's van, which is parked on Thin Kylie's drive, is rocking suspiciously.

**4.15 p.m.**
Conundrum solved. Thin Kylie has just emerged from the back of the van, closely followed by Liam 2. (Clearly he

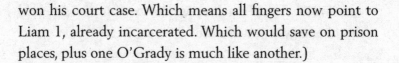
won his court case. Which means all fingers now point to Liam 1, already incarcerated. Which would save on prison places, plus one O'Grady is much like another.)

4.25 p.m.
And unsolved. Fat Kylie and Mr Whippy have just got out too. I hope they have not been swinging. The implications are horrendous.

## Thursday 25

And that Uncle Jim has taken to wearing Patchouli. It is vile. Even the dog is repelled. Mum is convinced he is back on the 'wacky baccy'. He was never off it. But he is so lethargic anyway and his room is so festooned with Glade PlugIns her suspicions have never been aroused.

## Friday 26

9 a.m.
It is D-Day. In just six hours' time I shall be another step closer to Hull, and, more importantly, the annual 'get drunk on the sheep field' post-exam party.

4 p.m.
Annual 'get drunk on the sheep field' party has been banned

# June

as the BTECers still have practical exams (bricklaying, nappy changing, vajazzling) and last year Reece Overall (real name, no neck, perpetually runny nose) was incapacitated for several days afterwards, and his wall was wonky and did not pass the 'kick it hard with a boot' test. I do not care though. I do not need a party to mark my success. I need only the satisfaction of knowing that the NHS was invented by Yuri Gagarin (trick question, as everyone thinks it is William Beveridge). And also that everyone is going to the Blind Monkey Fernando gig tomorrow at the Bernard Evans Youth Centre (moved from the ATC hut, which still has a charred weapons room) so we can get drunk then instead as, unlike Shorty McNulty and his minion Jimmy Nail woman, Darryl Stamp (works for Pelvis Presley, part-time barman, full-time idiot) does not follow underage drinking laws in the strictest, or indeed any, sense.

5 p.m.
James says Yuri Gargarin did not invent the NHS it was Aneurin Bevan. I said he couldn't have as he was too busy being the first human to orbit in space. He gave me a withering look and went back to laminating campaign posters

**(VOTE CALLOWAY (and win a free iPad)).**

Questioned the validity of this claim. He says it does not state a 'working' iPad and therefore does not breach any regulations.

Hurrah. Tonight is going to be seminal. Everyone who is anyone in the Saffron Walden music scene is going, which to be fair is not that many people, but suffice to say that Sad Ed, Scarlet, me, and Reuben will be there. Even Bob and Suzy are coming and bringing Harper. Suzy says a girl's first gig is a landmark in her journey to womanhood. Let us hope Harper does not follow her adoptive mother's example and snog the lead singer. On the downside Maya is going too. Scarlet says they have made up in the university versus university of life row and have agreed Jack can go to college but stay at hers in the holidays. Said what about coming home to Saffron Walden? She said he has secured Christmas Day and Suzy's birthday. Jack needs to stand his ground or he will end up in Maya's sway and will be wearing hipster glasses and red skinny jeans before he knows it. Though she does have a point. Who wouldn't rather spend their summer vacation (normally banned for being American but is official university term so am embracing in defiance of Mum's protestations) treading the gritty streets of Portobello, avoiding needles, rent boys, and vintage stallholders, compared to wandering the clean (bar Dogshit Alley) and crazy-paved environs of North Essex, where the only obstacle is avoiding Mrs Noakes and her all-seeing eye.

7 p.m.

Hurrah! Wilde has agreed to come to the gig. He says he wants to see how his replacement copes with the top C in 'Metal Kettle' (though he fears it will be as lamentable as the replacement of Jim Morrison with Ian Astbury for the Doors' reformation), plus the vodka is only £2 a shot. Am jubilant, as the Mayaness infesting tonight's festivities will now be counterbalanced by Wilde's superior vibes. He is bound to dislike her. She is too Kensington for his taste. I know for a fact she owns a Jack Wills vest top.

11.58 p.m.

A tragedy has occurred, on several levels, i.e. *a)* I am not drunk (Darryl temporarily incapacitated having run over his own foot in a Lancia, so temporarily replaced by Jimmy Nail woman) and *b)* not only does Wilde know Maya (they went to the same prep in Marylebone) but they 'partied' together in Rock last year. There were all sorts of shrieks of 'doll face' and 'sugar tits' (on both sides) and now she is backstage with him for a 'nightcap' and to laugh at the irony of living in suburbia. Ugh. This is typical. I finally get my very own borderline cross-dressing genuine Londoner, only to have him stolen back by his own kind. Worse, she is probably best friends with his first love Marlene and will try to oust me in an attempt to preserve the memory. The only consolation is that Jack is none too pleased either at having his ex-lead singer consorting with his chief groupie while he loads

drums into a plumber's van. I wouldn't be happy with the van full stop. The whole thing has an aroma of toilets about it. It is entirely unprofessional.

Also, on the subject of tragedy, and unprofessionalism, James and Mad Harry managed to infiltrate tonight's proceedings with Max Calloway. James said it is all part of their campaign to make their mathletic candidate look normal. I said encouraging Sad Ed to heave himself off the platform on top of four Year Eights was hardly normal. Three of them are now being treated for suspected fractures. Though why Sad Ed agreed is a mystery.

## Sunday 28

Mystery solved. Sad Ed says he was getting in some practice at launching into a void. He is going to leap off the Humber Bridge if Scarlet does not take him back by the time we all start uni. Also, more interestingly, the Walden arsonist has struck again, i.e. someone set light to the VIP room (aka the table storeroom) at the Bernard Evans Youth Centre in the early hours of this morning. Asked Sad Ed how he knew. He said his mum was due there at nine for Over-fifties Zumba but they got diverted to the Twilight Years Day Centre instead. Agreed this lacks foresight. The potential for hip injury is enormous.

Have texted Wilde to see if he knows anything. He

was backstage with the band so may have seen something untoward, e.g. a terrorist, or more likely, a rogue O'Grady.

2 p.m.
Wilde texted back. He said it probably blew itself up in protest at hosting such derivative amateurism. Asked if he wanted to come over and channel a dead film star in my bedroom. He said no, as he and Maya are going for ironic cream teas at The Bun in the Oven. Am not going to tell them it is closed on a Sunday. Ha. That will teach them to mock a Saffron Walden institution (renowned in five-mile radius for its malt loaf, and inability to serve anything above a temperature that can only be described as 'lukewarm').

2.30 p.m.
Though what if it being shut just adds to the whole irony thing and they bond even more over it? Oh God. It is like Sophie's choice again.

2.45 p.m.
Have texted. But too late. They were alerted to the Bun's curtailed hours by Suzy and have bought an ironic picnic from Mr Patel instead consisting of Skips, Cadbury Mini Rolls and Ritz crackers. I do not see what is ironic about any of those. They are delicious, hence being banned in this house.

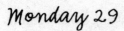 

# Monday 29

And so begins my first full week of officially having nothing to do. And it is completely legitimate so Mum cannot prevent me rejoining Jeremy Club for the foreseeable future. Not until she discovers the existence of ITV1+1 anyway.

10.30 a.m.

Mum has banned ITV1+1. It is Mr Wandering Hands's fault. She was lamenting the scheduling clash between *Upstairs Downstairs* and *Downton Abbey* and he suggested she watch the latter on 'plus one' (though why, as they are the same programme as far as I can tell). She then went through the *Radio Times* blacklisting this and all other channels of potential corruption. Dad is now limited to BBCs 1, 2, and 4, News24, and CBeebies. Am going round Scarlet's instead. They have no restrictions on television usage and a vast collection of French pseudo porn. Hopefully Maya will be too busy buying ironic tea cosies and ironic floral doorplates at Gayhomes (hardware shop, not ironic, just crap) to annoy us.

5 p.m.

Maya was not doing anything ironic. At least not in Saffron Walden. She has gone back to London as she says the country air was messing with her sinuses. I said she had spent six months in rural Guatemala, which made Walden look like Tokyo, but Jack said the main crops there were not oilseed rape and conker trees, which are her particular

hay fever triggers. Jack is obviously not taking her departure well as he then had the audacity to accuse Wilde of being involved in the Bernard Evans arson attack. I said he was just pathetically jealous of his talent, history with Maya, and custom Converse (cerise, with WILDE on the side in sequins). He said whatever (his insults are becoming incredibly predictable) but that Maya said he had got up to some 'crazy shit' back in 'The Hill' and that I should be careful. I said whatever (allowed as I did it ironically), his assumed concern is transparent and he clearly just wishes he was doing crazy shit, instead of just clearing up actual shit (Harper's, so fairly crazy as she has discovered how to take her own nappy off and use poo as a form of primitive paint. Suzy does not mind. She says it shows burgeoning artistic talent).

6 p.m.
Asked Mum if I had ever removed a nappy and tried to paint with my own poo. She said hardly, no one could infiltrate her double-pinned terry towelling. Also that it does not show burgeoning artistic talent, it shows the beginning of another bottom-focused pervert.

## Tuesday 30

10 a.m.
At least I can lie in bed in peace. That is one privilege of

post-exam leave that Mum cannot remove. In fact, I may lie in bed all day just to spite her.

11 a.m.
With a break for daring elevenses (Cheerios, admittedly not out of the packet, but without milk, so still under review).

12 p.m.
And lunch (more Cheerios).

1.30 p.m.
And a mid-afternoon snack (Cheerios).

2 p.m.
How can it only be two o'clock? Have just eaten tea (Shreddies, with a Cheerios topping). Am going to be gargantuan at this rate. No wonder Sad Ed has bingo wings with all the lying in bed and eating cereal he does. It plays havoc with your metabolism. I have probably compromised my pancreas irreparably.

2.10 p.m.
Though have realized I have no idea where my pancreas are and what they are for. Or my spleen for that matter. But they sound definitely damageable.

3 p.m.
Mum says neither my pancreas (blood sugar-regulating

glands containing excellent-sounding islets of Langerhans, according to James) nor my spleen (sort of washing machine for the blood, according to Dad) are irreparably damaged and has declined to book me an appointment with Dr Braithwaite as he is prone to writing antibiotic prescriptions and she is not wasting £7.40 on wilful malingering in such economically strained times. To that end she has also issued me with a new edict, i.e. I have to find a job, starting tomorrow. I said Dad has been trying for weeks and he has still not found one so what makes her think I can do any better. She said I am younger, cheaper, and I do not have a filthy semi-beard. This is true.

Though harsh.

## Wednesday 1

Trod the less-than-mean streets ceaselessly for an hour and a half this morning but to no avail. The shelf-stacking jobs are all taken up by gap-year students who have finished saving whales, etc. and are now desperate to earn money to fund their highly anticipated Pot Noodle and drug habits, or pensioners who are desperate to earn money to fund cats and cake. Plus my last resort job of official pasty warmer has already been 'snapped up' according to Pie Shop Pearce. This is an exaggeration. There is no way standing behind the counter in an overheated, doughnut-smelling fug can be that compelling, unless you are Fat Kylie.

I am now officially one of the jobless millions. This is yet another reason why moving from a mid-sized market town to an urban conurbation would be economically sensible, i.e. there is a distinct lack of jobs for the semi-skilled in the Uttlesford district due to restrictive planning laws concerning takeaway outlets and sweatshops, whereas London and Manchester are bulging with opportunities for burger flipping.

6 p.m.

James says I am not one of the jobless millions unless I sign on for benefits, I am just an unemployed student, which is not nearly as edgy or working class. On the plus side, I have kept up my part of the bargain and so can now luxuriate on the sofa ogling BBC channels and there is nothing Mum can say.

# Thursday 2

**8.50 a.m.**

I was wrong. Apparently there is a lot Mum can say and it mostly involves being compared unfavourably to Dad, i.e. we both give up feebly at the first hurdle. I said it is not our fault that the country is in economic crisis and the ageing population means people are holding onto their jobs with their liver-spotted fingers instead of giving them up to more youthful go-getters like me and Dad. But James said I need to do more 'thinking outside the box' and 'blue skies thinking', plus Dad can hardly be included in that description. He has clearly been watching *The Apprentice*, against Mum's diktat banning reality TV or anything with Alan Sugar on it, which I pointed out. But James said, *au contraire*, it is his new role as Campaign Manager for Max Calloway that has imbued him with shrewd-like business sense and a lexicon of executive speak. He then went on to talk nonsense about bottom lines and got sent to school without his second 'pudding' round of toast (i.e. with marmalade) much to both my and the dog's delight. But our jubilance was short-lived as I have been dispatched out onto the streets again with a list of potential employers, and the dog has a piece of peel stuck in its front teeth.

**3 p.m.**

Have crossed the following off my list:

1 Egg fryer at Chestnuts B & B (owned by Les and

Ying Brewster, also of Siam Smile fame), as Les's son Don (from his first marriage to non-Thai sex worker Denise) has moved back in, meaning they can no longer rent out their spare room as it is infested with the smell of body odour and Airfix glue.

2   Assistant Warden to Mrs Peason at the Pink Geranium Sheltered Housing Complex. This was down to the fatal error of taking the dog with me. She recognized its hairy face and moronic expression and has never forgiven it for consuming the communal Christmas lunch.

3   Games organizer at the Twilight Years Day Centre. Treena said that's *her* job and if anyone shows her up by actually doing some organizing (as opposed to smoking Benson & Hedges out of the office window and reading *Heat*) then she will be on the scrapheap too.

4   Lookalike for Mr Hosepipe (father of Mark Lambert, full-time fireman, part-time runner of crap stripping agency). He said I didn't really look like anyone famous, bar Brian May (it is the hair), and no one wanted to see *him* with his clothes off. Was tempted to cite CrazyJulie but thought better of it and left.

Also, have found out who 'snapped up' the job at Dorrington's. It is none other than Mrs O'Grady (mother of Fat Kylie, Stacey, Kyle, Paris-Marie, Whitney, two Liams, and potentially several other O'Gradys). This is an economic mistake on a colossal scale. She will eat any profit during her tea breaks plus she is hardly an advert for the health benefits of baked goods.

## Friday 3

Have had a genius idea. When I pass my driving test, I can set myself up as a taxi service using Dad's Passat (am not allowed to drive the Fiesta even when I pass my test as Mum is afraid I will over-rev the engine or use it for illicit sex). Will concentrate extra-hard in my lesson later, and use it to mug up on The Knowledge (cab-driver speak for knowing all the roads in the area).

4 p.m.

Mr Wandering Hands says The Knowledge has been rendered redundant by the advent of sat nav, plus if I carry on clutch cruising then it will be 'if' I pass my test, not when. Plus Mum has added the Passat to the list of vehicles I am not allowed to drive. I said I hoped she was planning on buying me a car for my eighteenth birthday otherwise my qualification will be nothing more than a piece of worthless paper. She said no qualification is worthless. I said what about a diploma in aromatherapy (banned for being made up). But she told me to stop clutching at straws and go to Waitrose to get some Febreze (dog has rolled in cat poo, or possibly its own poo, and then gone for a sleep in the airing cupboard).

5 p.m.

Bumped into Sad Ed, who is now back on trolley herding, having proved his mettle on the Chum aisle. Begged him to put in a word for me as an assistant herder. But he said

my driving skills are as yet unproven, and he cannot risk it, as if he fails his A levels then he is hoping to get the job on a permanent basis. I said this showed an astounding lack of ambition and was hardly Jim Morrisonesque. But he said all musicians have to do menial work as it builds character and angst into their oeuvre, and makes them hungry for artistic success. He is wrong. I bet Morrissey never worked at KFC.

11 p.m.
Have realized Mum did not actually rule out buying me a car, which is odd as she rules out most things on a daily basis. This is excellent news. I will not mention it again though, as it would spoil her joy at surprising me on the day.

## Saturday 4

James says there is no way Mum is going to buy me a car, given that it took her three years to give in to a mobile phone plus I am still waiting on the iPad. I said she always gives a clear indicator of intention (usually a resounding no) but had failed to do so on this occasion therefore I can surmise that she will, in fact, be heading to Platinum Motors to secure me a second-hand Ford (the only cars permitted in our family, and, if she had her way, the world. The Passat is on short shrift as it is. As soon as it dies she is hoping to replace it with a Mondeo) by the first of August.

11 p.m.

Jimmy Nail woman has a real name. It is Peggy, which is not very fitting for someone with tattoos and a mullet and who can bench press a hundred kilos. She looks more like a Wayne. Jack said it goes to show how you cannot judge someone by name alone. I said how true, as being called Rachel is completely misleading as I am not sensible and bespectacled as my name would suggest. I am much more of a Dolores or Lolita, which I have pointed out to Mum but she said the day there is a Dolores in the family is the day she renounces the name Riley.

Asked where his irritatingly named girlfriend was. He said he was surprised I did not know, as she has driven up to London for a party in the non-sick-smelling Car of the People and taken my ill-dressed sidekick with her. I said I assumed he meant Wilde, and we may be soulmates, but I am not his keeper. We do not need to spend every waking minute together to prove our commitment. He said when did I last spend any waking minute with Wilde. Said that is not the point. What is the point is that, as soon as I get my birthday car, then I will be driving Wilde to London to parties in Hoxton. He said it is not in Hoxton, it is in Hampstead, and also there is no way Mum is going to buy me a car, citing the infamous battle over the Twirly Curls Barbie. I said he had a depressing lack of faith in people, which is the root cause of why we are not together. He said the root cause was actually me snogging Justin Statham at which point I went and sat back down with Sad Ed and

Scarlet. It is not that he is right, it is that did not want to get back into the whole 'it was because I had accidentally taken magic mushrooms debate' as I have lost this no less than three times.

**11.45 p.m.**
Not that his lack of faith is of any interest to me at all. His opinions are no longer mine to debate. They are Maya's. Though they are clearly misguided anyway if they think Maya is his ONE. She is way too shallow. And her hair is the wrong sort.

## Sunday 5

**11 a.m.**
Scarlet has just texted. There has been a crisis chez Stone and I am to come immediately. Oh, the agony. It must be Harper. She has probably weed on a socket and electrocuted herself. Or maybe it is Jack. Not weeing (he has fully toilet trained) but fallen down the stairs after a row with Maya who has returned the non-sick-smelling Car of the People with extra dents in the panels because she drunkenly drove it into a wall in Hammersmith with half an indie band in the back. Am going immediately to tend to his injuries.

**4 p.m.**
It was not Jack. Or Harper. But it was utterly car-related. It is the sick-smelling Volvo! It has finally died. Apparently

the 'big end' fell out on the B1052 at Linton and it has been towed to its final resting place at Panel Paradise (scrap merchants, also Essex's premier dealers in Jacuzzis).

Scarlet says it is the end of an era, and a symbol of our lost childhoods. I said she was right. That car has been a major player in the theatre of our youth, and carries the indelible smell of vomit as proof. Sad Ed agreed, and said he could feel actual tears coming on. He could not, it was a ruse to win a hug from Scarlet. It did not work, but she did fetch him a Kleenex, which Sad Ed says is a clear sign she is close to breaking point.

Bob says he is minded to get a Midget (car not small person, though had to check) but Suzy says that smacks of mid-life crisis and is campaigning for a Touareg, which is definitely Labour-friendly because Jocasta has one.

Maya was not even back. She and Wilde ended up pulling an all-nighter and now they're crashing at someone called Assisi's. It is utterly unfair, and I do not care what Jack says, if I was called Dolores instead of Rachel this is exactly the sort of thing that would be happening to me, instead of attending the funeral of a Swedish estate car.

## Monday 6

Am going to school. It is not that I am so utterly bored that I would rather lurk in the orange glow of badly painted corridors with ill-behaved children than fester at home, it

is because it is the final week of the Head Boy and Girl campaign and Sad Ed has to go to invigilate campaigning. Me and Scarlet are going as political advisors/bouncers (there is bound to be fighting as the BTECers, i.e. Retards and Criminals, are fielding Noah Walker who is the uncontested headbutt champion of John Major High).

Plus I am bored.

## Tuesday 7

Am going to school again. Overseeing such a fiercely fought political campaign will be an excellent addition to my fast-growing CV. Plus there is a ready supply of junk food (the mathletes are running a delivery service from Mr Patel's) and a marginally comfortable sofa, i.e. I do not have to fight for my place with an overly hairy dog and an overly hairy man in pyjamas (Mum does not know. He puts his shirt and trousers over the top before she gets home), and Sad Ed has installed his portable TV in the common room for the week so he does not miss *Gilmore Girls*.

4 p.m.

The Calloway campaign has finally been graced with a first lady. Unbelievably, it is Charlotte Coston. James decreed her alliterative surname, solid farming credentials, and visible breasts would give Max the boost he needed and so has 'borrowed' her from Mad Harry. He said it is fine

as celebrities do it all the time to increase their popularity. Said he underestimates the electorate at John Major High who will see through this shallow ruse. He said I am wrong.

## Wednesday 8

I am wrong. Hustings declared a victory for Max Calloway. James said it was obvious Charlotte gave him the human touch he needed. Said it is more that Noah Walker got disqualified for 'offering Mr Wilmott out' when he refused to countenance a 'headbutt-off' and has now been replaced by Kyle O'Grady. Voting begins at 9 a.m. tomorrow. I predict a last minute swing to the O'Grady. Max may be clever, and have a girlfriend, but Kyle has several O'Gradys at his disposal to enforce compliance. Plus he can moonwalk.

## Thursday 9

9 a.m.
Voting has commenced, with Sad Ed and Thin Kylie casting theirs as outgoing Head Boy and Girl. Both have opted for the O'Grady. (Thin Kylie out of family loyalty. Sad Ed because he got a free Wham Bar, plus he thinks voting for the underdog makes him more attractive to Scarlet. It does not. It makes him look like a moron.) Scarlet said checking their papers was against all electoral commission guidelines

and we should start the whole process again, but I said it was only to make sure they had not spoiled them by adding lines from Bob Dylan songs (Sad Ed) or drawing love hearts (Thin Kylie).

3 p.m.

The votes have been counted (three times, due to a lost ballot box, later discovered in the Camilla Parker Bowles Memorial Crèche baby change unit, and Sad Ed's fat fingers dropping several piles on the floor) and, predictably, Kyle O'Grady and his sidekick Primark Donna have been declared the victors. Mr Wilmott is kicking himself for agreeing to go back to elections as opposed to his previous regime of 'just install who I want'. Though that is what landed him with Thin Kylie in his ill-advised attempt to breach the common room conflict, so it is swings and roundabouts as far as that is concerned.

## Friday 10

It is the end of our reign as superior upper sixth-formers. A new Head Boy and Girl have been crowned (not coronated, which is not a word according to Scarlet, though it should be) and we have been officially barred from premises until the prom next Friday. It should have been tonight, but Mr Wilmott says he cannot face two massive deep-cleans in a fortnight. Or sheep hunts. There is still one missing after

last year's shenanigans, suspected in the O'Gradys' shed. Grandpa insists he can hear strange bleating and banging noises there at night. It is more probably Liam 2 and Thin Kylie. They are always doing it in untoward places. So far she has notched up Mr Whippy's van, the toilets at Siam Smile, and Mrs Leech's desk. It is disgusting. When I do it, it will be in the traditional venue of the bedroom. That is one tendency I am proud to have inherited as a Riley. Unlike the mental hair, under-eye circles, and annoyance at the renaming of well-known household brands.

### Saturday 11

I was wrong. A Riley has fallen prey to the lures of al fresco groping, and unbelievably it is not Grandpa and Treena, but is Uncle Jim! Worse, the gropee was ailment-ridden Rosamund. I saw them outside the Goddard's meat bins on their lunch hour. Oh God, am traumatized by the sight. Though not as traumatized as Uncle Jim will be when he catches nits or some other hideous affliction. James is livid, as he had been hoping to woo him back to the charms of internet dating with the promise of Miss Mustard who has broken up with Mr Vaughan (she is probably too mature for him, being twenty-four). Asked how his John Major Matchmaking Agency was going (Charlotte Coston has defected permanently to Max Calloway, due to his superior academic skills). He said Mad Harry has tried Lucy Arbury

out for size, but she failed to meet his stringent 'talent' criteria. Next up is Lacey Prendergast who can spit a peanut five metres.

## Sunday 12

Mum is less than jubilant about Uncle Jim. It is because she fears a repeat of the Great Nit Infestation, when even the dog had to be Hedrined. She has warned him not to fall prey to the 'charms' of the fairer sex and to be led by his brain rather than any other body bits. There is no chance, he is the offspring of Grandpa Riley, chief thinker with his willy.

Am going to get Mum a birthday present at Scotsdales. Dad has been given special precedence to use the car. Mum is using reverse psychology on him, i.e. she is pretending to do him a favour, but in fact, it is a cunning ruse to get him out of the house as she is worried he is becoming hermit-like, and will lose the ability to wear normal clothes, drive, or discuss the finer points of a chip shot. It is since she discovered his pyjama concealment. It is Dad's own fault. He knows she can spot a hem of Marks & Spencer stripe at thirty paces.

4 p.m.
Have got Mum a monkey puzzle tree. It has no overambitious flowers, and the dog does not seem to want

to chew it, so it should pass all the vital tests. Dad, in a fit of uncharacteristic recklessness, has got her a novelty bird box. I advised him against his choice, but he insists that it is his own cunning ruse, i.e. the bird box will annoy the Drs Jones because it is a symbol of suburbia, and so Mum will actually be pleased. I fear he is taking Mum's ability to appreciate psychology too far. She gets most of her ideas from *Supernanny* as it is.

## Monday 13

9 a.m.

It is a momentous day in the Riley household, i.e. Mum officially hits middle age. James has been looking for signs of a crisis since breakfast but so far she has not tried to wear a Wonderbra, snog a toy boy, or buy tickets to a Take That concert. Dad says James is wasting his time as Mum has been middle-aged since the age of sixteen. He is right. Though maybe she will see it as time to relax her attitude, now that she is statistically halfway to death.

10 a.m.

Mum has put the novelty bird box in her 'things to return' pile of presents, also featuring a pair of overly 'fancy' knickers (Treena), and the autobiography of Carol Vorderman (James). So no change there then.

# Tuesday 14

WHSmith have refused to take back the Carol Vorderman book due to an unidentifiable sticky patch on the cover. It is not unidentifiable. It is Jesus's jam-smeared handprint.

Also saw Uncle Jim and Rosamund at Nuts in May. They were clearly snogging behind the savoury soya mince display. I am minded to tell Mr Goldstein as it is unhygienic, not to mention off-putting. Though I do not want to jeopardise Uncle Jim's job. He is the main breadwinner, even with Mum's Fiesta filing activity, as most of her money goes on my lessons, plus she must be saving the rest for my birthday present car and I do not want her having to divert it to groceries or water bills. It is an utter dilemma.

# Wednesday 15

11 a.m.
Have discovered excellent solution to conundrum, i.e. avoid town and pretend to know nothing. Instead, I shall sit in the front garden and read the entire works of Shakespeare in preparation for my immersion in the world of theatre come September. Plus I can monitor comings and goings next door. I have not seen Wilde for several days and I am worried Maya may be angling to usurp me as chief soulmate.

**11.30 a.m.**

Oh God, *Richard III* is impenetrable. Maybe *Twelfth Night* will be easier. It is a comedy, so will appeal to my soon-to-be-achieved working class tendencies.

**1.45 p.m.**

I do not see what is funny about Shakespeare at all. Compared even to Jane Austen it is hardly a riot. There is no sign of Wilde as yet. Maybe he is still languishing in bed, ravaged by poetic despair, or consumption, which is completely poetic, whatever James says.

**2 p.m.**

He is not ravaged by poetic despair or disease. He is 'hanging' with Olaf and someone called Petrova according to his text. I assume this means he is somewhere in west London with his Scandinavian best friend and the fur-clad daughter of a Russian oligarch. How enviably ironic. On the plus side at least he is not with Maya.

**3 p.m.**

Hurrah, have found someone who is ravaged by poetic(ish) despair. It is Mark Lambert! He has written Kylie a poem to win back her love. It is a thoughtful gesture, though I fear ultimately fruitless, given that it includes the lines: 'Liam don't have no Lamborghini. His knob is thinner than fettuccini.' Which rhymes, but the imagery is less than Blakeian.

Also, have given up on Shakespeare. It is clear that I cannot hope to appreciate the finer points of prose while I am trapped in such untragic surroundings. Have started on the jammy Carol Vorderman instead. She is essentially me. A working-class girl, thrust into the limelight by the enormity of her academic superiority.

## Thursday 16

Am racked with sorrow at the plight of poor fatherless Carol. I share her pain, even though Dad did not run off with another woman twenty-one days after I was born. More's the pity as then I would be the child of a broken home, and James would not even exist. As it is, he has gone to school with the naked Prince William doll. He says it will guarantee him success in his SATs. It will not. It will guarantee him a kicking from an O'Grady. Probably Paris-Marie.

Am glad I do not need to suffer those sort of indignities any more. University students will be above such prejudices, and will welcome such mannequins as ironic statements on the impotence of the monarchy.

11 a.m.
Have realized I have not been asked to prom tomorrow. It is utterly John Hughesian. Though I suspect that at any minute my Duckie, i.e. Sad Ed, will beg me to go with him.

**2 p.m.**

Sad Ed has not begged me to go to the ball. And in an ill-thought-out and possibly suicidal manoeuvre, he is taking Melody Bean (ex-fiancée, minigoth, owner of tarantula called Arthur) in a bid to make Scarlet jealous. It will not work. She is above such transparent tactics. Though will just check to see who she is taking to make sure it is not Trevor Pledger, as the potential Goth Corner fallout could be life-threatening.

**3 p.m.**

Scarlet says she is going 'stag', i.e. on her own, to prove that she does not need a man to have a good time. Suzy will be disappointed in her. She has devoted her life to the promotion of sex as the answer to everything. Plus Thin Kylie will just accuse her of being a 'lezzer'. Am also going to be tarred with the lezzer brush. Though I am not minded. Being a lesbian is de rigueur at university. I shall probably have snogged Harriet before the end of Freshers' Week. Ironically of course. As, disappointingly, minkies fail to move me.

**4 p.m.**

James is back and is unscathed. Said I was amazed an O'Grady hadn't threatened to compromise his genitals. He said clearly they understood it was a statement on the impotence of the monarchy. Plus he gave Paris-Marie packet of Quavers at first break.

## Friday 17

**9 a.m.**

It is the official last day of school EVER. Hurrah! I refuse to fall prey to the endless laments that it is the end of an era. It is not. It is the beginning of real life. And I for one cannot wait to get started. James is similarly demob-happy. He is wearing his 'street clothes' (skinny jeans, baseball cap (forward facing), Mole Hall T-shirt) and has taken in Dungeons & Dragons board game so the mathletes can 'go wild' at lunchtime.

**4 p.m.**

Oh it is utterly the end of an era. My sensitive nature cannot be bound. I was so struck by the moving sight of Mrs Leech chasing the sheep down corridor I burst into tears and had to be revived by Mr Wilmott (standing in on Peak Frean duty). Had a pink wafer, as is banned at home for promising a lot but delivering little.

Also, I am not going to be a lesbian after all. Which is disappointing, irony-wise. But I can forego this opportunity to be interesting, sexual preference-wise, as I have secured a date to the prom and it is Wilde! He is back from Olaf's and has agreed to go to the prom as an ironic statement on something or other. He is going to wear a ballgown (an ironic statement on gender, or beauty, I am unclear which, but it is definitely ironic). I cannot believe I doubted his devotion to me. In fact, I think tonight may be the night we finally add a pants-element to our unshakeable relationship. It is obvious

I have not been clear enough about my receptiveness to a snog, were he to offer one. He must be labouring under the misapprehension that I am an innocent ingénue who is averse to all advances, when in fact I have snogged several people, including a criminal. Hurrah. This is it. This time tomorrow I will be Bonnie to his Clyde, Fanny to his Keats. In fact I predict that, soon, it will be our names in the headlines: Wilde and Ray (will have to revive underused nickname as Rachel is not at all newsworthy).

1 a.m.
Have not snogged Wilde. In an ironic or any sense. Plus I smell of smoke, my ankle is singed, and I have to make a police statement in the morning. Which am too traumatized and tired to explain now. But suffice it to say that nothing went as planned.

## Saturday 18

11 a.m.
Am now revived enough by tea and Shreddies to make my official statement of the events of Friday 17th July, as witnessed by me, Rachel Riley.

7.30 p.m.
Wilde, dressed in pale blue taffeta and a tiara, crunches along gravel of 24 Summerdale Road in three-inch heels, and

shouts up at bedroom window to beg his Romeo (i.e. me) to take him to the dance. I oblige. Though not via preferred drainpipe method as is banned but by tedious normal method of stairs. Mum comments on my dinner suit arrangement and says she hopes I am not developing sapphic tendencies as my vegetarian phase was bad enough. Said had no idea what she meant but do not have any disease.

7.45 p.m.
Arrive to find prom in full swing, i.e. the mathletes pretending to be Kanye West, Mr Vaughan pretending he is not ogling sixth formers, and Fat Kylie backstage with her hand down Mr Whippy's trousers.

8 p.m.
Sad Ed arrives with Melody Bean. Scarlet wishes him the best of luck with his previously rejected child bride. But Sad Ed claims her platitudes are revealed as a hollow sham by the whizziness of the Throne of Magnificence towards the Fanta and crisps stall, and the fact that she deliberately ran over Melody's foot on the way.

9.30 p.m.
Sad Ed takes advantage of Melody Bean having drunk too much Fanta, i.e. on her sixth loo break, and walks provocatively past Scarlet and behind curtain at Goth Corner, i.e. temporarily declared snog corner.

9.35 p.m.

Scarlet follows him behind curtain in Throne of Magnificence.

9.40 p.m.

Throne of Magnificence wheels back out of curtain, with both Sad Ed and Scarlet seated in it, in more than compromising position. Melody Bean throws up can of Fanta and has to be taken to Mrs Leech for bourbons and a bucket.

10 p.m.

Wilde declares the prom to be a symbol of materialism, sexism, racism, and about four other isms that I have never heard of and says we should raze it to the ground in our own symbol of the inexorable rise of the freaks. I agree, and say we could send a letter to the *Walden Chronicle*.

10.05 p.m.

Wilde says the symbol is less symbolic than that, i.e. when he said raze to the ground, he actually meant set fire to, with matches, and the can of petrol he has stashed in his Birkin bag.

10.10 p.m.

Am rendered temporarily speechless by revelation. But then remember to channel Sylvia. She says it is a genius and worldly idea, but Rachel cannot actually hold the matches

or the petrol, because her mum will go mental. But she will be with him in symbolic spirit.

10.20 p.m.
Wilde sets light to bins of Rat Corner (thus minimizing threat to life, bar rats, which are endless source of annoyance anyway, so can always claim am doing Mr Wilmott favour if am found out). I say it is the end of an era. He says it is the end of a crap era and we should be celebrating. I see chance and say, 'This is true. And what better way to celebrate than with a kiss by firelight. It is our time, Wilde, time to seal our love that burns as bright as the flames currently creeping dangerously close to the Camilla Parker Bowles Memorial Crèche.' I close my eyes in anticipation.

10.31 p.m.
I open my eyes due to absence of anything romantic happening lip-wise. Note that Wilde's cherry-likes are pulled into rictus grin as he shrieks, 'Oh. My. God. I'm GAY, doll face. I thought you knew that. I mean, look at me for God's sake.' And he tosses his feather boa and shakes his drop diamante earrings as if to prove his point.

10.32 p.m.
I say what about Marlene, his first love? He says Marlene was actually Marlene Dietrich, and it was metaphorical love, not sexual love, as *a)* she is dead and *b)* she is a woman, which, like, ewww. I mumble something along the lines of

temporarily broken gaydar, plus also wrongness of assuming cross-dressing means gay (as had to be pointed out to Ying Brewster when she found Les wearing her pants). He says is not broken gaydar, is self-delusion i.e. I knew he was gay all along but was in denial and that I would benefit from some therapy on this subject. About to suggest couples counselling when note that fire is now definitely burning the crèche and possibly it is time to stop discussing gaydar and pants and go and press an alarm.

10.40 p.m.
Fire spreads to bike shed alerting several stoners, who are hiding behind a broken racer.

10.43 p.m.
Reuben Tull attempts to 'think' the fire into shrinking.

10.44 p.m.
Fire engulfs bike shed and heads towards farm. Reuben goes in search of marshmallows instead.

10.45 p.m.
Mr Wilmott evacuates everyone, including sheep, into the mobile science labs, and makes emergency calls.

10.55 p.m.
Mr Hosepipe arrives (in fireman mode, not stripper mode, much to Mr Wilmott's relief, and both Kylies'

disappointment) and extinguishes fire (much to Reuben Tull's disappointment who is back from Mr Patel's with four bags of Flumps and some skewers).

11 p.m.
PC Doone arrives to begin investigation into arson. Mr Wilmott says he will never get a confession out of anyone, as he is still trying to solve the mystery of who stole the school rabbit and that was ten years ago (was Lou the caretaker, who ate it, as everyone knows, bar Mr Wilmott).

11.05 p.m.
Wilde confesses everything, including the fires at the ATC hut and the Bernard Evans Youth Centre, and a bin behind Tesco that no one had even noticed. He is arrested and taken into custody. I beg to go with him, but Mum, alerted by James, his telescope, and his ability to tune into police radios, manhandles me into the Fiesta instead and ferries me back to 24 Summerdale Road where I am sent to my room with a cup of cocoa (Dad) and a shouting that it is about time I grew up and recognized who is boyfriend material and who is a homosexual criminal (James).

On the plus side, Wilde made the headlines. Though disappointingly for him it is not the *New York Times*, but the *Essex Evening Herald*. It says 'Goodness Gaycious, Great Ball on Fire', which is surprisingly witty for them, if predictably homophobic.

Oh how could I not see it? I have devoted several years to the acquisition of a gay best friend, and when he was under my nose, I was blind to his innate qualities and instead squandered my chance on the pursuit of a cheap kiss. Though maybe it is not too late. Maybe we will rise, phoenix-like, from the embers, and revive our friendship on a never-to-be-pants-based basis. I will go and see him in the morning to suggest this. If he is not being brutalized in a police cell by the notoriously anti-gay police force.

## Sunday 19

Have not seen Wilde. He was not busy being brutalized by PC Doone though. They released him last night according to Dr Jones (female). He is now in full-time psychiatric care, only I do not know where, as she refused to give me the location. I begged for her lenience, saying no one but me understands that he is a troubled gay genius. She said he is not, he is a born troublemaker who just happens to like penises, as his counsellor Dr Petrova Romanov and his probation officer Olaf Munt (how was I to know?) understood perfectly.

Went round to Scarlet's to commiserate. And also find out whether she has partaken of Sad Ed's penile delights. She says she could see it all coming a mile off and Wilde was just a well-dressed catastrophe waiting to happen. I said she was falling prey to the well-worn stereotypes perpetrated by the tabloid press in assuming that, just because he was

gay, he would be a troublemaker, because as any progressive thinker knows, it is impossible to be gay and violent. It is genetic. She says it is I who am falling prey to everything, and it is utterly homophobic to assume that just because someone is gay, they cannot also be everything a straight person can be, including an alcoholic arsonist. Changed the subject to Sad Ed's penis. She says she has partaken, but on a friends-with-benefits basis only, i.e. they are allowed to do 'it' but are not allowed to declare they are in love, soulmates, or telepathically connected. She says I should have taken a leaf out of her book and gone for convenience, i.e. the boy next door, instead of aiming too high and getting burned, Icarus-like. I said Wilde IS the boy next door. She rolled her eyes and went back to sexting Sad Ed.

I have no idea who she is referring to though. If anyone, Sad Ed is my boy next door. Or boy from just round the corner. I hope it is not him. I do not want to be involved in some kind of James-and-Mad-Harry-style love triangle.

Saw Jack on the way out (sans Maya who is still in London. She is obviously finding her health compromised by the sight of endless seventies estates). He said, 'That was a classic Riley stunt you pulled on Friday.' I said if he was referring to my near death experience in a raging inferno then I hardly think that is appropriate language, plus it was not mine, it was Wilde's. He said, 'I don't like to say I told you so.' I said, 'So don't', and walked off dramatically before he could get in any other words as was dangerously close to crying. Though the whole effect would have been improved

by me not tripping over Harper's Bugaboo on the drive and falling into the hedge. I do not think Jack saw though as I stayed in there for several minutes to ensure the coast was clear.

10 p.m.
Jack has texted. It says 'SORRY, RILEY. JUST DIDN'T WANT YOU 2 GET HURT.' Texted back to say 'THANX. ONLY PAIN IS BRUISED EGO. AND MINOR BURN ON RIGHT ANKLE.'

10.15 p.m.
Text from Jack: 'NOT BROKEN HEART?' Said 'AS IF. WHY WOULD I BE IN LOVE WITH SOMEONE WHO IS CLEARLY A GAY ALCOHOLIC ARSONIST?'

10.20 p.m.
Reply from Jack: 'YOU TELL ME. PS WHAT WERE YOU DOING IN HEDGE?' Curse his twenty-twenty vision. Said 'HIDING FROM AN O'GRADY.' Is utterly plausible. There are millions of them and they are all equally menacing.

10.25 p.m.
Jack: 'I WILL PROTECT YOU FROM O'GRADYS. AND DON'T HIDE AWAY, RACH. YOU BORN TO STAND OUT.'

Have not replied. 'Close to crying' is now actual crying and I do not want to get salt water on my phone. It has

only just recovered from a dose of Sad Ed's Fruit Shoot. It is clearly repressed terror from the fire. Or smoke damage to my retina.

## Monday 20

Mum has read my police statement. She says it is possible I need psychiatric counselling if I can hear Sylvia Plath talking to me about petrol. I said it was a sham. I could never hear Sylvia, which is yet another reason I am inferior to Wilde as he actually talked to Elizabeth Taylor. She said it is another sign that her strict, traditional child-raising methods are infallible and it is lucky PC Doone got baffled by the mention of another woman. As it is, I am grounded until my birthday. She says her only comfort is that no one could possibly bring more shame on the House of Riley after this weekend. I fear she underestimates James. And the dog.

I am not minded about the grounding anyway. I cannot face the over-scrutinizing eye of the gossip-crazed public (i.e. Mrs Noakes, Mrs Dyer, and Marjory) anyway. They are bound to ignore all facts and assume I am on drugs and pregnant.

## Tuesday 21

Mum was wrong. New shame has been wrought on the House of Riley, but thankfully it is nothing to do with me.

Unbelievably it is not the dog either, though it came close with wedging itself under the sofa. It is Uncle Jim. He has run away to India with Rosamund! There was a note on the Shreddies table this morning, begging forgiveness, and also asking someone to ring Mr Goldstein. I said it is utterly romantic and worldly. Mum said it is not. It is ungracious, and exceedingly annoying as he has taken her shampoo and the spare kettle. But on the plus side, they will both probably get dysentery, which will teach them a lesson about the perils of tourism in the third world, the spare room is now hippy-free, and there is a full-time vacancy in the world of lentil retailing. She has ungrounded me temporarily and dispatched me to Nuts in May to beg Mr Goldstein for my old job back.

1 p.m.
Have got job. I start tomorrow with staff training to learn what is new in world of lentils. I said this was unnecessary as the point about wholefood is that nothing is new. It is all old-fashioned and dependable. Mr Goldstein said I would be surprised.

### Wednesday 22

Am not surprised. Nothing is new. Also, saw Mrs Noakes (herbal laxatives). She asked if it was true I was pregnant by a transsexual who had paid me to carry his baby so

I could fund my addiction to Vicodin, only in my drug-crazed state I set fire to the school with a 'funny' cigarette? I sighed wearily, and said, 'If only life really were that exciting.'

Though thinking about it, it is the closest I have ever got to real life crime, and a genuinely gay man. I predict this will send me escalating the ranks of the worldly once I get to Hull. I don't suppose Harriet will have ever been party to pyromania whilst dressed as Fred Astaire.

Got home to find a For Sale sign up at the Drs Joneses. It was inevitable, I suppose. It is clear that not even moving to a supposedly uneventful, law-abiding tourist trap like Saffron Walden could keep Wilde's 'creative' tendencies at bay. I for one will be sad to see them leave though. Their intellect, wit, and appreciation of paint colours other than 'Hint of Barley' has brought a breath of fresh air to this stifling suburb.

Mum on the other hand is jubilant. She says incomers like them cannot hope to understand our traditional yet sophisticated ways. This is rich coming from someone who was brought up three hundred miles away in the land that time forgot.

## Thursday 23

Someone else is jubilant. It is Clive and Marjory. (Came into Nuts in May to ask if the story in the *Walden*

*Chronicle* was true that I am the unwitting victim of a serial arsonist who tried to bind me and rape me, and I am lucky to have escaped with my life. Said yes.) It transpires that life on Clancy Court is not all it is cracked up to be and they are desperate to return over the fence to their spiritual home. She is booking a viewing with Chilcott and Chilcott (Len and Don, moustaches, criminal striped shirts). I said surely a viewing was unnecessary, given that they only moved out of it a matter of months ago. Marjory said that's as may be, but if she has irreversibly destroyed the unique atmosphere then they may have to think again.

The dog will be pleased anyway. They may not have a philosophical cat to harangue, but they do have Hobnobs and a habit of leaving the back door open.

## Friday 24

Nuts in May is less depressing than I thought. On the downside, I emit a perpetual smell of beanburger, but on the plus side, there is an endless stream of John Major High students come to check I am alive. It is most heartening to know I am so loved. That or *Heat* magazine has been banned from WHSmith and they are starved of gossip. Today I had to retell the story to Dean 'the dwarf' Denley, five minigoths, and Mark Lambert. He said he doesn't remember me being tied to a stake like an unrepentant

Joan of Arc, but I said the smoke may have blinded him during that bit. He said he has good news on the Thin Kylie front anyway. I asked if his poem had done the trick. He said, no, it is better: Liam 2 has got 'knob rot'. Did not ask for details. I already know way too much about chav penises thanks to Thin Kylie's cousin Donkey Dawson (works in Halfords, penis 'like a saveloy').

## Saturday 25

James is mental with anticipation. It is because he, Mad Harry, and Mumtaz are off to Bury St Edmunds for a sleepover chez Shoebridge. I said I thought the love square had been dismantled now that Mad Harry was road-testing Lacey Prendergast. He said Lacey stalled at the first corner (she could only manage two metres with a dry-roasted) and so he is loaning him Mumtaz for the night. I said I refuse to believe Mumtaz, Mr and Mrs Mumtaz, or James himself are in any way happy with this arrangement. James said, *au contraire*, Mumtaz will just get a taste of inferiority and will be eternally in his mesmerizing power so it is win-win for him. Plus Mr and Mrs Mumtaz are still unaware of her 'pubescent charms', and think she is spending the weekend looking for curlews on Wicken Fen. He is revolting. And a moron. It is bound to backfire.

## Sunday 26

James is back from Bury St Edmunds and is bearing important news. On the downside, Mr and Mrs Mumtaz got wind of the non-curlew-related bonanza and she has been dispatched to Pakistan for the rest of the summer thus minimizing any contact with James or Mad Harry bar illegal Facebooking. But on the plus side there is an opening at Dauncy and Moss, Suffolk's foremost office supplies supplier because someone called Ted Nugent has got dropsy. (Which thought only goldfish got. Is fascinating fact.) But his pain is Dad's gain as Mr Shoebridge says he will put in a good word, which means it is in the bag!

## Monday 27

Mum is caught in a massive dilemma of her own making. It is Dauncy and Moss. On the one hand, it is paid work. On the other, it is too far to commute (four minutes over her one hour barrier), and she is not keen on moving as Bury St Edmunds falls short on all counts (academic results, crime levels, trickiness of Waitrose car park). Dad seems less than keen too. Though it is nothing to do with Waitrose but rather it will bring an end to his regime of daytime television, snacking, and watching Cherie Britcher sunbathing through the binoculars (he

claims he is monitoring their possibly illegal garden shed installation, but James has checked the specific angle and it is definitely trained on the sunlounger). James seems oddly unworried by the potential permanent separation from Mumtaz. Asked if he was putting on a brave face. He said, *au contraire*, if we move to Bury, he can resume relations with Wendy, so again, he has emerged victorious in all matters romantic. I am also unmoved. As come September I will no longer be a citizen of Saffron Walden, but of the world. And also Hull, which is not completely worldly but at least has a Waterstones and a Pizza Express.

## Tuesday 28

Clive and Marjory have made an offer on next door. It is less than they sold it to the Drs Jones for, but they say it reflects the nasty scratchy carpets (seagrass), depressing sludge coloured paint everywhere (Hardwick White), and replacement of the nice, modern avocado suite with weird second hand junk (roll top bath). Though this has now added to Mum's Bury St Edmunds dilemma, as, if she decides we are allowed to move, then Clive and Marjory are the ideal buyers, plus we still have a 1970s bathroom suite and barley shagpile.

Also, I note from Dad's binoculars that Liam 2 has not been a visitor in the Britchers' kidney-shaped swimming pool in these last days. Maybe Mark Lambert is right and

the knob rot has put Thin Kylie off. Though I would be surprised. I know for a fact she has been to the walk-in sexual health centre (i.e. clap clinic) at least four times and it is not just for the free condoms.

## Wednesday 29

Mr Wilmott came into the shop today. It was to buy chondroitin tablets (he is ravaged by arthritis in his left knee, which is yet another reason he should be phased out and replaced by a more dynamic super head as his hobbling is off-putting to prospective parents). I asked how the school was fairing, post-inferno. He said the damage is thankfully superficial, and the rats have gone, but the Camilla Parker Bowles Memorial Crèche will have to relocate temporarily. I said sorry. He said he does not blame me, more my pathological need to court controversy. I said it is lucky I am leaving then, and heading to a city that will understand my complicated soul. He said he understood far more than I think. I doubt it. He wears Hush Puppies. He cannot possibly understand someone who has dabbled with same-sex relations and once weed in a Pringles tube. It is true, I shall be glad to leave these environs. I am tired of the doubting Thomases and accusing whoevers. I need to go where no one knows me, or claims to. And whether that is Bury St Edmunds or Hull, I welcome it.

Today's top lentil-purchasing/gossiping visitor was Jack (also accompanied by Harper, who is teething, and so Suzy is trying to sleep in the day, vampire-like, so she can tend to Harper's night-time Bonjela needs. Asked if it was working. He said no she is just permanently minty and Bob is now sleeping on the sofa on a semi-permanent basis. I do not know why anyone has children. They are the death of romance, if not life itself). Jack asked if I had plans for my birthday yet. I said I had not thought about it, because I am worldly and above such petty celebrations, plus parties are banned at our house after last year's hoo-hah, and habitual venues, i.e. the ATC hut and Bernard Evans Youth Centre, are still fire-damaged. Jack said how about we all go down the Duke. I said that would be rather sad, and completely small-town. He said or I could think of it as ironic and nostalgic. Said I had thought about it and it was definitely ironic, and utterly nostalgic as it may be my last day in Saffron Walden, as come Saturday I shall almost certainly be driving towards the horizon, clutching my brand new driver's licence, which I will be gaining tomorrow. He said I should really put it in the glove compartment or I will crash. I said ha-ha and went back to pricing milkweed.

Also, Mum's house-moving dilemma is on hold. Clive and Marjory's offer on the Drs Joneses, has been rejected and they have agreed to hold off a 'more realistic bid' until Dad has had his interview next week. In the meantime they are coming to inspect the facilities at number 24. Mum has

put them off until next Wednesday so she can Cillit Band every surface and tackle the new and suspicious stain on the dining room carpet. It is not suspicious, it is the dog. It dropped a piece of beetroot there earlier (fetched from the bin in hopeless optimism, then rejected, as James and I had both done earlier).

## Friday 31

3 p.m.

It is less than an hour until Mr Wandering Hands comes to collect me and transport me to the Bishop's Stortford Driving Test Centre. Mum has given me the benefits of her cavernous knowledge on test etiquette and potential pitfalls. I am to:

*a*) Keep my hands on the steering wheel at all times, with the exception of essential gear changes and handbrake applications.

*b*) Keep to a steady twenty miles an hour, even if it says thirty. It is better to be late than dead or arrested.

*c*) If it is Audrey Cavanagh, hum a bit of the *Pirates of Penzance* as she is lead soprano in the Sawbridgeworth Gilbert and Sullivan Society.

At no point am I allowed to attempt to use my breasts as a decoy, not even if it is Roger Sullivan. I said, 'As if.' Though is annoying as that was Suzy's number-one essential rule. But Mum is right, I am a feminist, I do not need to use my

attributes, even if they are only 32C. I need only my innate skills, wits, and ability to navigate the notorious Hockerill one-way system. James said it is important I see this as more of a practice test as well. He is not using reverse psychology, he genuinely believes I will fail. He is probably right. It will be punishment for getting ideas above my station, i.e. Wilde, and the working-class northern university dream. I shall be reliant on lifts in the Passat for evermore, which will render me repellent pants-wise to anyone bar Sad Ed, who is repellent to me anyway.

Mum is hoping I pass. She says I will be a peril to all other road users, but Mrs Wandering Hands has given up Yogalates due to a row over downward dogs, so is back in the office, meaning she is out of work again.

5 p.m.

James's lack of confidence has proved ill-founded as I am now fully licenced to drive any vehicle on the highways and byways of Great Britain, if not the world (apart from minibuses, coaches, and HGVs). The examiner (Gordon Westerby, not interested in breasts but a fan of Gilbert and Sullivan) said he had never met anyone with such catlike reflexes (my emergency stop to avoid a dog caused minor whiplash) and I am a born driver. It is not that, it is because the dog was Fiddy (former lover of dog, mother of Bruce, on its way to Doggy Dos for a shampoo) and I did not want to incur the wrath of Thin Kylie. (Though thinking about it, the sorrow may have driven her back to the arms of Mark

Lambert for comfort. Maybe I should suggest he use dog murder as a last resort.) Begged Mum to let me borrow the Fiesta to go and tell Scarlet but she says not until I have proved, under her supervision, that I am capable of handling its tricky biting point. It does not matter. Tomorrow I will be exploring not just Debden Road, but the world, behind the wheel of my very own birthday present car.

I hope it is a vintage Morris Minor. I would look excellently retro in one of those.

I'm RACHEL RILEY
– welcome to my so-called life.

*August*

Birthday presents eagerly anticipated:

1   A car, preferably of the vintage variety.

2   A satnav to negotiate my way in the wide world, especially the gritty northern bits, which all look the same to me (or at least they do on *Coronation Street*, etc.).

Birthday presents received:

1   A cheque for £100 to 'set myself up for university' (Mum and Dad). Said I would not spend it all at once. I will. It will barely cover my new vintage wardrobe since Oxfam finally caught on to the vogue for retro and hiked up their prices.

2   An AA map of Great Britain including locations of Little Chefs and speed cameras (James, following Mum's lead).

3   *The Ultimate Student Cookbook* (dog). As if I am going to cook. The whole point of going to university is to live on black coffee, wit, and Pot Noodles.

4   A purple plush Build-A-Bear called Melanie (Grandpa, Treena, and Baby Jesus). Grandpa says it can be my lucky mascot at uni. It can not. It does not resemble any living creature, bar Fat Kylie in her ill-advised violet velvet minidress. Plus I know it was purchased in a fit of panic for Jesus after Shane went missing, but even he rejected it.

There is nothing from the Cleggs yet (Beefy Clarke in

Benidorm with his mum Sheila, and replaced temporarily by town albino Whitey Wilson, who is compromised by the sunshine and has to have several breaks for reapplication of factor fifty). Though knowing them it is bound to be *a)* useless or *b)* past its sell-by date.

James says I am shamefully ungrateful, and I should be filled with joy at the gifts being eighteen bestows upon one, like being legally allowed to binge drink Diamond White, play Grand Theft Auto, or join the library without parental permission. Mum said in fact I do not have permission to play 'clickety violence' or binge drink. I may however consume one or two alcoholic beverages, whilst adhering to government guidelines on sensible unit intake, and join the library. I said I am already a member, as well she knows. She said it is the being allowed that counts, not the act of doing. It is how she justifies never actually watching *The Shining* or *Sex and the City*. Just knowing she could if she wanted is terrifying enough.

5 p.m.

I take it back. The Cleggs' gift has arrived in the post, and unbelievably it is neither useless nor past its sell-by! It is the Cleggmobile! Granny has decided to bequeath the behemoth to her grandchildren. Though this is hypothetical as Boaz is forbidden from learning to drive in case he leaves the confines of Cornwall and falls prey to the deadly sins of lust, greed, and coveting his neighbour's bull. And James and Mary Hepzibah are both underage. Whereas I, Rachel

Riley, am grown up, with no religious restrictions, and a licence to drive!

5.10 p.m.
Mum has informed me that, while I may have a licence to drive, as yet I have no insurance. I said her persistent doom-mongering cannot dampen my spirits, as I shall get some, with my hard-earned lentil money. James said he hopes Mr Goldstein has introduced some kind of halva-selling bonus scheme as I will need £1,578 (he Googled it). Am now fully dampened. Though maybe a night of ironic nostalgia at the Duke will revive me. I doubt it though. It will probably only involve arm-wrestling competitions. Plus there is nothing ironic about Jimmy Nail woman.

## Sunday 2

Birthday presents received at the Duke:
1. Copy of *Endymion* (Scarlet).
2. Giant Toblerone (Sad Ed).
3. Mix CD of 'Walden anthems' (featuring 'Every Day is Like Sunday' by The Smiths and 'Don't Stop Believing' (original, not Glee cast, as Rachel is like me, only annoying, and with gay dads)) (Jack).
4. A colossal hangover (Jimmy Nail woman, and my own failure to adhere to Mum's/the government's guidelines).

James said I have proven I am not a grown-up at all (as Mum held out a bucket for me to vomit disturbingly orange sick into. What was I drinking? Lucozade? Also—why do mums always have buckets or bowls to hand? It is one of the great mysteries of life. Like swallows flying south in winter. Ooh am excellently philosophical, despite having bangy head and swirly stomach. Which is a sign I am grown-up after all, like Amy Winehouse being able to perform despite being high on vodka and hairspray). Said am impervious to his insults, as I am fully undampened at the news that Scarlet and Sad Ed are going to come on a Cleggmobile holiday with me. It will be our 'last hurrah' before the gruelling academic regime of university. James said university is mostly drinking games and writing rubbish about soap operas, as endless *Times* investigations have proven. Plus we cannot actually drive anywhere given that I have no insurance, Sad Ed has failed his theory test and Scarlet refuses to learn on environmental grounds. I said it is principle that counts, and we shall toast the symbolic end of childhood, and potentially life in the provincial hell that is Saffron Walden, whilst enjoying the view from the front garden of Pasty Manor. And would have said more, but the need to do orange sick proved greater than the need to disprove James.

## Monday 3

Have told Mr Goldstein that I will be leaving his employ in less than three weeks, as I am off on a gap fortnight trip

before 'going up' to university (excellent term gleaned from *Brideshead Revisited*). He was less distraught than I had anticipated (had imagined scenario with him on bended knee begging me to stay and wrangle lentils on a permanent basis). In fact he smiled encouragingly and asked if it was to Africa. I did not want to dampen his enthusiasm (clearly mere bravado) so said, 'Sort of.' It is not a complete lie as St Slaughter is similarly deprived in the toilet area.

## Tuesday 4

8 a.m.

The day of reckoning has dawned for Colin Riley, i.e. it is his interview at Dauncy and Moss (which sounds like ancient and very crap men's outfitters. But is merely ancient and crap stationery suppliers). James has warned him our entire future depends on it, and failure could mean poverty, homelessness, or, worse, Mum having to work on the tills in Tesco. Dad looked visibly nervous, unaided by Mum who reminded him not to swear, snort, or do 'that annoying thing with his fingers' (have no idea what this is, but feasibly anything as she is easily annoyed). Plus she is driving him there. She says he cannot be trusted not to crash, get lost, or decide to spend an hour in a Little Chef instead. James is going too. He is using it as an opportunity to 'spend quality time' with Wendy (i.e. do illicit snogging).

6 p.m.

Mum and Dad are back from Bury St Edmunds with mixed reactions. Dad says the job is definitely in the bag. But Mum says she does not like the look of the job, or the bag. James says the bag is fine, it is what you wear it with that matters. Went to my room as the conversation was threatening to become too unnerving even for a born philosopher like me.

## Wednesday 5

Dad got the job. Mum has capitulated and said the bag is do-able, as long as they can find a house that meets her specific needs, and a school that meets James's specific needs. James said his needs are simple: science club, maths club, and 'classy hos'. He has been sent to his room. But Mum has called Clive and Marjory anyway. They are coming round for a viewing tomorrow morning. Said again this was pointless as Marjory knows every nook and cranny, having spent half her life in here, banging on about June Whitfield and sausages, etc., but Mum says she has very stringent requirements on pine units and pelmets and needs to ensure it measures up. Though she is confident she will beat the Drs Jones in the battle of Summerdale Road, as we have retained our traditional 1980s fittings, whereas they have 'gone all fancy' with stripped oak and slate.

## Thursday 6

There has been a snag in the great bag (i.e. Bury St Edmunds) plan. Clive and Marjory have not jumped at the chance to purchase Chez Riley and are in fact in a quandary over which house to choose. Marjory says she is being torn asunder. I hope not. It sounds perilous, pants-wise.

More interestingly, the *Walden Chronicle* has reported the exciting news that Saffron Walden is being besieged by a flasher! According to the front page article, he exposed himself last Friday 'dangerously close' (i.e. the other side of the common) to the 'popular children's pleasure park' (aka slide of death and snog corner), 'leaving well-known and well-liked local business entrepreneur Barbara Marsh, 42' (runner of tedious and random fitness classes, 54, barely tolerated) 'fearing for her life'. Even Mum says it is an exaggeration as there is nothing terrifying about a penis. Said she has never seen Donkey Dawson's. She demanded to know if I had seen Donkey Dawson's. Said no (true), I did not need to. Its legend preceded it. She says it is one point up for Bury as they have not had an indecent exposure since the legendary summer of 1976, and that was mostly down to the heatwave. I said, *au contraire*, it is yet another annoyance that the minute I am about to leave Saffron Walden, it gets a bona fide pervert, as opposed to Barry the Blade who is just a bit dirty. And the O'Gradys who are just oversexed.

## Friday 7

The confines of 24 Summerdale Road are clouded with disappointment. Clive and Marjory have decided to buy next door instead. Their increased offer of the full asking price has been accepted, and they are hoping to be 'home' by September. James says they will regret their poor decision, as not only are they paying several thousands more than they sold it for, they are ignoring the benefits of our all-seeing eye hallway (allowing one to detect transgression in any wing of the house in one swivel-eyed panoptic movement). Mum is minty. She says it is a rejection of her supreme cleanliness and taste (it is not, it is like pigeons, i.e. those of limited imagination always go home in the end) but it is good news for diligent house buyers in the Uttlesford area as it will go on the open market as of next week. She has rung Chilcott and Chilcott, and one of them, hopefully Don (though the difference is barely discernible) is coming round to measure up on Monday. James says he does not need to, he has already done it, using his accurate-to-a-millimetre laser tape measure, and has also written some excellently persuasive particulars. Mum has checked said particulars. He has described the downstairs toilet as 'palatial'.

## Saturday 8

In a shock move, going against all her lentil-fearing tendencies, Thin Kylie has entered the temple of health-

giving snacks that is Nuts in May. To be fair she got the wrong door on her way to Pop-In (for all your skintight polyester needs), but to her credit, she did not scream and run out immediately. Though she did say, 'OMG, minging hell. I am in, like, the lesbian shop.' Pointed out that she was falling prey to lazy cliché and media stereotypes as no one in here was officially homosexual. She said, 'OMG, shut up, Riley. I am not lazy. I've been up since, like ten, innit.' Asked why she had risen with the lark, was it perhaps early morning sexual demands from Liam O'Grady (purveyor of knob rot)? She said no, she had had an appointment with Mr Hutchinson (bank manager, greasy hair, son once had a tryout for Tottenham) to get a loan for Ugly Ducklings. Was forced to retract my assumptions (based on lazy cliché and media stereotypes). Though do not know why she needs a loan. Cherie and Terry are former lottery winners. Plus she is renowned for her ability to extract money with menaces.

## Sunday 9

James and Mad Harry are consumed with potential flasher madness. Beastly Investigations is now fully operational, and they have gone down the common to lurk provocatively. Said they are wasting their time as a proper pervert is hardly going to want to display his wares to a pair of nerds with binoculars, a butterfly net, and a moronic dog.

5 p.m.

As predicted, the flasher has failed to make an appearance. James and Harry are undeterred though. They are going back tomorrow with the ghostometer (microwave radiation checker), hot pants, and wig.

If that doesn't deter him for good, nothing will.

## Monday 10

Mum is in a bad mood. It is because Mr Chilcott (Don, smaller moustache, louder stripes on shirt, so swings and roundabouts as far as Chilcotts go) has been round to measure up and he has expressed disappointment at the 'outmoded' kitchen decor. She said there was nothing wrong with Formica, it has served the Rileys perfectly well for nearly twenty years. Mr Chilcott said it was nothing a quick trip to Ikea couldn't fix. James said Mum nearly imploded with rage. She is of the opinion that there is nothing a trip to Ikea can possibly do other than herald the end of days. This is after Dad's notorious drive to Lakeside last year in search of a footstool to aid Jesus's toilet training. He came back with two hundred tea lights, a sack of Daim bars, and no footstool. James said even she would have bought the tea lights, it is a well-known fact that no one can resist them. But Mum says she is immune to marketing ploys of all kinds. This is true. She does not even overeat Pringles. Hence her letter to them arguing

with their advert which claims 'once you pop, you can't stop'. She popped, and stopped, and demanded her money back and a retraction of the slogan.

Also, there is still no sign of perversion at the play park, other than the usual quota of O'Gradys. James has conceded that the wig, hot pants, and ghostometer are not sufficient for this case's complex needs and that in fact he needs a proper (i.e. female, not cross-dressing Mad Harry) honeytrap. Have offered my services as have always wanted an encounter on a wild common with a penis-wielding pervert. It will be utterly *Wuthering Heights*esque. James has agreed. We are meeting at Barry Island after work and I am under orders to wear my most revealing outfit.

## Tuesday 11

Scarlet came into Nuts in May to get homeopathic remedies for Harper's ceaseless whingeing (Suzy says it is the teething. It is not, it is the genetically inherited violent tendencies rearing their ugly head) and to express profound disappointment in Sad Ed's inability to abide by their 'friends with benefits' rules. Asked what his transgression had been. She said he had made her a mix CD featuring 'Thank You' by Led Zeppelin, which is a sure sign of true love. Said Jack's birthday mix CD had that on it, and it was probably just similarly ironic. She rolled her eyes and asked why I was wearing Thin Kylie's boob tube to work.

Explained the honeytrap thing. She said it will not be like *Wuthering Heights*. It will be like *Shameless*. Said she is just jealous that James did not ask her. She said hardly, as I am merely perpetuating the sexual enslavement of women the world over. And if sex trafficking in the Essex area increases in the wake of this, then it will all be my fault.

It is probably exam results nerves getting to her. Her entire career hinges on her boffiny brain power. Whereas I am thinking of combining my acting prowess and honeytrap experience in a new role as a professional private investigator. I will be like Precious Ramotswe, No. 1 Ladies' Detective. Only white, and less enormous.

7 p.m.

My career is over before it began. The honeytrap has failed, and there has now been no official pervert sighting for eleven days. Maybe the boob tube put them off (or lack of boobs to fill it). Or possibly the presence of Jack who showed up just as I was reclining provocatively on the slide of death to demand an end to the 'madness'. Said it was not madness, it was a proven police method. Plus demanded to know why he was in the vicinity in the first place, unless—ta-dah!—he is the flasher! He said it is not ta-dah, and he is not the flasher, he was just checking I was not about to make an idiot of myself as Scarlet said I was up to my 'usual' tricks. Said he was wasting his worrying time and should he not be flexing his concerns over Maya who is probably much closer to perverts than

I, given that she is in London, which is pervert central according to Mum. He said that was exactly where he was headed tomorrow for the rest of the summer. Said I'd see him around then. He said not if I see you first. Which is pathetically clichéd.

James is not giving up though. He said maybe they just need someone with more 'obvious' allure. I am taking this as a compliment too. Given the pervert's previous preference, it is probably a bored housewife, i.e. Mum.

## Wednesday 12

The honeytrap is not Mum, it is none other than Thin Kylie! James has got her to do it in exchange for a packet of Embassy (borrowed off Treena) and a potential £500 from *Chat* magazine when they sell their story. This is an utter insult. Why would a pervert prefer Kylie to me?

Unless it is an O'Grady. Which is entirely feasible.

## Thursday 13

OMG. I was right. The flasher was Liam 2! He was caught red-handed, or red-penised, after only five minutes of Thin Kylie pole dancing in a bikini on the climbing frame. He panicked when he realized who the honeytrap was and claimed he was doing it for medical reasons, i.e. the knob

rot needed fresh air to heal, but Thin Kylie said she had heard that one before (from whom?) and chucked him immediately (as he was being handcuffed by PC Doone, which was excellently ITV Drama).

James is jubilant. It is his first real crime-solving. Though I pointed out that it is a hollow victory as *a)* he did not actually do the arresting, that was down to poor police procedure, i.e. PC Doone letting the Alsatians poo behind the public toilets, meaning he was conveniently in the area at the time. Plus *b)* he has broken up a loving relationship with his grim determination to seek the truth, regardless of romance. He said, *au contraire*, there is nothing romantic about knob rot or flashing, plus he has 'taken down an O'Grady' and is confidently expecting a reward from Mum, if not the Queen, for his services to society.

He will be disappointed on all counts.

## Friday 14

As predicted, the monarchy and Mum have failed to reward James with his preferred prize of an OBE and chocolate mousse for pudding for a week. Instead he has been ignored (by the Queen) and severely chastised (by Mum) for a list of misdemeanours too lengthy to actually remember (plus most of them were screamed at decibels only dogs and dolphins can hear). I suggested a good grounding would work wonders. But she said he will only

relish the solitude and use it to think up some other dog-based detective agency insanity. Instead she is setting him a list of brain-bending cleaning challenges to keep him occupied.

## Saturday 15

So far James has descaled the bath ring and polished out claw marks from the parquet. But jubilation eludes him as he has still to solve the mystery of how to remove beetroot from wool-mix carpet. He says he refuses to be defeated though and is on Mumsnet trying to get top tips out of someone called Shazza89. I predict disappointment. He would do better to ask someone like Janet64. Mum is in agreement. She is wearing a superior smirk along with her beige Marks & Spencer linen.

5 p.m.
Mine and Mum's doubting of Shazza has been ill-founded. The stain has gone as has the smirk, which has been replaced with thin-lipped mintiness. James is issuing withering glances willy-nilly. He says it is proof that sounding like a glamour model is no hindrance to success in life, and he shall be naming his first born Jordan Nikkala. Thin-lipped mintiness now replaced by open-mouthed panic that Mumtaz is pregnant.

5.10 p.m.

Mumtaz is not pregnant. James says he has only got to sixth base. Said there were only four bases. He said not in his book, there are eleven. Am now torn between wanting to work out what these might be, and throwing up at thought of James being involved in any of them. Mum said welcome to her world. Will ask Scarlet as she is bound to know.

## Sunday 16

Scarlet says she can only come up with seven, and one of them involves the bottom. Have decided to watch *One Born Every Minute* instead. It is far less traumatizing.

11 p.m.

Am never, repeat NEVER, having a child.

## Monday 17

Today marks the beginning of the end for my days at the lentil-face. When I am directing Greta Gerwig in a groundbreaking production of an all-female *Richard III* at the National Theatre I shall look back at this simple, honest toil with fondness.

6 p.m.

Or possibly relief that I never again have to encounter the Till of Confusion. I almost wish the Till of Doom were back. Bleeding fingers were preferable to it insisting that I give Mrs Denley (normal height) £43.70 change from a twenty-pound note.

### Tuesday 18

I do not know what is so noble about menial work. It is back-breaking and boring. I am glad to be leaving. Plus maybe Mr Goldstein will reward my loyalty over the years with a £500 bonus as a parting gift.

### Wednesday 19

Did not get £500 bonus. Or lifetime supply of mung beans. Got my pay packet and a packet of gluten-free lemon biscuits (broken). I am not minded; as James says, my true gift will arrive tomorrow when I elevate myself above his lowly station with my superior academic skills. Then I shall write an Olivier-award-winning play about health foods, starring a Mr Goldthwaite as the cruel but ultimately misunderstood hunchback of Saffron Walden.

Though my parting was not without sweet sorrow. It was the last time I shall have watched Dean Denley standing

on his box to reach the mincing machine at Goddard's over the road. And the last time I will have to eject Sad Ed for clogging up the herbal tea aisle with his hefty bulk and endless ponderings about Scarlet's needs. He is hoping tomorrow's results will be like a giant hammer to the head and she will remember that she is actually in love with him. I think he would be better off with an actual hammer. She is bound to get three A*s which will only remind her that she is batting way below her league with Sad Ed. Am starting to feel sick with nerves now. Have told myself that it is not the end of the world if I fail, i.e. I can do resits, or apply to less ambitious colleges. But Mum and James have made it clear that I am wrong, and that anything below three As is equivalent to a death sentence, future-wise.

## Thursday 20

Am jubilant. Have got an A (Drama) and two Bs (English and Politics)! Mum is trying to be pleased but it is clear that my lack of stars is yet another disappointment in a lifetime of misses. James is in agreement. He says according to *The Times* my qualifications are not worth the paper they are written on. I said they are worth more than the paper they are written on (though now realize this is meaningless) as they are my ticket out of Saffron Walden, and to the Time of My Life (everyone says university, not school, is 'the time of your life', it is well-known fact). James said it

is a ticket to a £30,000 overdraft and a lifetime of crippling debt (he is now eschewing university and is hoping instead to be the first sixteen-year-old to be invited to head the G8). Said it is not crippling debt, it is artistic poverty, which will only fuel my creative spirit, as anybody knows. Plus Scarlet can always bail me out with her MP's allowances. Unless Harper's endless wailing has taken its toll and she has actually failed all her exams and will be forced into a life of prostitution (it is that or burger flipping and she is vegetarian so predict that this would win, despite chance of venereal disease/getting axed by a madman).

10 a.m.
Scarlet got two As and a B so has avoided prostitution and a slow death from syphilis, and proximity to pork products and will be coming to Hull too. Sad Ed has not been so lucky. He only got two Cs and a D so he is on the phone to clearing in desperation. He is right to be desperate. He has no career as a rent boy, given his physique and morose expression.

5 p.m.
Sad Ed has secured his place at Humberside after all. He said it is his excellent bargaining skills and down-the-phone rendition of 'Little Drummer Boy'. It is not. It is because four other applicants got Es, one is dead, and one has opted for Bognor instead. We are off to celebrate at the Acropolis (fake Greek replica of the Parthenon, and habitual hangout

for stoners, so misleading on all counts) nonetheless. No doubt I shall not return until the early hours, having watched the sunrise in the company of my best friends, and bitterest enemies, who shall unite for this, our last taste of schooldays.

11 p.m.
Am already home. Sad Ed and Scarlet decided to celebrate by going back to Bob and Suzy's to find the elusive eleventh base. They are getting a lot of benefits for just friends. As are Lambo and Thin Kylie. She was so overwhelmed with emotion at him getting into his midwifery access course that she let him stick his hand down her hot pants.

I opted for the more traditional celebration of four ciders and a group rendition of 'Simply the Best'. Dean the Dwarf did offer to make it a 'night to remember', but snogging a midget is just not me any more. After Wilde, I have set my sights higher (both metaphorically and literally). And anyway, I am not a slave to my desires like Scarlet. I am far more cerebrally-based.

11.30 p.m.
Plus we are off to Cornwall on Saturday and I can always engage in a holiday romance with a fisherman's apprentice, who also surfs and reads Proust in his spare time.

*August*

## Friday 21

Or more likely a Jack Wills-wearing knob called Henry, according to Scarlet. She has set us strict criteria for our last hurrah, including 'no surfing, no swordfishing, and no Newquay'. I said it wasn't very hurrahish, but she said it is that or she will go and stay with Aunt Sadie in Westbury-sub-Mendip, so Sad Ed begged me to agree as Aunt Sadie is a witch and may have an irreversible effect on Scarlet's openness to conjugation. Have done so, if only for the sake of his penis. Have also added my own rule, i.e. no sex in the Cleggmobile. There is no privacy in there, plus the shaking is bound to overexcite Bruce or Grandpa Clegg, who may think it is gypsies, insurgents, or the Beast of Bodmin and try to shoot us with his air rifle.

Dad is taking us tomorrow. He is not happy about this, i.e. he says it is bad enough that in a few weeks he will be having to schlep up and down the A14 every day without spending his last days of freedom driving for seven hours with the Cleggs at the end of it. But Mum said *a)* schlep is not a real word unless he is Jewish which he is not, and *b)* she can't go as she has to take James to play minigolf unless he would rather do that. He would not. James shows no potential golf-wise. We are both a source of endless disappointment in that capacity.

She has not yet told him he will also be transporting the dog. Granny has offered it a holiday with its only son and heir, i.e. Bruce. Mum has said yes, on the grounds that the

292

less time that creature is in the house during prospective house viewings the better. She is right. Its hairy visage will only be a hindrance. Plus it is bound to wee somewhere it shouldn't, eat something it shouldn't, or throw up the thing it shouldn't have eaten in the excitement.

## Saturday 22

8 a.m.
Am packed and ready for the last hurrah. Though am also taking Stanislavski textbook and complete works of Chekhov to prepare me for rigours of Hull (also Carol Vorderman biography, as am reaching crucial denouement). Am already quite hurrahish as in just eight hours Scarlet, Sad Ed, and I will be ensconced in retro camper van, watching the sun set over the ancient Cornish landscape, as we sear freshly caught mackerel (or cheese-based vegetarian option for Scarlet) over an open fire, and discuss the meaning of life, the universe, and everything.

9 p.m.
Or eat Findus Crispy Pancakes in the front room of Pasty Manor while Scarlet and Pig argue about Davina McCall, and Bruce and the dog attempt to wrestle to the death in the spare room. Granny said she read it in *Reader's Digest*. It is the best way to let them decide who is cock of the

walk. Asked if it had been referring to chickens. She said yes. Thank God.

It is Dad's fault for taking so long to get here. Although he says it is the dog's for drinking too much water before we left and needing seven wee stops, including one at the banned Chieveley (no idea why, but is best not to question these matters). Although by that token it is actually James's fault for encouraging it to drink water in case Dad left it locked in the car in the blazing sun at Leigh Delamere and it desiccated to death. Dad said chance would be a fine thing as the one time he did leave the dog locked in the car (Taunton Deane, when it resolutely refused a wee) it ate the electric window button so that now it is wedged permanently open. Dad is devastated as now he is trapped in Pasty Manor for the night as Mum refuses to let him drive home in case he falls asleep at the wheel. He protested that there was no room but she is not taking no for an answer (she never does. It is one of her great achievements in life) so he is being forced to 'bunk up' with Pig. Pig is more than happy with this arrangement as he has been missing 'night-time company' since he and Mrs Pig began to have their differences. Dad is less jubilant. He is terrified he is going to be murdered, or worse, mistaken for a swarthy red-faced Cornish woman in the night. He begged to stay in the Cleggmobile but it is already more than cramped, what with Scarlet's gothwear, and the bulk that is Sad Ed. I said he needs to take a leaf out of my philosophical book (Carol Vorderman biography not Stanislavski, which have already rejected as being incomprehensible), i.e. tomorrow

will dawn a new day, when we can fulfil our open-fire fish-catching ambitions, and he can be back in the comfort of 24 Summerdale Road, listening to Mum frantically shampooing the shagpile and James and Mad Harry doing voodoo dances in their pants. He looked less than jubilant as he went to bed.

## Sunday 23

It is raining. Which means all fishing and fire activity is on hold. Have tried stimulating conversation but Sad Ed and Scarlet have ejected me so they can engage in 'beneficial' activity, and Pig does not know who, or what, Kant is. Have resorted to Carol in the hope she would have wise words, but I have checked the index and there is no mention of rain or inbred relatives. Dad is similarly displeased. His delight at escaping from Pasty Manor without being ravaged by Pig is tempered by the knowledge that he is going to get rained on for seven hours through the dog-damaged window.

## Monday 24

Still raining. Have now finished Carol Vorderman (shedding a tear at empowering ending) and so am started on Chekhov. Am sure it will be similarly inspiring.

4 p.m.

Clearly am in too inspired a mood for something so dry and Russian (what is the significance of the seagull? All they do is squawk endlessly and steal chips). Am now reading *The Murder of Princess Diana* instead, as borrowed from Grandpa Clegg's 'library' (non-extensive collection consisting of biographies of Margaret Thatcher and Terry Wogan, and a book about mines).

## Tuesday 25

Still raining. Have finished murder mystery book and am now on *The Claire Richards Story*, as purchased from Maureen Penrice (proprietoress of Spar, owns Alsatian called Arnie). Have also replenished food stocks, i.e. triangular cheese, crisps, and confectionery. Sad Ed is getting through several Mars bars a day, due to extra rain-induced benefits. He said the rain is Mother Nature's way of forcing Scarlet to realize the full power of his mighty penis and to pledge her eternal troth to him. I said not even judicious use of 'Mother Nature' (designed to appeal to Scarlet's feminist core) would persuade her to pledge any troth, eternal or otherwise.

## Wednesday 26

Still raining.

## Thursday 27

Still raining.

## Friday 28

Still raining.

## Saturday 29

Still raining. Oh God, when will this weather torment end? Have now read three biographies (Claire Richards, Chris Evans, Denise Welch) and all Maureen has left is Hattie Jacques who have never heard of. Plus am going to get scurvy from malnutrition as Cleggmobile cooker is out of bounds due to no one knowing how to connect up the gas canister without exploding things, and the only other source of hot food is Granny Clegg who does not 'believe' in vegetables, bar baked beans, and mostly subsists in ready meals and Viennetta. How the Cleggs are still alive is a medical miracle. Maybe there is some hitherto undiscovered vitamin in Fray Bentos pies that could actually save disease-ravaged African nations.

Plus the Cleggmobile is less than retro chic. The ceiling leaks and the windows rattle eerily at night. It is more like being trapped in a low budget slasher movie. Any minute now the rain-distorted face of a serial killer is going to

loom through the plastic, and lick his lips at the thought of dismembering me with a Trago Mills meat cleaver. Scarlet says I am overreacting, and it is a mere symptom of cabin fever from the confinement. Said how come she was not suffering. She said because she is doing what all prisoners of war do when wrongly incarcerated, i.e. engage in frustration-relieving intercourse with a fellow internee. Said if she was suggesting I 'borrow' Sad Ed then she clearly does have cabin fever after all. She said no, he is her internee and I need to find my own. Serial killer now looking attractive as an option as the only non-related man on the premises is Pig.

1 a.m.
Oh God. Can hear a noise outside. Maybe it is Pig come to claim me after all. Will not look at window. If I do not look at the window, then nothing bad can happen, it is a well-known fact.

1.05 a.m.
Aaaghhh. Could not resist temptation (horror films clearly more realistic than have given them credit for in past) and looked at window and there is definite rain-distorted visage of a serial killer outside. But is not Pig. Is younger. And with no ganglions. But is definitely murderous as has been mouthing evil obscenities and knocking on door in ominous axe-wielding manner. Am not answering. Will wake Sad Ed and make him answer. He can distract the menace while Scarlet and I flee to the safety of Pasty Manor.

**1.10 a.m.**

Scarlet is going to answer door instead as she says Sad Ed lacks any self-defence skills and is notoriously slow-witted, i.e. will die instantaneously, whereas she is panther-like and trained in advanced anti-rape self-defence skills. Sad Ed says he is not insulted, it is just further proof of her devotion that she will risk her life to save his. He is right, she is utterly brave. Any minute now she could be skewered on the end of a poker while her killer laughs, hyena-like, at the storm-ravaged sky.

**1.15 a.m.**

Or dries his hair with a David Beckham towel (Sad Ed's) while he drinks comforting chocolate Yazoo. It is not a serial killer. It is not even a slightly deranged local who is protesting about incomers. It is worse, i.e. it is Jack, who has no doubt come to gloat at our non-retro situation with his newly found edgy London ways and he and Maya can laugh about it with Binky and Cags while they drink espresso vodka shots and listen to sub-Mumford and Sons new folk. Am going to sleep. Hopefully he will be gone by first light, back to the comfort of civilisation.

## Sunday 30

**10 a.m.**

Jack is still here. On the plus side, he and Maya have broken up, so he is less gloaty than I imagined. In fact he is not

really gloaty at all, is more a mixture of depressed and tired, having driven through the night after the row at Binky's (actual person), which he says is too traumatic to discuss. Though am not going to comfort him in case he assumes it is because I am overcome with cabin fever and want to snog him. Which I do not. Because also on the plus side it has stopped raining, so at least I can leave the confines of the Cleggmobile and go for a walk to the Rec to admire the view from the vandalized climbing frame. He will probably be gone by the time I get back.

11 a.m.
Am back from the Rec (view from climbing frame less than inspiring, i.e. vandalized roundabout and bog-eyed youths smoking roll-ups, i.e. signs of rural economy in sharp decline and education system in tatters) and Jack is still here. Said is he intending on gatecrashing our last hurrah on a permanent basis, because if so, he will need to ask Granny Clegg to get in more cheese (her only vegetarian dish) and to let him bunk up with Pig as there is no way he is squeezing onto my bench (Sad Ed and Scarlet have the penthouse, i.e. mezzanine level contraption that threatens collapse at any moment). He said actually he had a rather different proposal, and a two-man tent. Asked for details of said proposal. He said it is to take advantage of him actually having insurance, and take the Cleggmobile on the open road! Agreed immediately. Not only will it infuriate Mum (who will be self-flagellating for not thinking of this before) but the story of our summer on the

road will make an excellent scene in my Carol Vorderman/ Rachel Riley life story drama. And will not even notice Jack if he is driving all day and sleeping in tent at night. Sad Ed is the only person who is unhappy with this arrangement. He fears the change in weather and the excitement of the highway will remind Scarlet that there is more to life than him. He is right. She is bound to fall for an itinerant socialist with a beard, a Che Guevara T-shirt, and a dark secret. That or she will take up Wicca again. Aunt Sadie is unnecessary in this respect as Cornwall is full of witches. Granny Clegg insists her bunions are down to a curse from Ada Polgoose up on Goonhilly Drive. But I cannot deny our destiny for the sake of Sad Ed's mojo. We are off, across romantic moorlands and past legend-infused tin mines to the very end of England. Hurrah!

5 p.m.
Have not quite reached the end of England. Nor have witnessed any romantic moors or tin mines. We are stuck outside the giant Matalan on the A30. Something has fallen out of the bottom of the Cleggmobile, and it is very possibly the entire engine. Am devastated. The dream is over before it even began. We are now waiting until Denzil arrives with his pickup truck and drags us back to Pasty Manor.

6 p.m.
No sign of Denzil as yet. On the plus side have bought three dresses, an iPod dock, and a shoulder massager from

Matalan. Scarlet says I am funding the exploitation of Chinese sweatshop workers, and the death of the British high street. I said it is not my fault, I am merely the victim of the financial crisis, and Mr Goldstein's crippling wage packets, but I promise to buy something from over-expensive artisan shop when I get my first student loan to make up for it. Plus she is welcome to borrow the shoulder massager if she wants. She has declined.

9 p.m.
Still waiting for Denzil. Have rung Granny Clegg to urge him to hurry but apparently he cannot be disturbed during *Gossip Girl*. Am going to go to bed, i.e. bench, with the philosophical thoughts of Hattie Jacques, until he arrives. Scarlet has taken the shoulder massager and Sad Ed up to the mezzanine. I do not know what she is going to do with it, but I doubt I shall want it back later.

## Monday 31
*Bank Holiday*

9 a.m.
Must have fallen asleep. But we are definitely no longer outside Matalan as the distinctive hum of the wetsuit factory next door has disappeared. So it is Pasty Manor for us for the rest of the hurrah. Which is about is hurrahish as a Sunday in Summerdale Road. Will go and beg some

Nimble toast from Granny Clegg. Am starving and there is nothing but a Double Decker and half a Laughing Cow in here.

9.10 a.m.

Something odd has occurred. Walked out of Cleggmobile and instead of being faced with the stone-cladded and Cornish-flag festooned exterior of Belleview, found myself staring at open expanse of Atlantic ocean from edge of precarious cliff. Is lucky am easily stunned into stasis or would be lying dead on pointy rocks right now. Which would be edgy and romantic. But if I end up doing that, I need to leave tome of meaningful poetry open on suitably impenetrable entry, rather than page ninety-two of *Here's Hattie!*

9.30 a.m.

Apparently, in a stroke of hitherto very well-hidden genius, Denzil suggested towing the Cleggmobile to Lands End, as opposed to St Slaughter. He is considering it as a new money-making venture. Jack said he did point out that it was possibly illegal, plus the paucity of tourists in possession of broken motorhomes would render it somewhat unprofitable. But Denzil was stumped by the word paucity and thus ended the conversation, bar him saying he'd be back at 8 a.m. on Saturday to collect us. Said that was a bit early. Jack said Denzil needs to be home in time for *Dick and Dom*. Said fair enough. Plus it is not so bad, as we still have six full days of hurrah to enjoy. Jack said that was very

philosophical. I said I WAS very philosophical, and it is all thanks to my rain-induced confinement reading. (Did not tell him actual philosophers were stream of B-listers and dead obese woman. He will only do gloating, and am quite enjoying the non-gloaty old Jack.) Anyway, we are off for a reviving morning swim, once we have roused Sad Ed and Scarlet, and worked out how to climb in the cab from the living quarters to avoid falling a hundred metres to our gory deaths. Jack has sensibly pitched his tent several metres away. Though knowing Sad Ed he will still manage to trip over a guy rope and fall perilously close to the drop.

11 p.m.

This is what vintage glamping *Famous Five*-style life is supposed to be like, i.e. have swum in secluded cove (albeit one crammed with ill-dressed and sunburnt families from Wolverhampton), have eaten knickerbocker glories (albeit at deplorably overpriced café run by badly tattooed woman called Stacey), and have fried fresh fish (and cheese-based kebabs) on an open fire as we watch the twinkling of fishing boats bobbing in the distance (albeit purchased from the Spar in St Just, as none of us know how to actually fish or have any equipment other than orange plastic crab line purchased for princely sum of £5 from Stacey). All that is missing is Timmy the dog. Aka dog. Though given his un-Timmy like tendency to lick suspected smugglers joyously, and then trip over, this is probably a good thing.

I'm RACHEL RILEY
– welcome to my so-called life.

September

Hurrah. A day at the beach stretches out before us: lounging on the rocks in an enormous hat reading mind-improving literature (me, Scarlet, and Jack)/overdosing on Nobbly Bobblys and attempting to conjugate in smeggy caves (Sad Ed). Jack has asked to borrow mind-improving literature as he left his analysis of the Iraq war at Maya's. Suggested he try Scarlet or Sad Ed but he said Scarlet will not let him sully her feminist handbooks with his man fingers and Sad Ed only has last week's *NME*.

He has gone for the Carol Vorderman (with no discernible gloating). I said she went to Cambridge so it will be an excellent guide as to what he can expect as a lower middle-class comprehensive student, in this unfamiliar world of mortarboards, rowing blues, and high tables. He said, 'Yeah, sure.' He is surprisingly blasé about his future at one of the world's most rigorous and elitist academic institutions. Maybe he is still in mourning over Maya. Or more interestingly, is secretly addicted to beta blockers like Kenny from Watford (*Jeremy Kyle* addiction special) and is unable to feel raw emotion.

5 p.m.
Jack definitely not on beta blockers as he has just called Sad Ed a knob for dripping Mr Whippy (actual ice cream, not boyfriend of Fat Kylie) on his chest (Scarlet has had to mop him up with a wet wipe before the wasps get him. I

offered to do it but she said I cannot have my cake and eat it. I do not know what she means. No one has had cake since Granny Clegg's past-its-sell-by Battenburg two days ago and I didn't want that in the first place) plus am sure I saw him shed a tear at Carol's tribulations. He claims it is sand in his eye but I know it is the bit about her lifelong battle with weight and post-pregnancy comfort eating.

## Wednesday 2

Am slightly bored with the beach now. There are too many wasps and Mr Gallucci (like Mr Whippy, only obese and with possibly fake Greek accent) has run out of orange Calippos. I am clearly more of an intellectual city-break based person, e.g. New York, where I can wander elegantly round the museum of Modern Art, and get swooned over for my British accent and kooky dress sense. Jack is in agreement (about the beach, not getting swooned over). He has suggested a walk to look at a tin mine and tea at Stacey's, but Sad Ed insists that a healthy tan is slimming (he has finished *NME* and is now on a *More* magazine he found at Stacey's) and he is hoping to have visually lost a stone by the end of the week. He will need to be Black Ash on the Cuprinol scale for that to happen. Said I would go with Jack. Scarlet gave me another cake-based lecture and withering look. I really do not know what her problem is. I am not going for the cake. I am going for

the historical interest, and opportunity to admire Stacey's heavily tattooed neck.

5 p.m.

Maybe Scarlet knows something I do not, as I have eaten cake (coffee and walnut) after all and liked it. Plus have had long and interesting conversation with Jack about his break-up with Maya. It was not her dumping him for his refusal to wear red skinny jeans or lensless glasses, it was him dumping her for her attitude to Saffron Walden, i.e. she said it was 'pointless' and was refusing to attend the Stone family anti-religious left-wing Christmas. She said he needed to shake off the shackles of his past, and look to the future more, whereas he said he would never betray his middle-class Essex roots. I said Maya has a point, (though not about shaking off shackles, as they need actual unlocking, otherwise slavery would have ended a good few centuries earlier), which is why I for one am glad to be leaving its stifling suburbanity for good, i.e. life is about where you are going, not where you are coming from (excellent philosophical motto, as gleaned from Carol). He said surely there were some things I'd miss. I said maybe. But not enough to count on more than one hand. He said, 'Try it, you'll be surprised.' I said no thanks as we needed to get to the Spar to buy kebabable goods before it closed. He is wrong though. The only surprise would be if I managed to think of two.

Also, Scarlet and Sad Ed are back from the beach. Sad Ed is now Tomato Soup on the colour scale, which is not

in any way slimming, it just highlights his idiocy and man boobs.

10 p.m.
Mini Babybel and Wotsits have been taken off the list of kebabable products, due to tendency to over-melt/burn in puff of orange smoke.

## Thursday 3

Sad Ed has been banned from leaving the Cleggmobile until sundown. The pain stage is over, but any further exposure to bright lights may cause irreparable damage and embarrassment. Plus, he cannot do any conjugating as his skin falls off when he rubs against anything. Scarlet is going to stay behind and read excerpts of Christina Rossetti's poems to him. He does not look in any way pleased about this, but she refused to read an article about Adele as it would compromise her goth ways. She is scared she might develop a sudden liking for rousing ballads.

It is probably a good thing he is staying in. He has nearly fallen off the cliff five times since we arrived. Denzil should offer his perilous clifftop-towing service to those contemplating suicide. It could be like a giant game of Russian roulette. Maybe there is a TV show in that? Will note it in brain for when I am a high-flying media type.

Am going out again with Jack. We have not decided

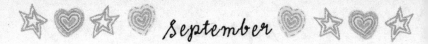

September

where. Mainly because we are being utterly spontaneous. Plus there is not that much to see anyway, unless you like caravan sites or appalling theme parks which we do not. Have pre-empted Scarlet by saying if I want cake, I shall have it. Particularly if it is lemon drizzle. She just rolled her eyes as she rubbed aftersun on Sad Ed's muffin top.

5 p.m.

Have spent fascinating, if complicated, day walking to villages by only turning right. It is partially spontaneous, and partially so that we could only feasibly go in a large circle, thus reducing the chances of getting lost. Which sort of worked as we ended up at Stacey's four times.

Jack asked if I'd counted the things I'd miss in Walden yet. Said no as I was too busy spontaneously having my cake (Victoria sponge, with surprising, though pleasing, Nutella filling). He said I was chicken. I said I am not the dog, and insults and reverse psychology would not work on me (though to be fair they do not work on the dog either. It just continues on its idiotic path). Plus I am not on holiday to spend time moaning about my deprived childhood and uninspiring home life. This is supposed to be a last hurrah, and therefore we should do something hurrahish, e.g. a clifftop bonfire party. Amazingly Jack agreed. We have purchased a crate of lager from Spar and a quart bottle of highly suspicious cider from Stacey's boyfriend, 'Pikey Benson'. Sad Ed says he may be too weak to attend, but Jack has given him a four-pack of Snickers and a promise

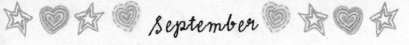 

to drag him the few metres to the fire on a bodyboard. He will not be able to. Sad Ed is heavier than he looks, and he already looks huge.

9 p.m.
Jack is actually stronger than he looks as he managed to drag Sad Ed and Scarlet (claiming benefit-induced ankle injury) to the fire. Though Scarlet fell off twice on the way and had to be treated with Pikey's cider. It is surprisingly drinkable, with an interesting aftertaste of metal. Scarlet said I should stick to the weak lager as too much of the scrumpy could lead to cake eating. She is cake obsessed. Maybe she has developed anorexia by proxy and is determined to shrivel me up.

10 p.m.
Scarlet is wrong. Have had eight plastic cups of Pikey's cider and am not even tempted to open the Mr Kipling almond slices. Am far too busy talking to Jack.

11 p.m.
Fire has gone out due to prevailing winds (according to Sad Ed) and crapness of fire-starter, i.e. me (according to Scarlet). They have gone to bed to do sex talk (still no conjugating until he has lost his flaky epidermis, snake-like, and grown a new, more resilient layer that can cope with polycotton abrasions). Jack says I can sleep in his tent if I want. Said yes as do not want to overhear Scarlet

fantasizing about licking Sad Ed's buttocks or similar atrocities. He said cool. Though now he is bound to start fantasizing about buttocks, though not Sad Ed's. I said we are both adults (officially, with library card to prove it) and can therefore suppress urge to fantasize about buttocks or any other body parts.

11.15 p.m.
Am now fantasizing about Jack's buttocks. Wonder if he is fantasizing about buttocks. Will ask.

11.20 p.m.
He also fantasizing about buttocks. Probably Maya's. Will check.

11.25 p.m.
Not Maya's. Said who then. He said you first. Could say lifeguard on Porthcurno, as is feasible. He has very shapely buttocks in his Speedos.

11.30 p.m.
Or I could tell truth. Maybe I will tell truth. Honesty is always the best policy. And it does not mean I have to then go near said buttocks. Could stay quite happily in separate sleeping bags wedged against orange canvas with at least ten centimetres of space between us. I am grown-up after all.

# Friday 4

10 a.m.
Or I could do that.

Oh my God. I did that. I mean 'it'. And it was perfect.
Like everything and nothing I imagined. And I had definitely
imagined it. Even with the nappy and the voting Tory.
Though luckily they did not make an appearance last night
as gagging would not have been appropriate mid-'it' noise.
Not that could even consider what was appropriate as was
utterly transfixed by the wonder of Jack. I mean, this was
Jack! Jack who I have known since I was the one in nappies.
Jack who I used to play Connect Four tournaments with
when Scarlet had glandular fever. Jack who fixed my bike
and told me who The Smiths were (i.e. not a Canadian boy
band).

Jack who kissed me so hard last night I thought I would
buckle and break. Jack who made me feel like the world
had stopped, and nothing else existed, just me and him,
turning silently in the centre of everything.

Jack who put his hands, and thingy, where not even Dr
Braithwaite (huge hands, lazy eye, bottle of whisky in desk
drawer) has had a good look.

Aaaagghh, we did 'it'. WE FINALLY DID 'IT'!

Brain now melting with implications. Is complete world-
changing event. Like discovery of fire. Or sliced bread.

Have to speak to Scarlet immediately. Am going to
Cleggmobile before Jack wakes up and tries to do 'it' again.

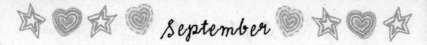 

Not that I don't want to do that again. Do I? Oh God, am confused. Which is why I need Scarlet. She is unflappable when it comes to matters of the flesh. It is having a sex guru for a mother instead of a repressed former accountant with a cleaning obsession.

10.05 a.m.

Something more brain-melty has happened. The Cleggmobile has gone! I fear the worst. That Sad Ed's heaving bulk dislodged the hand brake and they have plunged to their deaths trapped inside a giant plastic coffin. Cannot bear to look over edge. Oh, and now phone has gone off. Is probably text from media needing a tear-strewn interview over tragedy.

10.10 a.m.

Was not media. Was Lambo saying he has beaten the 'twat with the knob rot' (too many corrections needed so did not bother) so the wedding is back on and we need to be at St Regina's by eleven tomorrow. Have said it is unlikely as I fear I will be filling out police statements. (Did not mention incongruity of church-based wedding, given their combined sexual histories.) Oh God cannot look over edge. Inevitable carnage would be too much to bear.

There is nothing for it. Will have to wake Jack. And thus end our brief but torrid affair, as it is plunged into the mire of family tragedy.

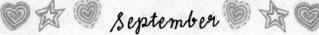
10.20 a.m.

Have woken Jack, who immediately made a move to grab me, or at least part of me, but being a selfless heroine in the face of utter devastation, I declared, 'We have to forget about last night, I already have (which is not true but cannot tell him am thinking about his penis rather than his dead sister), and something more life-changing and earth-shattering has occurred.' Jack, who immediately paled into state of visible shock, then checked over edge, but declared he could not see any carnage, and that maybe I am overreacting, as usual, and not focusing on the facts, and important things. I said what could be more important than a tragic caravan accident, and clearly it must have sunk into the briny depths, like so many ships before it, and now it is buried for evermore in Davy Jones's Locker. Oh God, phone is going again. Is probably Thin Kylie this time. Can I not be left to grieve in peace?

10.25 a.m.

Was not Thin Kylie. Was Scarlet to demand to know why she had woken up with Granny Clegg hovering over her with a bowl of All Bran. Thought it might be some kind of out-of-body hallucination from an air pocket under the water, but Jack commandeered phone (admittedly I was wailing incomprehensibly) and it seems Denzil got the days wrong (this would not be the first time) and towed them back to Pasty Manor. Jack has told her about chav wedding emergency and demanded that Denzil come back and fetch us in the non-sick-smelling Car of the People. Denzil has

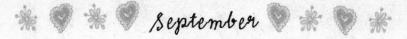 

agreed, but we are having to wait until after *DIY SOS*. Which means am alone with Jack for at least an hour. What if he wants to do it again? Though maybe he will be too tired. Or will be belatedly rendered mute at shock. It is possible, I have seen it on *This Morning*.

11.00 a.m.
Jack not rendered mute. Has just struck tent and offered me an almond slice.

11.15 a.m.
Still no sign of rematch, or even discussion of rematch. Despite eating four almond slices, which are quite phallic in their appearance. He is being very blasé.

11.17 a.m.
Or maybe it didn't happen at all but was just a very lucid dream induced by Pikey Benson's cider.

11.20 a.m.
No, it definitely happened. There is no way I would feel like that, down there, after normal sleeping activity. Not even after dream involving Jim Morrison. Plus have checked bin (Spar bag) and condom wrapper very much in evidence.

11.25 a.m.
Can reflect no longer on lack of post-coitus communication as Denzil is here with Sad Ed and Scarlet and our worldly

possessions (i.e. rucksacks, ill-advised purchases of plastic beach tat, and the dog). Jack has pointed out he cannot squeeze Denzil in to drop him off en route but Denzil says he will get a lift from Monkey Penhaligan and his potato lorry later. So this is it. Our last 'hurrah' has been sounded, and is lost on the last of the summer breeze. The harvest is reaped and an autumn chill creeps in. Just as our blossoming, carefree childhood is replaced by more sober times.

I am enviably poetic, even in the face of almost tragedy and sexual mortification.


**7 p.m.**
Am at Stortford services while Jack buys petrol, Sad Ed buys condoms (skin is showing sign of renewal already. He says he is thinking of patenting his diet as it is clearly the key to eternal youth. It is not. His liver will give out before he is thirty), and Scarlet cleans dog sick off her flip-flops.

Am oddly looking forward to welcome home. Am like prodigal daughter returning from arduous travails. Maybe there will be a celebratory supper and a technicolour dreamcoat.


**8 p.m.**
No celebratory supper. Had Shreddies as Mum and Dad were too busy arguing over whether or not curtains are included in house price. The dog got more of a welcome. James had made it a new collar with glow-in-the-dark

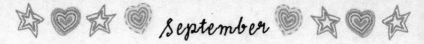

stickers and compass attachments. It is a waste of time. It will only lose them or eat them. Plus no dreamcoat. Though admit may have got my biblical references confused.

10 p.m.
Still nothing from Jack. So have come to devastating, but only feasible conclusion, that I am but another notch on his futon-post. He has used my body mercilessly to help him get over Maya, then flung me aside, like a dirty sock, or the used condom. Actually with less ceremony than the used condom, as he put that neatly in the Spar bag.

How utterly depressing.

11.15 p.m.
Though worldly.

11.20 p.m.
In fact, maybe he has done me a favour. Maybe I will meet someone superior at Hull. Someone who is truly open to my unique tendencies. Someone who isn't two hundred miles away or my best friend's brother who have known since was five and has seen me wee in a paddling pool.

11.25 p.m.
But then, someone who doesn't make me feel like I am all that matters in the world. Who doesn't make me melt every time he touches me.

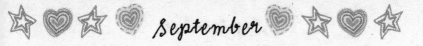

**11.35 p.m.**

But someone who doesn't just ravage me because I happen to be sharing his tent and have had a crush on him since I was thirteen. No. It is definitely for the best.

**11.55 p.m.**

Isn't it?

## Saturday 5

If there is one thing to remind me of the perils of forming a lasting relationship with someone from Essex it is the horror of today's historic Lambert–Britcher nuptials. Predictably, the ceremony did not pass without several mishaps, as follows:

1  Seven crèche inmates, led by Jesus, escaped during Beyoncé's 'Crazy in Love' (inappropriate choice allowed by temporary and progressive vicar Reverend Metcalfe (rainbow jumper, pierced ear, insane smile of drug addict/zealot). Am minded to write to Archbishop of Canterbury to complain. Though Sad Ed delighted as he says he is having 'You're the One for Me, Fatty' when he marries Scarlet. He is surprisingly self-aware if nothing else). Inmates, minus Jesus, rounded up in toilets. Treena says not to bother waiting for him, he always turns up eventually. Ceremony proceeds.

2   Whitney O'Grady removed from church after trying to use font as paddling pool.

3   Stacey O'Grady removed from church after trying to use font as urinal.

4   Liam O'Grady removed (unconscious) from church for failing to forever hold his peace, and instead brandishing note from sexual health walk-in clinic declaring he is now knob-rot free and begging Thin Kylie to take him back (Fat Kylie punches him. Mr Whippy proposes on spot. She punches him too for failing to do romantic candlelit proposal at TGI Friday's).

5   Mother of the bride, Cherie (in traditional fascinator, and non-traditional strapless skintight leopard print), passes out in aisle in assumed display of overexcitement. Later revealed to be actual display of effects of seven Bacardi Breezers.

6   Father of the groom, Mr Hosepipe, called away to emergency at museum next door.

7   Mr Hosepipe returns with causer of said emergency, Jesus Harvey Nichols Riley, who had climbed into sarcophagus and got trapped inside with mummified cat.

Obviously, were I to marry Jack, which I am not, it would be in Chelsea Register Office, following in the footsteps of Mick Jagger, Judy Garland, and Patsy Kensit, and everyone would wear vintage Dior and retire for dinner at the Ivy, as opposed to hula hoops and a prawn ring in the back room of the Axe and Compasses. But that is not the point. The point

is that marriage, like Saffron Walden, is utterly provincial and I do not want any part of it.

Also have not told Scarlet about loss of virginity. There is no point disgusting her pointlessly for something that was so trivial. At least to one of us. I should have used aversion tactics after all. Picturing Dad with a mullet would have saved me time and bother.

And mild cystitis.

## Sunday 6

It is yet another historic day in the House of Riley, as it has witnessed the departure of Dad for Bury St Edmunds, and his new temporary home, Four Cats Bed and Breakfast (seven cats, two parakeets, and one cross-eyed owner, Mrs Menzies). He did beg to wait until tomorrow morning but Mum said she did not want him getting stuck in the notoriously heavy rush-hour snarl-ups on his first day and getting sacked before he has even started. She has placated him by pointing out it is only temporary because as soon as the house sale goes through she and James will be joining him. James said she had mistakenly omitted the dog from this sentence. She said it was not a mistake, the move could be too traumatic for him, and she is hoping tomorrow's prospective buyers (Alan and Anthea Copping, provenance unknown) will fall in love with him and adopt him. This is a lie. She just does not want new carpets getting soiled habitually, or new dog-owning

neighbours getting minty when he tries to conjugate with their pets, despite his lack of genitals.

James is outraged. Have pointed out the unlikelihood of anyone, let alone Alan and Anthea, swooning at the sight of the dog, but he and the creature in question are now locked in his bedroom having a sit-in protest. I give them until tea. It is toad in the hole. There is no way James or the dog will miss out on the chance of consuming pork products.

3.45 p.m.
The dog is out. It savaged Prince William and James is not talking to it any more. He says the Coppings are welcome to it. He is just sulking as school starts tomorrow. Said he only has six years to go and then he will be like me. He says if he is like me in six years he will give up on life itself.

## Monday 7

Asked James how school was. He said, '*Plus ça change.*' Said to be more specific. He said Billy Wilson (cousin of Whitey Wilson, not actual albino, but with definite corpse-like pallor) has dyed his hair black over the summer and is now attempting to unite Goth Corner and the mathletes tables in one colossal domain of geek. Said he would fail, as had countless others before him. The goths are just not clever enough, and the mathletes will tire of their inability to name square roots in the end.

Also, the Coppings have been to see the house. They did not fall in love with the dog, as predicted (unsurprisingly as it was engaged in some sort of battle with a sock at the time), but did express delight at the neutral decor. Mum is confidently expecting an asking price offer by tomorrow morning. I share her optimism for once. Although mine is tinged with the dirty taint of desperation at wanting to never ever see Jack Stone and his willy nilly again. Unless he wants to see mine. Which he does not.

7 p.m.
Not that I have one.

## Tuesday 8

No offer on the house as yet.

## Wednesday 9

Still no offer. Mum says no news is good news. Said this was a U-turn on her usual policy of no news means that someone is either guilty or dead. She said she is giving them the benefit of the doubt. This is odd. She never gives anyone the benefit of the doubt. It is one of her great rules in life, along with never go to Spain, and don't trust anyone with a beard.

## Thursday 10

Mum has caved under endless questioning from James (who is keen on hurrying along his reunion with Wendy) and rung a Chilcott. Apparently Alan and Anthea have found a three-bed in Sawbridgeworth instead. Mum says it is their funeral but they will regret it when they are having to do their Waitrose shop with a hoard of footballers' wives. She is just sulking that Saffron Walden only has one celebrity left (i.e. the not-so-famous McGann) now that Marlon Dingle has moved to Emmerdale environs on a permanent basis.

Though I note that despite her comment, she is remaining remarkably circumspect about this downturn of events. I fear she has got a taste for the high life now that Dad is not here to clean up after/shout at about shoes in the house. She is quite enjoying the arrangement.

Unlike Dad. He rang during *Hairy Bikers* to complain about conditions at Four Cats. Apparently there are mice, or possibly rats, and he has run out of toilet roll. Mum said he needs to take this up with Mrs Menzies. He said he had but according to her, the mice/rats/possibly shrews are not a real menace as they only come out at night, and toilet roll day is Sunday. Mum has dispatched him to Tesco Express for some emergency Kleenex and gone back to moaning about abundance of saturated fats, lack of hairnets and beardnets, and incomprehensible accents.

## Friday 11

1 p.m.

The downturn has about turned. Alan and Anthea have changed their minds (it turns out they are more afeared of vajazzling than Mum gave them credit for) and have offered full asking price. Mum said she is minded to ask for more to compensate for their hesitation but Dad has overruled her, accepted the offer, and demanded her presence in Bury St Edmunds immediately to look for a house. Clearly conditions are untenable at Four Cats as he is never this forthright at 24 Summerdale Road. Unbelievably, Mum has done as she has been told (though I suspect she is just letting him think that, and it is more the opportunity to have words with Mrs Menzies about her lackadaisical attitude to vermin and bottom cleanliness), and has left me with a twenty pound note for emergencies and full parental control of the house. This is unprecedented. As well as rash on Mum's part. Which James pointed out. But she says she has left Post-it note instructions on all household appliances requiring any degree of skill and in doubt I am to phone her or the police immediately. Hurrah. This is my first test of living alone. Or at least without someone who categorizes carrier bags according to size, colour, and how embarrassing it would be to put the recycling out in (Waitrose fine, Mr Patel's under no circumstances). It will be excellent practice for university.

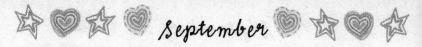

**2 p.m.**

Have checked house for Post-it notes. There are fifty-seven, including 'Do NOT use "supersuction" mode' on the Hoover, and 'Squeeze out THOROUGHLY or it will go smelly' on the Spontex sponge.

**4 p.m.**

Have tested Hoover supersuction mode to see if Mum just over-worrying. She is not as nozzle has created alarming bald spot on stair carpet. Have covered it with decorative basket. She will never notice.

**5 p.m.**

Dog has partially consumed basket and hawked it up four stairs down. Hopefully she will be too distracted by purpleness of stain (dog has been at beetroot again) to notice bald spot.

## Saturday 12

**11 a.m.**

Have got my confirmation of accommodation letter through from Hull. I have been allocated to 66 Auckland Avenue, i.e. a student house, which is a complete relief as halls are invariably peopled by tedious maths and language students who think university is one long *American Pie* movie, according to Scarlet. Maybe she will be in halls. It will be

good for her not to be surrounded by bohemian splendour for once.

**11.15 a.m.**
Scarlet has texted. She is in 59 Auckland Avenue, which she says is the dedicated goth house, infamous for its late-night parties and being the birthplace of several bands. She asked where I was. Said I am in 66. She says it is all overkeen Japanese students and faux Cath Kidston cushions. This is typical. Though is not as bad as Sad Ed who is somewhere called Wilberforce Heights. Knowing his luck it is an old people's home.

**4 p.m.**
Scarlet has texted again to ask if I want to go down the Duke for old time's sake. Asked if Jack was going to be there. She said yes, but will not be able to join in old time's sake activities, as he is working, as Jimmy Nail woman has gone into hospital to have a hysterectomy. (Am amazed she had a womb in the first place. Her chromosomes would be of scientific interest.) Said no anyway, as am firmly looking to the future (even if it is floral furnishings). Plus Mad Harry is over and he and James cannot be trusted not to experiment with drugs/ alcohol/bombs. She said I have the wrong attitude and should follow Suzy's example, i.e. give children their freedom, then they will be imbued with a sense of responsibility, like her and Jack were. She is right. I will

leave the boys home alone. It will be a test of their mettle. They can even make their own tea.

11.30 p.m.
Am at Scarlet's for a quick nightcap to toast arrival of Bob's new car. It is another Volvo. Scarlet says it is a sign he is getting old, i.e. he is refusing to try out new things. Suzy is in agreement. Though I suspect her concerns are more sex-related than brand of car. But could not be sure as she then burst into tears due to non-presence of Jack at family ceremony (he was clearing glasses still at the Duke). Suzy says it is a sign of things to come, i.e. her pitifully empty nest. Scarlet said nest in fact full, i.e. with Harper and her many mental issues, plus Edna who is now living in, but Suzy said losing Jack and Scarlet may be too much to bear. She does not mean suicide. She means she needs to open another bottle of Merlot. Have declined glass as am responsible adult, and must go home to check responsible boys are in bed responsibly.

12 a.m.
James and Mad Harry are not in bed responsibly. In contrast they are up, wearing bras (mine) and pants (Dad's) and insane grins (theirs). They say they cannot sleep, they are too excited. Have checked kitchen. Four bars of cooking chocolate and a packet of icing sugar are missing. Have instructed them to put on pyjamas (to combat horror) and drink vinegar (to combat excess sugar. Delia is always suggesting it for oversweet pasta sauce).

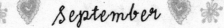
**12.15 a.m.**
Both boys have been sick. On plus side all sugar now ejected from bodies and they are now sleeping off trauma. On downside, their utter lack of aiming skills is evidenced by sick all over the bathroom walls and splash mat. James said it is what a splash mat is for. It is not. It is for looking like the John Lewis catalogue, as well he knows.

**1 a.m.**
Have come over all Suzy and am feeling a bit empty nest. Is not James and Mad Harry. The sooner they are out of my nest the better. It is Jack. I will miss him. Even if he is a heartless Lothario who takes advantage of impressionable teenagers. The thing is, Hull just won't be the same without him. I do not understand why he didn't take up his place there. It is far more suitable to schooling the first ever anti-war Foreign Secretary. Plus the beer is only £2.20 a pint.

**1.15 a.m.**
Unless it is to avoid me, because looking at me reminds him of a night filled with experience so revolting he would rather have sex with a Spice Girl with a mullet wearing a nappy (latest aversion tactic). In which case I am kicking him out of nest and would rather it is empty than hosting cuckooesque charlatan.

## Sunday 13

Am not leaving house for fear of further sugar/vomit-based hoo-hah. Instead am spending entire day Googling useful facts about Hull to aid my orientation and integration with locals (according to Scarlet, knowing the price of beer is not sufficient). Have sent James to kitchen to reorder the dried goods drawer according to salt content and told him he is not to speak unless spoken to. He has agreed. He sees it as an opportunity to best Mum at her own game.

10 a.m.
Have stopped Googling Hull facts. It is less riveting than I anticipated. Am watching T4 instead. Being able to endure hours of trash television is essential to student life. Plus film adaptation of *Merchant of Venice* is on this afternoon, which will save me several days attempting to read it.

11.30 a.m.
Why did nobody tell me Grandpa, Treena, and Jesus were coming to Sunday lunch? Have rung Mum to chastise her for failure to pass on essential information regarding invitation. She said they were not invited. Asked Grandpa if this was true. He said yes, but it is because they will miss us when we are gone and it is essential we spend quality Riley time together. Asked Treena if this was true (using Mum's deadly

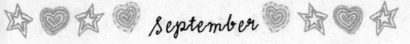

thin-lips plus menacing frown combination) she said no they had run out of Micro Chips. Am better at being Mum than I thought. In fact will prove it by cooking excellent traditional family meal of shepherd's pie. There is mince in the meat compartment of the freezer. Will defrost it in microwave.

1.15 p.m.
Microwave has failed to defrost mince. Instead has burnt outside to crisp and left inside as solid ice. Which is odd as followed user manual, and there was no note attached to advise me otherwise.

1.20 p.m.
Dog has hawked up yellow Post-it. Asked James if he had seen said dog in vicinity of microwave this morning. He said yes, it was eating a Post-it note off there, which he would have told me, only he was sworn to utter silence. Have dispatched him to Mr Patel's with Mum's emergency twenty pound note and instructions to spend it wisely. Used combination move again so am confident of success.

1.30 p.m.
James has come back with nine toilet rolls, a frozen turkey, and a four bags of Doritos. Clearly he has had more opportunity to build up his anti-lip defences, unlike Treena. Though he says the Doritos were two for one and the turkey was £5 cheaper than in Waitrose so in fact he has spent very wisely.

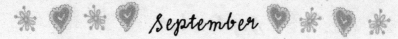

We are having nachos for lunch. Depressingly the Nichols-Rileys seem quite content with this arrangement. Jesus says it is his favourite Sunday lunch, after McDonald's and cereal.

## Monday 14

8 a.m.
The dog has managed to lock itself in the toilet. Have called Mr Hosepipe to rescue it. Thank God James is at school today. It is one less moron to worry about.

11 a.m.
James been sent home from school together with a note from Mr Wilmott saying he was prepared to forgive last week's string of offences, given his previous exemplary record, but calling Mrs Leech 'grandma' is a step too far. Demanded to know what last week's offences were. They are: refusing to dissect a frog, deliberately spoiling his chemistry homework, and using the staff toilet (female). Asked if he was on drugs (Mum's immediate response to unusual transgressions). He said only the habitual Sanatogen multivitamin, and teaspoon of demerara for brain function, but what is the point in making any effort when he is going to be leaving in a few weeks anyway? Am ringing Mr Wilmott to beg for a rethink. Once have worked out a way to screw the bathroom door back on.

Firemen are more than happy to knock a door down, but less keen on getting out their Dremels and putting it back with no visible interference.

1 p.m.
Have given up on door. Will just say it fell off. It is feasible given the presence of the dog, and known visit of Jesus. Also, James is back in school. Told Mr Wilmott that there were extenuating circumstances at home, i.e. Dad had left. Is not a complete lie, just did not add details about new job and temporary B&B arrangement.

2 p.m.
B & B is even more temporary. Mum just rang. They have had an offer accepted on a 1970s detached with an all-seeing hallway. She is jubilant, and will be back by teatime. Have not told her about projectile vomit, bald and purple carpet, or broken door. Her joy at seeing her two children will override her fury. Though I note she sounded less than joyous on the phone. Maybe it is being apart from us. She is like Suzy and her empty nest.

5 p.m.
It is not empty nest. Mum has found and catalogued all three known transgressions plus an incredible seventeen unknown ones (including lid off toothpaste, toilet roll on wrong way round, suspiciously low hot-chocolate supply).

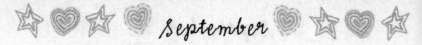
Have been sent to my room to reflect on meaning of word 'responsibility'. James is smiling the smug smile of someone who has played a blinder.

5.15 p.m.

James is no longer smiling. She has found the twenty-first transgression: a picture of a not very dressed Cheryl Cole under his pillow. He has been sent to his room to reflect on the meaning of the word 'adult'.

## Tuesday 15

10 a.m.

Mum is in a weird mood. You would think she would be irritatingly jubilant given her success in replicating 24 Summerdale Road in the guise of 72 Betty Driver Drive (*Coronation Street* reference luckily lost on her. She thinks it is wholesome councillor type), complete with essential all-seeing eye hallway, but she is silently Cillit Banging the bathroom for the fourth time (James did some sort of radial movement and splashes have been detected on the light fittings). Said to Dad maybe she is disappointed in herself for not seizing the day and going for something built before 1970, i.e. she has become Bob-like (explained the new Volvo thing). Dad said she was born Bob-like.

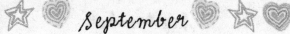

11 a.m.

A postcard has arrived from Mumbai. It is from Uncle Jim who says he and Rosamund have caught dysentery but are engaged to be married, so it is swings and roundabouts romance-wise. Have shown it to Mum. She has stopped Cillit Banging and is now studying postcard scrupulously for any clue as to their specific whereabouts so she can write and remind Uncle Jim he is still married. She said she does not want another bigamist in the family, not after the Treena hoo-hah.

Am going to Sad Ed's. It is marginally less depressing.

8 p.m.

I will almost miss Mrs Thomas. She may be practically a pensioner and Deputy Chair of the Aled Jones fan club (Essex branch) but her ability to make high tea is admirable. Sad Ed ate twenty-four sausage rolls (not mini), six packets of iced gems, and half a cheese and pineapple hedgehog. Thought it might be an overdose of nostalgia but he said it was essential energy as Scarlet had promised a benefits meeting later. She says the arrangement is only until they are at Hull and then it is back to academic resolve and masturbation. Sad Ed is begging her to reconsider though. He says he has done his best musical work since they got together. If this includes 'Purple Sock Lady' then she should end it now and spare us all.

# September

## Wednesday 16

10 a.m.
It is all change at 26 Summerdale Road. Or rather it is some change and some reversion to the status quo, i.e. the Drs Jones and Nietzsche are off to London to join their pyromaniac homosexual son, and the less controversial and annoyingly non-homosexual Clive and Marjory are unpacking their Waitrose boxes. BUT instead of welcoming them back with open arms and a plate of plain chocolate digestives, Mum is in the bedroom having some sort of mental breakdown. Albeit in a Janet Riley manner, i.e. there is no renting of clothes or hair, she is writing a list of all the plus points of Saffron Walden. On the upside, it will surely not take her very long.

11 a.m.
Mum is still writing.

12.30 p.m.
Mum is still writing. Have left health-giving Marmite on toast and an apple outside door. Do not want to go inside lair for fear of a shouting. Even the dog has sensed the ill mood and is sitting freakishly upright on the kitchen floor, where it knows all accidents are at least wipe-clean.

2 p.m.
Mum is out, armed with a 173-point list of why Saffron Walden is an unsurpassable place to live. Asked what she

336

was going to do with list. She said she knows what she would like to do with the list, but it is unmentionable. Besides, it was the therapeutic writing of said list that was ultimate point (all list-writing therapeutic in her book, in fact should be compulsory subject at GCSE), and now she is going to put it away in a drawer, get the digestives out, and go next door to help Marjory with her pelmets.

2.15 p.m.
Have got Mum's list out of drawer. Am disturbed to note that she has included giant pants shop Patricia. Also Mr Wilmott. Who, in my book, is utterly replaceable.

2.20 p.m.
Though she has a point about the excellent library service.

2.25 p.m.
And the cleanliness of side streets.

2.30 p.m.
And the extensive stationery section at Harts.

   Maybe Jack was right. Maybe I will miss things after all. It is too late though. We have set our course on different paths. Him to Cambridge. Me to Hull. And Mum to Betty Driver Drive. It is her destiny and she cannot be swayed off course now.

## Thursday 17

Mum has been swayed and Betty Driver Drive has been downgraded from destiny to last resort. It is the *Walden Chronicle*, which for once has interesting news as opposed to residents' parking 'good or evil' and photos of Brownie revels, i.e. Mrs Wainwright Mark II has decided she doesn't want Wainwright and Beacham after all so it is reopening under the guise of Wainwright, Beacham and Manson (i.e. Malcolm from IT). Mum has rung Mr Wainwright and asked about Dad's chances of getting his job back. Said that there is no way Dad will agree to having Malcolm as a superior (he is not, in any sense) but Mum says she will gloss over that bit and he has got an interview at the golf club on Saturday afternoon. Mum has demanded his presence at the Shreddies table this evening, and told him to bring his wits and his nine iron. Dad was only too willing to oblige. He said another night with Mrs Menzies could kill him. Mum's defences have failed and the shrews are back, plus he had a takeaway curry and has run out of toilet roll again.

## Friday 18

6 p.m.
So this is it. My final day in Saffron Walden. And I can declare that it is has been an utter let-down. Was expecting last hurrah (non Cleggmobile-based) but Sad Ed and Scarlet

went to Cambridge to get new duvet covers (she says he cannot go to college with David Beckham on top of him unless it is ironic, and he is gay, which it is not, and he is not) and then they are getting an early night to road-test said purchases. Jack has probably gone with them to acclimatize and even as I write is spending his first evening at High Table in a mortar board and cloak. How different our paths in life will be. Though not as different as mine and Thin Kylie's. Went over to say goodbye but she is still in Mykonos with Mark Lambert. Or rather Lambert-Britcher. They have both gone double-barrelled. She thinks it will woo customers to Ugly Ducklings. It will not. Any misapprehension that it was run by landed gentry will be dispelled the minute they see her orange face and black roots.

Am somewhat disappointed by less than nostalgic attitude from my own family at my impending departure. Dad has been too busy on the fairway practising his chip shot under Mum's supervision and now they are round at Clive and Marjory's playing Jenga and eating cheese. James called in sick for him. He told Wendy to tell her dad he had had an allergic reaction to shrew secretions. I said it is worrying how easily he lies to women. He said I should know, I have been lying to myself for months.

He is an idiot. I shall take him off my list of things I shall miss. Which, I will stress, I have only started to while away boredom until the doorbell sounds with the first of the last-minute well-wishers. Am now up to seventeen. Am aiming for eighteen, to signify my childhood years here, which

are now ending. Was going to go for twenty-four, i.e. the number of this house but will never think of that many.

8 p.m.
Have got thirty-two and doorbell still hasn't gone. Though am not sure 'Cheap lemonade sparkles from Mr Whippy' really counts. Especially as they always run the risk of cross-contamination from Fat Kylie's backside.

10.30 p.m.
Now up to forty-four. Remembered Barry the Blade, potentially philosophical tramp/installation artist (actual madman) who once took up residence on a disused mattress on Clive and Marjory's drive. Ooh doorbell. Maybe it is Barry the Blade come to bid me adieu.

11.59 p.m.
Was not Barry the Blade. Which is a good thing. Given what has just happened.

It was Jack, who had not been at High Table (what IS High Table? Is it somehow suspended in air, Hogwarts-like?), he had been down the Duke (Jimmy Nail woman still compromised uterus-wise), arguing with Kev Banner about fenders.

I say, 'Ah, Saffron Walden's number twenty-nine: Kev Banner.' He says Kev had never played for Saffron Walden FC, plus since when had they ever managed to get more than eleven players. I say that is not the point, and anyway,

if he is supposed to be filling in for sterilized Peggy, what is he doing here? He says he walked out. Immediately felt funny. Realized I was hoping I knew the reason why. But I have made mistakes in this area before, so I actually ask why. He says, 'Because I needed to see you.' I say, 'Score', which now realize was possibly not the best choice, but was utterly pleased to be right for once. Though then had panic that he only wanted to see me because he had been diagnosed with a colossal tumour and only had days to live. Ask him if this is case. He says no. Then it all goes awkwardly silent, until I remember something and say, 'Have made list, ta-dah', and wave piece of A4 paper at him. He does not read list (which is a shame as had included Car of the People and Blind Monkey Fernando) but says, 'I'm glad, I'm glad you'll miss this place.' More awkward silence follows. Then more funny feeling. And I realize if I don't say it now, I will never say it. Because tomorrow will be too late. So say, 'Made another list too. About things I'm going to miss. I'll read it to you: Number one. Your hair. Which is not too short or too long, but just long enough to be poetic, and also clean. Number two. Your original band tour T-shirt collection. Number three. That you know loads of clever stuff, like the order of Led Zeppelin albums, but it never sounds like showing off when you talk about it. Number four. That you do not, and have vowed never to, wear red skinny jeans. Number 5. The way you always check up on me, in case I have pulled a 'classic Riley', even when we are not actually speaking to each other.'

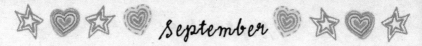
And I never got to Number six because he kissed me. And I kissed him back. And it was exactly as I described in Number ten: perfect.

When we finally stopped (rogue hair in teeth) he said, 'But I thought you wanted to forget it; what happened in Cornwall.' I said why would he think that? He said because that was the first thing I said when we woke up the next morning. Did mental check of conversation and realized that he was right. Said I made poor choice of words but mind was addled due to thingummy, and also potential caravan tragedy situation. Plus I thought HE was the one who wanted to forget it, and that he had only used me like dirty sock, to get over Maya, then cast me aside ready for his next, prettier, cleverer, more worldly conquest. He said he does not use dirty socks for anything, despite what Scarlet might say. But Maya was to get over me, not other way round. I am prettier and cleverer by far. I said, 'Not more worldly?' He said, 'No.' I said, 'But that is why you like me, ha ha?' He said, 'No.' And was about to curse self for trying to be amusing and self-effacing even in dramatic situations when he said, 'That is why I love you.' And then heart definitely on verge of exploding, but managed to breathe out, 'I love you too.' Because I did. I do. And then we kissed again. And I felt like the world, my world, was complete, that in those few seconds, in his arms, I could not possibly want for anything ever again. Not even to be Bob Geldof's illegitimate love child.

Until I remembered that this was it. This really was our

last hurrah. I said, 'I'll miss you, you know. And now it's too late. Why, oh why did I spend so much time trying to escape, when what I wanted was right here all along? Is like utter Richard Curtisesque romcom. Starring Julia Roberts. Or Sandra Bullock.' He said it is not like a romcom. It is real life. And it's not too late. It's never too late. Not for love. Or thingummy. Though I should really stop calling it that. And then he gave me one last heart- and brain-melting kiss and ran off to non-sick-smelling Car of the People.

But he's wrong. It is too late. I could have been having the Time of My Life, instead of waiting for my life to start. It is like Joni Mitchell says in her seminal song about overdevelopment of multistorey car parks: 'You don't know what you got till it's gone.'

And it's gone.

I am a moron.


12.05 a.m.
Worse, I am moron who has not packed yet. Mum is going to go mental.

Accommodation Department
University of Hull
Cottingham Road
Hull HU6 7RX

Jack Stone
198 Debden Road
Saffron Walden
Essex CB10 11AX

Ref:BA (Hons) Politics

Dear Mr Stone,

This is to confirm you have been allocated a place in one of our student houses at 59 Auckland Avenue. If you do not wish to take up this offer, please notify us by return post or email.

Yours sincerely,

Norman Bray

Norman Bray

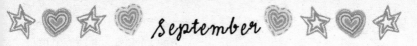 

last hurrah. I said, 'I'll miss you, you know. And now it's too late. Why, oh why did I spend so much time trying to escape, when what I wanted was right here all along? Is like utter Richard Curtisesque romcom. Starring Julia Roberts. Or Sandra Bullock.' He said it is not like a romcom. It is real life. And it's not too late. It's never too late. Not for love. Or thingummy. Though I should really stop calling it that. And then he gave me one last heart- and brain-melting kiss and ran off to non-sick-smelling Car of the People.

But he's wrong. It is too late. I could have been having the Time of My Life, instead of waiting for my life to start. It is like Joni Mitchell says in her seminal song about overdevelopment of multistorey car parks: 'You don't know what you got till it's gone.'

And it's gone.

I am a moron.

12.05 a.m.
Worse, I am moron who has not packed yet. Mum is going to go mental.

Accommodation Department
University of Hull
Cottingham Road
Hull HU6 7RX

Jack Stone
198 Debden Road
Saffron Walden
Essex CB10 11AX

Ref:BA (Hons) Politics

Dear Mr Stone,

This is to confirm you have been allocated a place in one of our student houses at 59 Auckland Avenue. If you do not wish to take up this offer, please notify us by return post or email.

Yours sincerely,

Norman Bray

Norman Bray

From: ColinRiley@WainwrightBeachamManson.co.uk
To: RachelRiley@hulluniv.ac.uk
Date: December 1st
Subject: Christmas

Hello!

Only a quickie (ha-ha), but Mum says she needs definite numbers now for Christmas lunch so she can let Marjory know whether or not she needs to borrow the clover-pattern side plates. So, is it just you, or will Jack be coming? And if he is, does vegetarian include turkey, as Mum says there's no gristle or visible blood.

It is a shame you missed James's performance in the Year Eight production. His rendition of 'Over the Rainbow' was quite the sensation. Mr Wilmott says he has all of your talent.

Anyway, must go. Malcolm is clamping down on private phone calls, emails, and thinking. I was going to protest but Mum is in agreement. She says she does not want a repeat of the Bury St Edmunds debacle because we cannot control our urges to play Minesweeper or order golf shoes.

Hope you are having fun. The Carol Vorderman thing sounds fascinating. Though I agree that casting you as Piers Morgan is a little left-field. See you in a few weeks.
Dad

Joanna Nadin grew up in the small, and tragically normal town of Saffron Walden in Essex. In a bid to make her life more like it is in books, she went to university to study Drama and become a famous actress. Instead, she somehow ended up as a Special Adviser to the Prime Minister. The Rachel Riley books are based entirely on these failed formative years, and her own peculiar family (she sends apologies to James for not even bothering to change his name).

As well as this bestselling series, Joanna has written numerous award-winning books for younger readers, has been shortlisted for the Roald Dahl Funny Prize, and thrice shortlisted for Queen of Teen. She now lives in Bath with her daughter Millie.